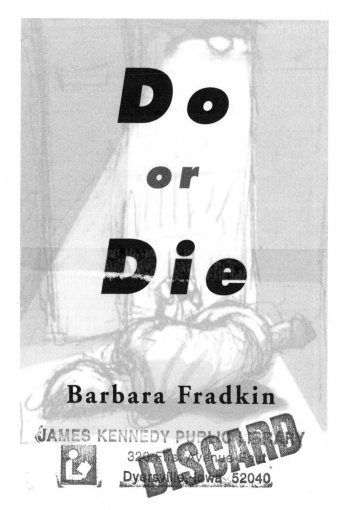

Do

or

Die

Barbara Fradkin

RENDEZVOUS
PRESS

Cover and title page art: Christopher Chuckry

Le Conseil des Arts du Canada depuis 1957 | The Canada Council for the Arts since 1957

We gratefully acknowledge the support of the Canada Council for the Arts for our publishing program.

Napoleon Publishing/RendezVous Press
Toronto, Ontario, Canada

Printed in Canada

05 04 03 02 01 00   5 4 3 2 1

Canadian Cataloguing in Publication Data

Fradkin, Barbara Fraser, date—
    Do or die

An Inspector Green Mystery
ISBN 0-929141-78-4

I. Title.

PS8561.R226D6 2000   C813'.6   C00-931968-9
PR9199.3.F65D6 2000

In loving memory of Arnie

I am grateful to the many people who provided support and assistance to me in this endeavour over the years. I'd particularly like to thank the members of the Ladies' Killing Circle, my critiquing group, Madona Skaff, Jane Tun and Marguerite McDonald and *Storyteller Magazine* for their support of my work, as well as my publisher, Sylvia McConnell, and my editor, Allister Thompson, for their belief in me. A special thanks to Constable Mark Cartwright of the Ottawa Regional Police and Professor Claude Messier of the University of Ottawa for their advice and expertise.

To my family and my children, Leslie, Dana and Jeremy, thank you for your patience, your enthusiasm and most of all, your love.

One

Later, Carrie MacDonald wondered why she had heard nothing, but in the bustle just before closing, she had been too busy to pay much attention. Photocopiers whirred, pages crackled and students hustled past. She heard the hollow ping of the elevator bell and the rattle as the door slid closed, but she did not look up from her stacking. The library closed in ten minutes and she knew that unless she got all the books back onto the shelves, she would face Margot's wrath in the morning. The wizened prune wielded her puny power with the zeal of an SS officer, always after Carrie for sketching when she should be working. As if that were all she was good for.

A big lout in a studded leather jacket and cowboy boots shoved past her and lumbered to the elevator without so much as a glance in her direction. He jingled change in his pocket, wheezing as he waited for the next elevator. I'm invisible, she thought. Just hired help, only useful when you have no quarters, or the photocopier has run out of paper. She wanted to shout "I'm a student too, you know. I'm one of you. I sit in classes and take copious notes and think great thoughts, just as lofty as yours. But unlike you, I don't get an allowance from Daddy, and I have a ten-year old to support."

When the elevator door slid open, the fat man barrelled in and punched the button. At the last minute, a girl shoved past Carrie, frizzy hair flying. She paused at the entrance to the

1

elevator for one last anxious look behind her, then flung herself through the closing doors.

Everyone was gone abruptly in a final flurry of excitement before the late-night hush settled in. Carrie went back to her books, placing the last of them on the cart in proper sequence by call number. Wheeling the cart, she set off down the nearest aisle.

She knew the entire library by heart—the busy sections with the well-worn titles in English literature and social science as well as the remote corners whose riches hadn't been explored in years. The blonde had come from the education section, the lout probably from the literature section. Although he didn't exactly look the sonnet-spouting type.

The first four books on her cart were from the law section. After disposing of them, she wheeled the cart past obscure shelves bearing esoteric titles she barely understood, all long undisturbed and thick with dust. She was scanning the titles as she walked, relishing the impossibly long words, when a misplaced book leaped out at her well-trained eye. It was stuffed into a gap, askew and half hidden in the dark. She stopped, grumbling to herself. This was how books were lost, misplaced by some careless student and not found again for months. This book was on the wrong floor miles from home, a book on neuropsychology in a section on Victorian novels.

She placed it in her cart and was about to move on when she heard a moan. On second hearing, more a gasp than a moan. Abandoning her cart, she followed the sound around the corner to the next aisle. The sight stopped her short.

A young man lay curled on the floor, his arms clutching his stomach. His sleeves, his chest, the once-grey carpet were all soaked in blood. She recognized his face immediately. Just the week before, she had sneaked a sketch of him hunched over a stack of books, staring into space. She was always on the look-out for special faces, and his look of bewildered sadness had captured her. He had looked like a young man with a burden far too great for his years.

Now his face was drawn tight in a grimace, his eyes squeezed shut and his mouth gaping in a silent scream. He was deathly pale, and this, even more than the blood, galvanized her to action.

Shouting for help, she dashed across the library to the emergency phone to call security. As she returned, she caught sight of a red plaid jacket, dark hair and widened eyes by the elevator.

"There's a man hurt up here! Go meet the ambulance guys downstairs. Fast!"

Barely had she turned in the aisle when the fire alarm began to clamour.

"No! Not the fire—" She spun around just in time to see the red plaid shirt disappearing into the elevator. Cursing, she ran on.

By the time she reached the young man again, he was unconscious and lay inert in his pool of blood. As she flung her sweater over him in a vain attempt to combat the shock, he stopped breathing.

"No!" she cried and flipped him onto his back to begin CPR. It was only then, as she applied her fists to his chest, that she saw the wound.

*   *   *

At six-twenty the next morning, Inspector Michael Green lay sprawled across his bed with his pillow over his head. Heat glued the sodden sheet to his back. The baby was crying, and his wife clattered irritably around the kitchen preparing a bottle. In between howls, the baby kicked his overhead toy with his feet, causing the bell to clang and the crib to thump against the wall. In their tiny apartment, it sounded like World War III.

Oh God, Green thought, the start of another day. A day in the life of middle management in the new bigger, better, amalgamated police force, a day now spent sitting in boring committee meetings, drafting service models and pushing papers around his desk. Murders were up in Ottawa, thanks to government cutbacks to social services and health, which drove people to increasingly desperate solutions. But it was all routine stuff, easily handled by the regular field detectives of the Major Crimes Squad. Not a serial killer or a mystery assassin in sight. Nothing that required his deductive powers or intuitive ingenuity, only his woefully inadequate supervisory skills. Not that he wished for a real murder to sink his teeth into, exactly, merely some new spark in his life. What the hell had possessed him to become an inspector anyway?

Clamping his pillow more firmly over his ears, he burrowed further under the sheets until the baby was reduced to a distant whine. He did not even hear the phone ring; Sharon yanked the pillow off and shoved the cordless phone in his face.

"Sounds like Jules."

Shaking sleep from his head, Green took the phone. The Chief of Detectives' dry voice crackled through the wires, unusually urgent.

"Michael, something important has come up. Be in my office for a briefing in half an hour. Oh—and Michael, wear a decent suit."

Green stared at the phone. Jules had hung up before he

could even rally a protest. Decent! In the old days, Jules had never told him what to wear. Hinted, sometimes, when the media were going to be around, but never ordered.

"I don't even have a decent suit," he muttered to Sharon when he emerged from the shower five minutes later. "Both my court suits are at the cleaners."

"Three nice suits wouldn't exactly kill you," she retorted without looking up. She was slumped on the bed, dark eyes haggard, giving Tony his bottle. "By forty most men own a few decent suits."

No support from that end, he thought with more sympathy than annoyance. She's all tapped out. In their early years, she'd found his fashion ineptitude endearing and would have been ready with a wise-crack retort, but now she couldn't even muster a smile. A good jolt of Starbucks French Roast might help, but he didn't have time to make it for either of them.

Instead he appeased her with a brief kiss on the head before turning his attention to his cramped corner of the closet. He did in fact have a few proper suits, the most promising being a mud-brown, double-breasted tweed that had served him well at funerals and weddings over the years. The cuffs were faded and the pants seat shone, but it still fit, if he could survive tweed in a June heat wave. He didn't notice the odour of sweat until he had climbed into his car and headed across the canal to the station. Serves Jules right, expecting a decent suit on half an hour's notice.

Jules' clerk leaped to her feet as Green burst into the office. Despite the obvious gravity of the summons, she couldn't suppress a smile but quickly wrestled it under control as she ushered him into Jules' office.

To Green's surprise, the Chief of Detectives was not alone. Seated with him at the small round conference table was a familiar, bull-necked figure in a too-tight suit. Jules rose to greet him, but Deputy Police Chief Doug Lynch did not.

Adam Jules was a tall, reed-thin, silver-haired man in a crisp cotton suit. His eyes flickered briefly, and his nostrils flared, but otherwise he betrayed no hint of reaction to his subordinate's attire. He extended a manicured hand.

"Michael, thank you for joining us."

Playing along with the formality, Green returned the handshake and then took the only remaining chair at the table. His pulse quickened. Something big was in the air. Maybe the answer to his prayers...

Belatedly Lynch shoved out a broad, callused hand. "Mike, good to see you."

I'll bet, Green thought to himself. I'm about as welcome a sight as a cockroach in the vichyssoise. Unless you want something from me.

And sure enough...

"We're hoping you'll be able to help us with a very difficult case."

Us? Green thought ironically. As in the force, or you and your buddy the Police Chief, who's wily enough to let you play frontman for him? If you think that will get you into his shoes someday, you're deluding yourself. There are no letters after your name, no useful friends in the wings. You're his pit bull, nothing more.

Green raised an eyebrow. "Oh?"

Perhaps sensing trouble, Jules moved in. He took a thin file from his desk and held it out. "A student was stabbed in the University of Ottawa library last night. Young man by the name of Jonathan Blair."

After fourteen years in Criminal Investigations, very little surprised Green any more, but murder in a university library was a first. The second eyebrow shot up before he could stop himself.

"Marianne Blair's son," Lynch cut in. "Name ring any bells?"

Obviously it was supposed to, but it didn't. And it was really too early in the morning to play one-upmanship with a pit bull. Especially before even one cup of coffee. Without much hope, Green glanced around Jules' office. As usual, not a pencil out of place, not a hint of human habitation. And of course, no coffee.

"Should it?" he grumbled.

Lynch smirked, but Jules was faster. "Marianne Blair is the head of the Lindmar Foundation, a major funding organization that underwrites charities, research, the arts."

Ah! Suddenly the fog began to lift. One of Chief Shea's famous "connections". The Police Chief had come to power the new, corporate way, attending management courses and cultivating connections that could serve him well on the way up. Now, at the apex of his career, he had a fair network of expectant friends. Among them, no doubt, the rich and generous Marianne Blair.

"Mrs. Blair is understandably very upset," Jules was continuing in his dry monotone. "When she called this morning, I told her we would be assigning our best men."

Green eyed Lynch warily. "Is there anything I should know?"

Lynch held his gaze a moment then broke into a smile and leaned back in his chair, hitching his pants up. "I'm just an observer in this, Mike. This is Adam's and your show. You know my policy on non-interference. But I just wanted to let you know who we're dealing with here. This is a high profile case. The spotlight will be on the department. If we don't deliver, Marianne Blair will make enough noise to be heard at City Hall, and I'm sure none of us wants that. I want you to know I have every confidence in you—that's what we made

7

you an inspector for, isn't it? To handle tough cases. Hell, it's the only thing you're good at. I know you won't let us down. And it goes without saying that you'll have the full cooperation of the force. Anything you need, you let me know."

Green fingered the file before him, trying to figure out the hidden agenda. He hated politics and had no talent for it, preferring to plough straight ahead like a bloodhound on the scent. Yet now he had the sense of waiting for some other shoe to drop. Lynch could have applied his pressure without having to meet him personally. Jules knew—in fact all the brass knew—that Green loved the thrill of the hunt. Unlike most managers, he preferred the trenches and when he took over a case, he drove himself and everyone else on the case to exhaustion till it was solved. This little pep talk wasn't necessary. There must be something more at stake.

He sent out a feeler. "What does it look like so far?"

"No idea," Jules replied. "There were no eyewitnesses, no murder weapon, no known motive. The victim was twenty-four years old, single, lived with his mother. Just a hard-working graduate student, according to her."

Lynch waved a casual hand as if to dismiss all other speculation. "My guess is it was some undesirable who went to the library to meet someone else, and the Blair kid was unlucky enough to get in the way. That's where I'd start looking, Mike. And I'd cooperate with university security on this. They know the territory. I wouldn't bother too much with the university staff."

Green raised his head in surprise. "But I certainly have to—"

"Check it out, sure. I'm just saying be careful with the university types. Remember, this isn't a back alley someplace. These are educated, liberal-minded people who know their rights. And their lawyers."

Green chilled. "I'll handle it the way I handle all cases. I'll ask the questions that need to be asked."

Lynch raised a soothing hand. "Of course you will. But I know your reputation for thoroughness, Mike. Some might say bull-headedness. Ask your questions. Just don't ask questions you don't need to ask. Don't ruffle more feathers than you need to."

Finally, Green thought he heard the echo of the other shoe. He feigned confusion. "You don't want me asking too many questions of people at the university?"

The pit bull stiffened slightly. Beside him, Jules had turned a faint shade of fuchsia. "I didn't say that. I just want you to remember they're on the same side as us. Everyone wants to find the killer. Just you focus on that, and don't make things more complicated than they need to be. The sooner this is cleaned up the better, so let Adam know what you need to do the job."

I need the freedom to operate, Green wanted to shout at him. I need to know what the fuck is going on. A major homicide case has just been handed to me. New, hot, begging to be pursued. And here I am, playing twenty questions with you.

But for the sake of his wife and new baby, he counted to ten and slowly raised his eyes.

"Ten men, for starters."

"You can have thirty."

Green shook his head. "If I need gofers, I'll let Superintendent Jules know. But for now I'll take ten good detectives from the Major Crimes Squad, including Sergeant Sullivan and Detective Gibbs."

The Deputy Chief nodded. "Sergeant Sullivan is already on the case. He took the initial call. Anything else you want?"

"The rest of the details I can work out with Superintendent Jules." Green picked up the file and pushed his chair back.

"Now, if there's nothing else, sir, I should get started."

* * *

Green had barely begun the file when Jules walked into his office five minutes later, flicking lint from his jacket as if to cleanse himself.

"Thank you, Michael—" he began but got no further. Green thrust the file aside.

"Adam, I can't work like this! I'm not allowed to ask too many questions, I'm supposed to defer to university security! Since when! How the fuck am I supposed to solve the crime?"

"Don't worry. The Deputy Chief just has to keep an eye on City Hall."

"You mean on the Chief's pals! In case I probe too deeply into their love lives or their bank accounts. Either he trusts me and lets me do my job, or he lets the staff sergeant handle it just like any other case. I won't have him second-guessing me at every turn!"

Jules drew his lips in a thin line. "Michael, Lynch would never obstruct a criminal investigation. He may be more…pragmatic than you or I, but he's not unethical. He's seen the preliminary reports. The crime needs you and he knows it. Forget about him. Just proceed as you usually do." He hesitated and gave his dry approximation of a smile. "Well, try to follow procedure a little more often. He'll be watching."

Green was silent. Adam Jules had always been his greatest ally, encouraging him up the promotional ladder so that he would have the freedom to set his own course and running interference for him when his quest took him outside the bureaucratic box. But the name "Jules" no longer commanded the same respect and influence in the bigger pond of the new force, and Green could see defeat and disillusionment creeping into the man's eyes.

"I'll do my best, Adam," he replied. "Kick me if you see steam starting to come out my ears."

Jules' smile faded. "For all the good that's ever done. Just solve the case for me, Michael. Brian is waiting for you outside."

*   *   *

Sergeant Brian Sullivan was a former high school linebacker who took up most of the free space in Green's little office, particularly when he paced. His blonde hair stood in tufts, and his square jaw was set.

"What a fuck-up!" he exclaimed as soon as he shut the door. "Everything that can go wrong in a homicide case went wrong in this one, and who does it turn out to be? Some friend of the goddamn Police Chief!" His expression changed abruptly as he registered Green's suit, and he burst out laughing. "You look like a bargain basement shoe salesman!"

"Don't start." Green grinned as he stuffed the reports back in the file and pocketed his keys. "Let's go over to the crime scene. You can fill me in on this stuff as you drive."

Outside, they found themselves in the crush of the morning rush hour. The June sun glared off chrome and glass, making Sullivan squint as he bulldozed the unmarked blue Taurus into the traffic. In front of them, traffic oozed along the elevated Queensway which bisected the city. Exhaust fumes shimmered in the rising heat. Another scorcher, Green thought, wondering how the city's tempers, frayed by unemployment and government cutbacks, would handle yet another stress. He glanced at Sullivan, who was fuming at a red light.

"So tell me about the fuck-up."

Sullivan rubbed his face wearily. "First of all, some moron sounded the fire alarm, so when the fire trucks arrived, there was near-panic on the main floor. Firemen rushing in, students trying to get out. Any hope our suspect was still in the building went up in smoke. Then the security guard who called in the 911 only asked for an ambulance, said someone was hurt. Didn't say stabbed. Didn't know, apparently. So the dispatcher sent a routine patrol unit along with the fire ambulance. One constable—a rookie who hardly even remembered the procedure book. He tried his best. I mean, the victim was still alive, so I know his first concern had to be…anyway, he got there about two minutes after the firemen, who were giving CPR, so he rushed in to help them. But meanwhile, they trample all over the scene, they move the victim. Nobody takes pictures, nobody secures the scene, a whole bunch of other people—firemen, rubberneckers, university security—come up in the elevators and get in the way."

The light turned green. Sullivan squealed the tires, accelerating around the corner, only to stop short at the next light. He sighed.

"Finally one of the firemen takes charge and, thank God, he has a brain. He asks the rookie if Ident's been called, and the kid says Jeez, I forgot, and he starts remembering his guide book. So he calls for back-up. I get a call and so does Ident. Lou Paquette was on—one lucky break. There were a dozen cops on the scene when I got there, but the paramedics took off to the General with only one patrol officer. Nobody thinks to take fingernail scrapings or bag the hands. Nobody thinks to stop the emerg doctors from tossing all his clothes into a bag. We got them back, but, oh Jesus, Mike, they've got to be contaminated as hell."

Green had listened to this rambling tirade without

interruption, but now he looked across at his colleague, who had stopped for air. In the silence, their police radios chattered in mindless bursts which they no longer heard. Brian Sullivan looked beyond tired. His normally ruddy Irish farm boy face was white with fatigue, and new lines were beginning to pull at the corners of his eyes. It seems like yesterday we were rookies together, Green thought, but look how this job has battered him.

Green's first wife had stomped off in disgust with their baby in tow after only three years of marriage, leaving him without ties or obligations for nearly ten years, but Sullivan had married his first love, had three children in rapid succession, and now struggled to keep his life compartmentalized. He was too much of a professional to bring his home worries onto the job, but sometimes, as now, the stress seeped through. As they inched over the Pretoria Bridge across the Rideau Canal, stuck behind a line of cars doing an illegal left turn onto Colonel By Drive, he drummed his fingers and cursed. Green wondered what else was eating at him.

"Does it get any worse?" he asked gently.

"Can it get worse?" Sullivan countered. "Put it this way. It doesn't get better. I leave Lou Paquette and his Ident team to get what they can from the mess in the library, and I rush off to the hospital, but the victim's in surgery. No instructions to anybody to listen for dying declarations. And worse, the guy has no ID on him. Not even a library card!"

"His wallet was probably lifted."

"I figured that." Sullivan broke off long enough to accelerate around a red Honda waiting to turn left. The car beside him blasted its horn, and he raised his middle finger. "Unless of course it fell out while the guys were moving him. Anything is possible in this fiasco. But as a result, we didn't know who the John Doe was. I ran a description through missing persons and checked recent reports, but it was only a bit past midnight by then, and who the hell reports a fully grown man missing at that hour? Probably not even at four a.m. Anyway, the victim comes out of surgery and into recovery, but he hasn't regained consciousness and it doesn't look like he will in a hurry, so I post a uniform by his bed and I go back to the scene. No—first I checked his clothes. Expensive, so I know the guy's not starving. Conservative, so I figure he's not a punk, but that's no surprise. He was stabbed in the Shakespeare section of the university library. Not your average street punk's stomping ground. That's why dispatch screwed up so badly on the 911 call, by the way. Sergeant Jones says 'Who the hell expects a stabbing in a library, for God's sake! If the call had come from a parking lot in the Byward Market, we'd have sent four experienced teams down there right away. Not one poor rookie.' And it's not the kid's fault, after all. There was a lot of blood around, and he just wanted to save the boy's life. I'd have forgotten all the procedural shit myself fifteen years ago."

Sullivan pulled the Taurus to a halt behind a police van near the entrance to the library, and the two jumped out. A police officer was posted at the entrance to the library and another at the elevators. One elevator had been commandeered for use in the investigation, and the fourth floor button had been taped on the other elevators. Students gathered in whispering clumps, gawking curiously.

Sullivan led Green into the elevator and punched four. "Looks great now, doesn't it? Everything according to procedure, every 't' crossed. The Ident team has cordoned off the entire fourth floor, and they're probably still there."

The elevator door slid open, revealing yellow plastic tape

across the exit. They logged in with the uniform on guard, and ducked under the tape. Ahead of them, half a dozen men were crawling around on the floor with magnifying glasses.

"Yes, they're still here."

"And we'll probably be here till Christmas," came a gravelly voice from behind a bookcase. An instant later the senior Identification Officer, Sergeant Lou Paquette, emerged around the corner, red-faced from crawling. "We haven't found a damn thing yet." He peeled off his latex glove and held out his hand to Green. "Glad to see you, Mike."

"You've got nothing?" Green echoed in dismay.

"Oh, we've got tons of shit. Fingerprints, hair, fibres, bloodstains. There's blood all over the place. The witnesses tracked it around, the paramedics tracked it around. The only thing I can't tell is if the killer tracked it around. And this is a public place. There could be fingerprints and fibres from half the city of Ottawa here. The half that doesn't have prints on file downtown." Paquette grinned at his own attempt at humour. His mustache quivered. "I've sent a guy to collect the shoes from every fireman and paramedic who was at the scene. That'll be fun."

Green took out his notebook. "Can you tell us anything?"

Paquette sighed and grew sober. "As far as I can tell, there was no struggle. No books were pulled down, nothing kicked out of place. It's a narrow space. It would be hard to fight without knocking the bookshelves."

"And the young woman who found the victim heard no sound of an argument, no screams," Sullivan added. "Libraries are pretty quiet. She would have heard a violent scuffle."

"Did she see anything unusual that evening? Anyone suspicious or out of place?"

"Nothing that she remembered, but she was pretty shaken

15

up. She got covered in blood, and all she could think about was getting cleaned up. After the preliminaries, I let her go home."

Green nodded. "We'll get to her later."

They had walked to the far end of the library along the path Ident had laid out and now stood in front of the large, browning pool of blood where the body had been.

"The victim was stabbed once in the abdomen," Sullivan said. "According to the emergency room surgeon, the weapon pierced the stomach and lacerated the liver, nicking an artery as it went by. It sounds like a horizontal thrust directly forward, made by a knife held at waist level."

"I suppose nobody took photographs of the wound before they sutured it all up?"

Sullivan grinned. "You got it."

Green looked up from his notes with a snort. "Jesus. Jules said the case needed me, but what it really needs is a goddamn miracle."

*   *   *

The two detectives stayed at the scene another fifteen minutes reviewing the meagre forensic harvest. No murder weapon, no signs of disturbance or misplaced property, hundreds of latent fingerprints which would take days to analyze and could not be tied definitively to the murder anyway. Blood had been tracked up and down the aisle leading to the elevator as well as the two aisles on either side, but the traces were consistent with bloodstained shoes rather than with drops of falling blood. The only spilt blood was the large pool where the body had been and a fine spray of arterial blood on the bookshelf nearby.

"The perpetrator would have got blood on himself,

without a doubt," Paquette said. "On his hand and sleeve, probably also on his shirt, pants and shoes. The body fell forward. The perpetrator would have had trouble jumping out of the way in time, especially since he was trying to pull out his knife. Some of these bloody footprints may be his, once I eliminate all the other assholes who were on the scene."

Green sketched the scene, noting the rows of floor-to-ceiling bookshelves which effectively blocked any overview of the area. Jonathan Blair's killer had trapped him in a remote corner, where the chances of anyone witnessing the crime were even fewer. By luck or design?

Green glanced at his watch. "Brian, I want to meet with the mother before she calls the Chief again, and I need you to tell me what else you've got. Come on, I'll buy you a coffee. I missed having mine this morning."

Seated over two mugs of scalding coffee at Harvey's, Green mustered a smile for his weary colleague. There was no one he respected more. The two had been friends since they started together on the streets twenty years earlier, and although Green had risen further through the ranks, placing strain on the friendship in sensitive moments, he secretly considered Sullivan the better cop. The Deputy Chief was right. He, Green, was only good at detective work. Sullivan was good at everything, paperwork and organization as well as handling people and crises. And in the middle of a case, you couldn't ask for a more careful, thorough investigator.

"How did you finally identify him, by the way? You didn't get that far in your depressing tale of professional incompetence."

"His mother called in, finally. Actually, her personal assistant called in, guy by the name of Peter Weiss. Apparently the victim was the quiet type, no wild parties, no late nights, a bookworm. Never stayed out all night. Maybe he'd have one drink with friends after the library closed, but he was usually home by midnight. Certainly by two. So when his mother woke up at five in the morning—she's some kind of early morning freak—and saw he never came home, she heard on the early morning radio about a stabbing in the library, and she got worried. So Weiss called the station. By then Blair was dead. He died at three fifty-six a.m. without regaining consciousness. When the assistant called I was just trying to wake MacPhail and get him down to the hospital to take over the body. I let him have all the beauty sleep I could spare, but I didn't want the ordinary doctors screwing up the evidence any more than it already had been."

Sullivan took a sip of coffee and cradled his chin in his massive hand. Some life suffused his reddened eyes as he grinned. "That old Scot is a bugger to wake up. I always have to hold the phone two feet from my ear when I call at night. But he came through for us. He got to the hospital in half an hour, reeking of whiskey but at full steam. He ranted up and down about the suturing, but after he'd examined the body and looked at the medical records, he came out with his theory. Sharp, smooth-edged knife, at least six-inch blade, he guessed about an inch to an inch and a half wide. He'll know more after the autopsy. One smooth horizontal stroke in and out."

Green whistled. "Neat job."

"Yup. And into the middle of all this, without any warning, just as MacPhail is loading the body bag into the elevator to go down to the morgue, along comes the little rookie again wanting us to unbag the body so mummy's assistant can have a look."

"In the middle of the hospital hallway?"

Sullivan laughed. "That was my reaction. I was tired and I was mad about all the mistakes people had made, especially him. So I told him to follow proper procedure and take the assistant down to meet us at the morgue."

"Nothing wrong with that, Brian. Rigid, maybe, but by the book. No one can fault you for that."

"Oh, yeah? Well, the Deputy Chief did. Showed up twenty minutes later with this Weiss guy in tow, ripping a strip off me for caring more about procedure than about the decent citizens of Ottawa. I saw my whole career flashing before my eyes. My mortgage, my three kids, tuition for college—all bye-bye."

"Ach! Political grandstanding to impress the Chief, that's all. You've done the right things, Brian. You were the first person to act like a professional in this whole mess."

"Yeah. We'll know soon, won't we? When I've been assigned to permanent traffic detail."

Green grinned. "You've been assigned to me. So let's get on it. Did you have time to find witnesses or interview anyone?"

Sullivan rubbed his bloodshot eyes. "Besides the young woman who found him? Are you kidding? I was so busy chasing the body and mopping up everyone else's mess, I had no time to investigate! We don't have one lead, we don't have shit, but every 't' has been crossed."

Green felt the caffeine from his second cup beginning to spread through his system, bringing with it a return of optimism. He glanced at his watch. Nine oh-five. "Right now I'm heading over to interview the mother. That's going to be a tough one, so I'll be turning off my radio, but you can reach me by cell if you have to. Arrange a briefing for ten-thirty with all the men Jules gave me." He pushed back his chair and stood up. "We'll find a trail, Brian, once we start talking to Jonathan Blair's friends and family. A nice kid who studies Shakespeare and lives with Mummy can't have too many enemies."

Two

The Village of Rockcliffe Park was not a village in any normal sense of the word, except perhaps in exclusivity. It was a tree-lined enclave perched on a bluff above the Ottawa river, surrounded by the bustling city and boasting the highest per capita income of any municipality in Canada. Mercedes and Volvos sat discreetly on shaded drives, and massive beds of peonies and irises framed the old stone mansions. Even the heat was tempered.

The living room of Marianne Blair's Rockcliffe mansion was painted Wedgwood blue, perfectly offsetting the rose floral love seats which framed the Persian rug. A discreet, old-monied room, perfect for a rich benefactress, Green thought, except that the designer had neglected to take a good look at the owner. Marianne Blair contrasted harshly with her surroundings, at least in her current raw state. She hunched on the edge of a love seat, dressed in a shapeless brown sweat suit, her gray hair askew and large jowls quivering.

Her personal assistant stationed himself at her side, glaring at Green. Weiss had met the detective at the front door, wrinkling his nose visibly at Green's suit and inspecting his ID for a conspicuously long time. Green knew that at five feet, ten inches, with mousey brown hair and hazel eyes, he was remarkable only for his nose. It was the only visible trace of his Semitic heritage, which was generally honoured more in the breach than in the observance.

His parents were both Holocaust survivors who had lost their first families to the ovens, and they had an almost paranoid fear of public exposure. They had met in a displaced persons camp in Cyprus after the war, but it had taken them nearly fifteen years to risk having a child, and even then the Jewish festivals had been muted, secretive affairs. Green had grown up with Hasidic folktales and Klezmer clarinets ringing in his ears, but outside the family walls, his parents cautioned their sandy-haired, hazel-eyed boy to keep his Jewishness to himself.

In the modern, urban world into which he moved, that proved seductively easy. He belonged to no synagogue or Jewish groups, worked in an entirely non-Jewish environment, had almost no Jewish friends and none of the previous women in his life, including his first wife, had been Jewish. His recent marriage to Sharon Levy had been as much of a surprise to him as it had been to his father. Although Sharon had been trying to introduce some Jewish traditions into their family life since the birth of their son, Green's identity still found its main outlet in his commitment to smoked meat, bagels and Nate's Delicatessen.

But for some, the nose was enough to fire up old myths and prejudices, and whether Weiss had reacted to the nose or the odour of his suit, Green couldn't be sure. Weiss had swivelled on his heel without a word and led the way across the vast marble foyer into the mercifully air-conditioned interior. He moved with impeccable grace, but his blue linen suit was buttoned wrong, and his toupee dipped over one ear. Not quite recovered from this morning's excursion after all, Green thought with some satisfaction.

On the drive over, he had tried to plan his interview

strategy. Marianne Blair, he had learned from Jules' briefing file, was the only child of a wealthy British Columbia shipping magnate who had made his fortune as a young man shipping timber from the virgin forests of the young province. He had diversified into oil and real estate later in life and had established the Lindmar Foundation as a means of purchasing immortality, as well as tax relief. To groom his daughter for her role as elegant patroness, he had sent her first to Eastern private schools and later to universities in British Columbia and Europe. But rumour had it that beneath the civilized veneer, Marianne Blair was her father's clone: willful, self-indulgent and stubborn as a mule.

Green had expected to find her raging mad and demanding vengeance. Judging from the way the law enforcement top brass had jumped to attention earlier, he had thought he would be bullied and threatened. But seated opposite her now, looking into her eyes, he saw no fire in them. Only bewilderment. She was a mother like any other at this moment, he thought, and felt himself relax. With her permission, he set his tape recorder on the table so that he could give her his full attention.

"Mrs. Blair, I'm sorry," he said simply. "I need to know about your son. Are you up to answering a few questions?"

She nodded, and he began. She had last seen Jonathan at breakfast yesterday, she said. They lived alone with a housekeeper; Jonathan was an only child, his parents divorced. It had been just like any other morning. Jonathan was an early riser, and she had a busy schedule ahead of her so they had eaten about seven. They had spoken little, but that too was usual. They liked each other's company but did not feel compelled to talk. She had reports to read, and he was absorbed in a journal article. He had always been a voracious reader and never sat at the table without a book in hand. He had commented that he would be at the university all day and wasn't sure when he would be home. This too was usual. He spent much of his time in his lab or the library.

"Did he tell you what he planned to do yesterday? Anyone he planned to meet?"

She shook her head. "We didn't really talk."

"To your knowledge, did your son use drugs?" He saw her stiffen. Weiss started to protest, but Green cut him off. "It's confidential, Mrs. Blair, but I have to know."

"Not to my knowledge."

"I need the names of all known friends and associates."

"Peter said you'd need that information, so we've prepared a list. We haven't got all the phone numbers, I'm afraid, but we'll keep working on it." She glanced across at Weiss expectantly, and he slipped out of the room.

"Thank you." Green watched until he had disappeared, then leaned forward. Without Weiss, he had a much better chance of reaching her. "Do you know of anyone who might have had reason to kill your son?"

She sighed, and some of the stiffness seemed to dissipate. "I have racked my brains over and over, and I can't for the life of me think who might have done this. Or why. It makes no sense."

"Did he have any enemies?" She was shaking her head. "Any conflicts, any fights with anyone?"

"No! Jonathan avoided conflict. He was too nice; people walked all over him. He never seemed to get angry—something he certainly didn't get from me." Unexpectedly, she faltered. "But he was a wonderful boy. I'm not criticizing him. He was generous, sensitive, forgiving. Sometimes I was afraid of what life would do to him. And look what it's done."

"Was there anything out of the ordinary about him

yesterday? Anything he said? His mood? Behaviour?"

She breathed deeply to collect herself. "Actually, he did seem tense. Distracted. He poured juice into his cereal." A smile trembled on her lips. "I asked him if anything was wrong, but Jonathan is a private person. He's used to solving his own problems—a casualty of having a busy mother, I guess. If something was troubling him, he became even quieter until he'd worked it out." She cocked her head thoughtfully. "In fact, he's been quieter the whole past week or so."

"Did you get the impression something was troubling him?"

She pressed her large, coarse hand to her lips. A faraway look had crept into her eyes. "I think he was going to tell me. The night before he died. He came downstairs from studying about eleven o'clock, and he asked me if I wanted tea. I said I was going to bed, so he went back upstairs. But…he looked upset. Oh, God." She put her face in her hands.

Green hated tears. He panicked at the thought that he might have to provide solace. Watching her quiver on the brink, he plunged ahead.

"Do you have any idea what it might have been? Was there anything going on in his life that might have been on his mind?"

She rallied with an effort and rubbed her eyes on her sleeve. Green glanced around the room for a kleenex, but the tables held nothing but china figurines. He wondered what room they really lived in.

"I don't know," she replied when she could speak. "He's been working very hard in his lab, but he loves his work. Jonathan leads—" she stumbled, chin quivering "—led a quiet life. He just had his studies, a small circle of friends, cycling on the weekend. I worried it was too quiet, too restricted a life for a young man. He takes after his father that way, not me."

"Any girlfriends?"

24

"Not now, but Jonathan attracts girls. Partly his money, but also his gentleness. And he's a very handsome man. He's always been a little bewildered by what his looks do to women."

"Any recent break-ups? Any vengeful women?"

"A fairly recent break-up, yes. But I believe it was amicable. I can't imagine Vanessa being vengeful, she's far too bright. Too much her own woman."

He sensed an edge, but perhaps it was just natural maternal jealousy. His own mother had never considered any of the many girls in his youth good enough for him either. Of course, considering the girls he had picked…"Vanessa?" he probed gently.

"Vanessa Weeks, one of his classmates. They'd been dating for almost a year, but they broke up last month. I don't know why, actually, because I had the feeling Jonathan still cared for her."

"Maybe it was her idea."

"I don't think so." Mrs. Blair drew her brows together. "She called here one night a few weeks ago looking for him, and we talked. She seemed very fond of him. Said he was shutting her out, and she was very worried about him. I'd say she was upset, but certainly not angry. Jonathan is so nice he's hard to get mad at." She looked rueful. "Something else he gets from his father."

"Where is his father?"

"Vancouver. Jonathan hasn't seen him in some time." Her voice was flat, but she reddened slightly, and Green sensed a surge of hidden feeling. Bitterness? Fear? Or something else.

"Mrs. Blair, do you have any enemies, anyone who might want to send you a warning or punish you for something?"

"Punish me?" Her eyes widened as the connection hit her. "You're thinking of Jonathan's father? Ridiculous. Henry adored Jonathan, would lay down his life for him. I am by far

25

the less important person in Henry's life."

Something else, Green decided. Maybe regret. He filed the observation away. "How about other enemies? Disgruntled business associates, psychotic artists?"

A shadow passed over her face, gone before he was even sure it was there. She squared her shoulders and jutted out her chin. "Sure, I have enemies. You can't deal in money without angering someone. Peter Weiss handles them."

"Anyone threaten you? Threaten your family?"

She scowled, the softness of a moment ago quite gone. "You're barking up the wrong tree, Inspector. I can be abrasive, but no one hates me that much."

"Believe me, Mrs. Blair, there are all kinds of nuts out there. Would Mr. Weiss even bother to tell you?"

Her eyes hardened, and she stared at him for a moment. Then colour suffused her face. "If he didn't, there would be hell to pay."

Weiss hustled back into the room, paper in hand. Green had heard no footsteps approaching on the marble and wondered if Weiss had been listening at the door all this time.

"Peter!" she snapped. "Have there been any threats against Jonathan that you haven't told me about?"

Weiss stopped in his tracks. "Certainly not, Marianne. Our investigators don't tell me all the details, of course—"

"Bullshit!"

Weiss coloured. "But I'm sure anything as important as that—"

Mrs. Blair swung on him, eyes blazing. The fighter had returned. "I want you to tell this officer everything! If I find out you're withholding information that he needs to find my son's killer, you'll be pumping gas in Flin Flon!"

The sight of Weiss' face was repayment enough for the

pompous aide's earlier disdain, and Green was hard put to keep a smile off his own. Returning to more neutral ground, he spent ten minutes trying to trace Jonathan's movements on the three days before his death. He learned that Marianne Blair knew very little about her son's daily life, a discovery which distressed her but did not surprise him. How much had he let his own mother know about his activities in the years before she died?

Afterwards, Weiss showed him upstairs so that he could search Jonathan's room. It took little time. The small room contained nothing but a single bed, dresser, desk, computer and shelves and shelves of books. His closet held a modest collection of conservative but expensive leisure clothes, as well as two dress suits and a Harris tweed sports coat. His desk was crammed with notes, articles and papers, but there was no diary, address book or appointment calendar to shed light on his activities. If Jonathan Blair kept any personal records, he kept them elsewhere.

On the desk lay a computer printout of a complex statistical analysis which Jonathan had obviously been studying. Red underlinings and asterisks peppered the pages. Was this what Jonathan had been working on the night before his death, when he had come down to his mother, upset and wanting to talk? Green examined the printout curiously but could make little sense of it. He had been forced to confront statistics for his forensic science course at the police academy as well as his masters thesis in criminology, but he had avoided them when possible ever since.

He was puzzled, however, by the array of numbers on the desk of an English literature student, and became even more so when he turned to the books on the shelves. He expected Chaucer, Dickens and an entire shelf of Shakespearean plays.

Instead, he found formidable tomes on disorders of the limbic system and the neuropsychology of memory. Suddenly he remembered Marianne Blair's use of the word 'lab' and cursed himself for failing to pick up on it. In the excitement of Sullivan's tale earlier, they had both made the leap from the place where Jonathan was stabbed to the subject matter he was studying. A rookie's error in logic, which neither should have made.

Pulling out the nearest book on the brain, he headed back downstairs and found Marianne Blair on the phone in the living room, looking all business.

"What was Jonathan working on at the university?"

Startled, she swung on him and pressed her hand over the receiver. "He was doing his Masters in cognitive neuroscience, conducting research on auditory channels in the brain."

"Does he have an office at the university?"

"A lab. At least he has a desk, computer and files somewhere. I've never been there."

"Did he have an associate? Was he working with anyone?"

"Oh yes. There's a whole group of graduate students, most of whom are on the list I gave you. They're all working under Dr. Myles Halton."

There was respect in her voice as she uttered the name, as if her accomplishments were nothing compared to his.

Green had never heard of him. "Is that supposed to mean something?"

"To a neuropsychologist, yes. He's one of the up-and-coming experts on language and the brain. Students from all over Canada, even the world, would sell their souls for the chance to work with him."

* * *

The ten detectives from the Major Crimes Squad had been waiting for half an hour by the time Green barrelled through the door of the conference room. Sullivan had installed them in the unrenovated briefing room walled in blackboards and cork, for which Green secretly thanked him. How he hated the high-tech flash that passed for progress in modern meetings. More time was wasted fiddling with control buttons than it took to fill an entire chalkboard with facts.

Sullivan had used the waiting time to brief them on the background of the case and to pin sketches and photographs of the scene to the cork board on the wall. It took Green an additional ten minutes to report on his visit to the Blair house.

"You are to keep the procedural screw-ups strictly to yourselves," he admonished in the most inspectorish tone he could muster. "I've looked at the case, and I don't think the crime scene would have told us a hell of a lot more anyway. Jonathan Blair was a quiet, law-abiding kid with no priors, not even a speeding ticket. There aren't any obvious motives for his murder, and we certainly have no ready suspects. But we've got more than enough leads to follow. As the facts stand now, and ruling out robbery and psychos, there are three possible motives. The first two, given the age of the victim, are predictable."

Green turned to the blackboard and wrote a word in block letters. "Drugs. Was a deal going down in that remote section of the library? Jonathan Blair had no wallet in his possession. No money was found at the scene. But Ident has vacuumed every inch of the carpet in the vicinity, and if some drugs spilled, they'll find them. The forensic pathologist is working on Blair's body now, and he'll tell us if Blair was a user. Meanwhile, we use our standard investigative techniques. Ask his associates, check his bank accounts."

He jotted the words "forensics, autopsy, interviews, bank" under "Drugs" and moved over to write a new column. "Passion. Blair attracted girls. His mother says there was a recent break-up; check into it, check into jilted lovers and jealous rivals. According to his mother, Jonathan never got angry and never treated people badly, a rose-tinted view of her boy. Let's find out the truth. He was twenty-four years old, single, rich and handsome. There's got to be some skeletons."

Green studied the men around the conference table. He had worked with most of them in the fourteen years he had been solving major crimes. Jules was no fool. He had given Green the ten best officers on the Squad. Sometimes when Green took a personal interest in a case, he ended up doing much of the field work himself because he doubted the competence of anyone else. It didn't make him popular with the staff sergeant who managed the squad or with the brass, who liked their pigeon holes, but it felt good to be on the streets again.

The men before him were all solid, experienced investigators who needed little direction, but Deputy Chief Lynch's personal interest added an extra twist. Thoughtfully Green turned to the third column on the blackboard and wrote "Innocent Bystander", debating how much to let his own disdain and suspicion show through.

"That's the third motive in this case, the one that Lynch believes most likely. Jonathan Blair may be dead simply because he was in the wrong place at the wrong time, standing in the medieval literature section of the university library while a heavy drug deal went down. Or while some freshman got mugged for his bus money."

There was a cautious ripple of laughter. The detectives generally shared Green's view of the top brass, but they never knew who the spies might be.

Green shrugged, deadpan. "It *is* possible. So check it out, get the help of university security, ask the drug squad, poke around to see if anyone saw anything suspicious last night."

Green dusted chalk dust off his hands and stepped away from the board. "That's it. I don't have any idea which motive is right. Maybe it's something else entirely. I don't think it was robbery, but his wallet was missing, so ask his friends how much money he usually carried around with him. I also don't think it was a psycho. Too clean. So we have five things we need to do." Green picked up the chalk again. "One team— Watts and Charbonneau—you search for possible witnesses to the crime. I know the guys last night did a routine canvass of people who were at the library, but I want us to do it again. Set up a hotline and advertise it on the radio stations and in the newspapers, on the University's PA system. Another thing you can do is check the computer records of books taken out or returned on the evening of June 9, especially with call numbers from the fourth floor."

Watts and Charbonneau exchanged grimaces. It was like looking for a needle in a haystack. Lots of work and very little payoff.

"The second team—Jackson and Laplante—find out all you can about the victim, including his friends and his recent movements." Green paused as a small inconsistency niggled into his thoughts. "Blair was studying neuropsychology, which is on the fifth floor of the library. He was killed on the fourth, plus he was killed in a remote corner, not a place you'd usually pass going from one part of the library to another. Find out what he was doing in the literature section.

"The third team—Gibbs and O'Neil—get the autopsy and forensic results, bug them until every last detail is in, and follow up any lead they give. If there are none, help Watts and

Charbonneau. Don't bug me for every little thing. You guys know your job, but if anybody gets a major break, radio me ASAP."

He paused a moment, scanning the scribbling on the board. "The fourth team is to conduct a search of Blair's university lab and interview all his professors, fellow students and associates who aren't on Jackson's list. That's a big job. Goodwin, you better work with Perchesky and Proulx on it." He grinned at the last remaining detective unassigned. "Brian, you're coming with me."

"And what are we doing?"

"We're going to start with the woman who discovered the crime."

*   *   *

Carrie MacDonald had been given the day off to recover from the shock, but it didn't seem to Green that she needed it. She had just washed her hair, and it was piled high on her head in a pink towel when she greeted the two detectives at her door. Her blue terry cloth robe gaped slightly over her breasts, and her cheeks were pink from the shower. Her eyes lit up at the sight of Sullivan.

"Hi, Sergeant! Are you on duty again?"

"Still," he muttered.

"You'll need some coffee, then." She stepped back to allow them to squeeze past her into the narrow hall. "I sure need it. Boy, what a night we had!"

Green bristled. Carrie MacDonald seemed to have overlooked him completely as she turned to lead them down the dimly lit hall. Sullivan was five inches taller and fifty pounds heavier than he was. He looked like a cop, and people responded instinctively to his authority. His ruggedness appealed to women, evoking some primal suppliant need in them, but all this was wasted on him. Sullivan had loved his wife since he was sixteen and seemed impervious to the fire in other women's eyes.

Green, on the other hand, drifted through a crowd unobserved. His boyish freckled face evoked nothing except the occasional urge to mother him. At times it was an advantage, when he wanted to be unnoticed or underestimated, but there were times when it was a curse.

"I'm Inspector Green," he said sharply at her retreating back. "I'm in charge of the investigation."

"Oh!" She turned her blue eyes on him in surprise. "Sorry, I thought you were..." She let her dismissal of him go unvoiced and gestured him into her kitchen. Standing on tiptoe, she rummaged in her cupboard for two mismatched mugs, one with the university crest and the other featuring the slogan "World's Greatest Mom". She poured two coffees, then pulled her robe over her breasts self-consciously.

"Do you guys mind if I get some clothes on? I'll be two minutes."

True to her word, she emerged two minutes later, barefoot but clad in blue jeans and black t-shirt. Her hair tumbled damp and honeyed down her back, swinging as she prepared her own cup.

Joining them at the table she smiled. "How can I help you guys today?"

Her frank smile and the honey hair falling over one eye unnerved him. Control was essential during an interview, and this one was starting off all wrong. To regroup, he dropped his gaze to his notebook and riffled the pages officiously. Normally, he would have let Sullivan take the notes, but this time he sensed he was going to need the prop. "I'd like to review the information you gave Sergeant Sullivan last night, and see if there's anything else you've remembered since."

Dutifully, she related the events leading up to her discovery of the body. By the time she had finished, Green felt back in full control.

"Did you see anything out of the ordinary? Hear anything? Any voices? Signs of a struggle? Any items on the floor—money, a wallet?"

Her eyes were grave as she searched her recollections. She's no fool, Green thought. Sexy, but sharp. She knows what she saw, and she'll be good on the witness stand.

"It's strange, actually," she said, "that I didn't notice anything. I mean, how does a guy get stabbed only a hundred feet away in a deserted room and you don't hear a thing? Of course, my cart squeaked—I was meaning to fix it—so I only heard the guy groaning once I stopped my cart to get this book."

"How long was it from the time you left the elevators till you found the victim?"

"Only two or three minutes. I had only returned half a dozen books."

Green studied the diagram he had constructed. The bank of elevators in the centre was the only exit route from the fourth floor except for the fire stairs at each far corner. It would have been impossible to get into an elevator without being seen by Carrie MacDonald as she sorted books. The paramedics and other medical personnel estimated from the nature of the wound and the amount of blood lost that Blair was stabbed no more than half an hour before the paramedics arrived. If the information in the logs could be trusted, the paramedics arrived on the scene twelve minutes after the 911 call. Allowing a few minutes for university security to relay the call, that meant Blair was stabbed less than fifteen minutes before she found him. Probably a lot less.

To escape, the killer had three options. He could have taken the stairs, in which case he would have escaped unnoticed. He could have walked directly past Carrie and got on the elevator, which meant that he had to wait for it in plain view of her, covered in blood from his shirt sleeves to his shoes. Or he could have hidden in one of the side aisles until she set off with her cart and then slipped to the elevator. It was a mere two or three minutes before Carrie discovered the victim and returned to make the call.

"Did you see anyone around when you called security?"

"Just one student waiting at the elevator. I yelled at him to go meet the ambulance, but he was so freaked, he pulled the fire alarm instead."

Green's antennae quivered. "Can you give me a description of this student?"

She searched her thoughts, chewing her lip. "It happened so fast, and…I was so shaken up. Things are just a blur. All I remember is thick dark hair and a red top. Plaid, I think."

"You said 'he'. What makes you sure it was a male?"

"He was kind of tall. And there was something about his face…" She shut her eyes, remembering. "I think he had a mustache. Yes, a big, dark mustache."

Green leaned forward, willing her to focus. "Did you notice anything unusual about him? Was he breathing hard? Seem scared? Did you see anything on him that could have been blood?"

She was shaking her head firmly. "He looked more…bewildered than anything else."

"Did you actually see him pull the fire alarm?"

"No, but it's right by the elevator."

Green turned to Sullivan. "Did you get a lead on him, Brian? Did the rescue guys get a name?"

"I haven't checked with them yet. I ran out of time."

Green tossed his notebook down. "What? Call over there and tell them to find him right away!"

"Watts and Charbonneau will be—"

"They'll think you did it! Who the hell wouldn't follow up a potential suspect and one of the two witnesses in the case?"

Sullivan flushed red. Pushing away his cup, he glanced at Carrie. "Is there a phone I can use?"

Her eyes were sympathetic as she smiled at him. "In the bedroom. Just ignore the mess."

With a twinge of guilt, Green watched Sullivan stalk across the room and bang the door shut behind him. When he turned his attention back to Carrie MacDonald, he found her eyes on him appraisingly. There was no sympathy in them now, and he felt his annoyance return.

"Hard taskmaster, aren't you, Inspector?"

"I expect competence from my men," he said. "Especially him."

"He was very competent last night, I assure you. But by now I'd say he's been without sleep for quite a while."

"He should be used to that," he replied, his eyes on his notes. Her level tone, and his own resentment, unsettled him.

"Most of us are a long way from perfect, Inspector."

"A man has died, and we not only have to find out who did it, but we have to prove it in court, so mistakes are not an option. Now, can we get on with this?"

Chastened, she got up to pour herself another cup of coffee, which gave him time to chastise himself. Jealousy, professional or personal, had no place in police work. By the time she returned to the table, eyes averted, he felt he was back on track.

"Okay, let's go back to the few minutes when you were sorting books by the elevator, just before you left with the cart. Can you remember who came to the elevator?"

She searched her memory for a long moment, shaking her head. Just as he was about to intervene, she held up her hand. "Give me a minute." She sat back in her chair, folded her hands in her lap and shut her eyes. She remained immobile, breathing deeply. Without her gaze to unsettle him, he allowed himself to study her. There was a peace and control in her expression that surprised him. An unusual woman, he thought, full of unexpected twists. He found himself looking at her chest as she breathed, watching it swell as she inhaled, stretching the black T-shirt. He felt himself stir in response and hastened to return to his notes. Not that he was upset by his response, which was familiar and harmless, only by the scattering of his thoughts, which he could not afford yet again. He was still trying to collect them when she resumed.

"Only one man stands out in my mind. He was the last one to take the elevator before I began shelving." She remained with her eyes shut, scanning.

Green hoped his voice was neutral. "Describe him."

"He was gross. Huge and fat. He wheezed as he waited. At least 275 and six-foot-two. He reminded me of John Candy— you know, the movie star?—but his hair was lighter brown, and he had a silly little mustache. He was into leather, but if he was hoping to score points with it, no woman in her right mind— Oh!" Her eyes flew open, intensely blue. "There was a woman too! Dashed in at the last second. She seemed kind of worried, like she was looking for someone."

"Any physical details?"

"Kind of hard looking. Blonde, but out of a bottle and with one too many perms. Bony face. Full of angles. It's hard to describe people in words." For the first time, she smiled at him, her eyes crinkling and two dimples framing her cheeks. His lustful thoughts took wing again. "I could draw them if you like."

"You draw?"

"One of my many talents, Inspector. I've always doodled, and sometimes the hours at the library are long and boring. I draw sketches of the people I see, just for fun. In fact, I drew a picture of Jonathan Blair last week."

He stared at her. "You're kidding!"

She jumped to her feet. "I'll show it to you. I look for special faces, unique expressions..."

She skipped out of the room, and Green found himself looking around for clues to her many facets. The apartment was small and crammed with cheap furniture. In the corner of the room stood a ten-speed and a child's bike. Bunched into the cushions of the sagging sofa was a young girl's jacket, and a pair of children's rain boots stood by the door. Stacks of notes, books and old newspapers covered most of the surfaces. A busy woman, he thought, full of curiosity and ideas, but not enough hours in the day for them all.

She emerged from the other room holding up a sketchpad in triumph. He was struck by how vividly blue her eyes were. It was an effort to force his down onto the paper she held. Then he received a second surprise. Jonathan Blair gazed out at him from the sketch, sad and contemplative. His face, partly cast in shadow, was breathtakingly handsome. The drawing was brilliant.

"Was he really this handsome?"

Reverence glinted in her eyes as she studied the picture. "Yes, he was. Thick dark hair and blue eyes you could die in. That's why I noticed him. He was reading this journal article and taking notes, just like any other student on the floor. But then he set down his pen, rested his chin on his hand and stared into space. There was such profound despair on his face! Like he had the weight of the world on his shoulders. He stayed that way for the entire fifteen minutes it took me to draw him."

"Had you seen him before or since?"

"I had, in fact. He was a regular, and once you see that face you never forget it."

"Ever talk to him?"

She smiled and shook her head, suddenly sheepish. "No, I keep my fantasies to myself. The last thing I need is a man in my life."

I don't know about that, he found himself thinking and pulled himself firmly back on track. "Ever see anyone with him?"

"A few times he had a girl with him. Hung all over him. She was gorgeous, too."

Green's pulse quickened. "Describe her."

"Mediterranean-looking. Maybe Arab or even a light-skinned Indian. Thick, wavy black hair that framed her face like a halo. Large black eyes, long-lashed. That satiny milk chocolate skin that doesn't have a flaw in it."

"I can tell you hardly gave her a second glance."

She laughed. "You're much nicer when you're human, Inspector. I can draw her for you too."

He felt himself flush. "Could you? I'm serious. These are important witnesses. Could you draw all four? The guy who pulled the fire alarm too?"

"No problem. I've got the day off and my daughter's not back from school till three-thirty. I can have them ready for you by tonight."

He knew there was no further reason to stay. Not with a

dozen leads to follow up and his report to Weiss already two hours overdue. He was reluctantly closing his notebook when the bedroom door yanked open and Sullivan emerged, tight-lipped and grim.

"Mike, you're not going to believe this. Another problem. No one in the rescue crew remembers even seeing a kid in a red plaid shirt!"

Three

"I talked to the paramedics, the firemen and the rookie patrolman who took the call," Sullivan reported. "No one remembers a student coming to meet them."

Green leaned against the wall outside Carrie MacDonald's apartment, shaking his head. The warm flush of a moment ago had vanished. "I don't believe this is happening. A potential eyewitness, maybe even a suspect, and he slips through our fingers. Didn't you seal off the building?"

Sullivan inspected a spot on the far wall, and for a moment Green thought he wasn't going to answer. When he did, his voice was tight. "Of course we sealed off the building. But the student would have been long gone before that, in the madhouse created by the fire alarm."

"Which is why he pulled it in the first place, Dummkopf! This is probably our guy!"

On the way back to the police station, Green suffered through ten minutes of stony silence and screeching tires before he finally sighed.

"Brian, I'm sorry I called you a Dummkopf. We can't let this case get to us. We've got to pull together."

"You also humiliated me in front of a witness."

"I know. I was wrong."

Sullivan stopped at a red light, and Green saw him gradually deflate. "Yeah, but you were also right. I should have

41

followed up on that student right away."

"You should have. But then you would have just had one more failure to report to me." They exchanged glances and laughed. "It's good we can joke about it. Let's hope the other guys are luckier."

Back at the station they dodged cameramen and crime reporters as they made their way to the second floor. The death of Jonathan Blair was no longer a secret; it had become front page news. Shutting the door to his little alcove office, Green seized his radio even before he sat down.

"Now to get the reports from the troops," he muttered as he called. Two minutes later, Detective Jackson responded to his page. Traffic roared in the background.

"Have you come across a guy with thick black hair and a big mustache?" Green asked.

"Mustache? No."

"Keep looking, it's important. How about a gorgeous dark-haired woman?"

"Not yet. But I'll be glad to start looking for her."

"Ask Blair's friends if they know her. Arab-looking, wavy hair, big eyes. If you find her, call me."

"Will do."

"Got anything useful yet?"

In the background, Green heard a car engine roar, and Jackson raised his voice over it. "Lots of background, no leads. Everybody's in shock, can't believe somebody would do that to such a nice kid, that sort of stuff. Nobody knows any enemies."

"Seen the ex-girlfriend?"

"Vanessa Weeks? She wasn't at her office. Do you want us to go out to her home?"

"No," Green said impulsively. "Give the address to me."

When he hung up, he swung on Sullivan. "Passion—that's what I'm betting on. A handsome guy and too many women. I've got to check this one out myself."

Sullivan was halfway out of his seat. "What do you want me to do?"

"Stay put so you can field the calls. Get a media plea out on the dark-haired student in the red shirt. Then man the radio and get progress reports from everyone. I'll be back in an hour."

* * *

The young woman who answered the door after almost three minutes was neither dark-haired nor gorgeous, at least in her present state. Vanessa Weeks' face was puffed and blotchy, her eyes webbed in red. Oily blonde hair straggled across her forehead and down her neck. She clutched a cotton dressing gown around her with one hand and pressed a kleenex to her eyes with the other.

Oh God, Green thought. Tears.

He followed her into a small studio apartment strewn with papers, dirty dishes and cast-off clothing. The building was not air-conditioned, and the steamy air smelled faintly of sweat. Beyond the mess, the room was sparse, with no pictures or other personal mementos to warm it up. No portraits of doting parents or goofy siblings. A girl without a past, or at least without one she cared about.

"I thought you'd probably come," she managed as she folded her tall, willowy frame amid the sofa cushions with a sob. "None of his friends has even called me. It's as if I don't exist any more. As if, just because we broke up, I don't have feelings any more."

Green debated how to proceed. The woman clearly needed

to talk, and he had no idea what might be important. Experience had taught him that letting witnesses ramble often yielded unexpected dividends. He set his tape recorder on the table and eased back casually into an armchair opposite her.

"Tell me about you and him."

Her eyes filled again. With a grimace, she leaned over and made a half-hearted attempt to pick some papers from the floor. "I wish I could. I don't know what happened to Jonathan and me. I thought he loved me—he said he did—but then he started giving all these excuses about working late and being busy. Usually I helped him with his work, but this time he wouldn't tell me what he was working on. Then a couple of times when he'd said he was working, I saw him with another woman."

"When was that?"

"It started about a month ago. Jonathan and I had a big fight over it, and he said I had to trust him. But I'm not a fool. I can't compete with a woman like that."

"Do you know who she was?"

Her mouth quivered. "Raquel Haddad."

Haddad, he thought. Lebanese name. "Jet black wavy hair, olive skin?"

She glanced up in surprise. "You've seen her?"

He shrugged, non-committal. "Who is she?"

She lowered her eyes and twisted the kleenex around her finger like a noose. "An undergraduate troller. She hung around our floor, looking for prey. She started with another guy but quickly moved on to more promising prospects. At first Jonathan denied she was even in the picture. Then he said she was just a research assistant. Yeah, right."

"You didn't believe him?"

"She was all over him." The noose tightened, then she

released it with a small gasp. "I...I don't mean he lied." She pressed her hand to her forehead and took deep breaths, striving for composure. "It was just his way of letting me down easy. Jonathan hates to hurt anybody. But sometimes being wishy-washy hurts more than an honest yes."

"How did he seem recently? Anything different? Was he troubled?"

"He felt bad about me, I could tell. He avoided me at the university. He'd leave the room if I came in or pretend he was engrossed in a book. Jonathan was never very extroverted, but he seemed quieter than before."

"Sad?"

She put the shredded kleenex aside and smoothed her bathrobe, in control again. "You know—" She raised her eyes thoughtfully "—sometimes he did look a little sad. I thought maybe she was giving him a rocky ride. She looked a little too...hot-blooded for his temperament."

"Did you notice anything different between him and his friends or classmates?"

"He didn't hang out with them as much as before. He seemed buried in his work. They made snide little comments like 'Blair thinks he's going to find a way to make cats talk'."

"That sounds jealous. Were others jealous of him?"

"Jonathan had no airs. He was handsome and brilliant, but he was also modest and unassuming. I think some guys were even jealous of that. They'd like him to be an arrogant creep, so they could put him down without feeling guilty."

"Are you saying jealousy was a major problem?"

"Jealousy is always a problem in the academic world, Detective. That's one of the first things my father warned me about." She smiled wryly. "But then, my father would say jealousy makes a good incentive."

Or a good motive for murder, he thought to himself, but did not say it. He wanted to keep her soft and pliable. "Any particular person more jealous than the rest?"

Suddenly, she unfolded herself from the sofa and drew herself up to her full height, careful to arrange her dressing gown. "I'm sorry, do you want a cold drink? I didn't realize this would take so long. I should fix myself up a bit."

Gone was the moment for pliability. She glided into the kitchen, head high and back straight. Unlike the living room, the kitchen was spare but spotless, every pot neatly stacked on the shelf. She plucked some items from the fridge, tossed them into the blender, and disappeared, giving Green a chance to snoop. He could tell a lot about a person by the way they arranged their kitchen. In his own home, three half-empty boxes of Cheerios and a lidless ketchup bottle were likely to fall on your head when you opened a cupboard door, but there was no such danger here. There certainly wasn't much money either, but the neat, organized inhabitant was making the most of it. The kitchen table doubled as a desk, and a painted bookshelf held cans and boxes neatly arranged by type. The food was simple and utilitarian—no spices or exotic grains.

Green revised his initial impression of Jonathan's ex-girlfriend. The mess in the living room was superficial, created in a day of shock and grief. Marianne Blair was right; Vanessa Weeks was very much her own woman, practical, organized and used to being in control. True to this insight, she returned a minute later dressed in shorts and a pink T-shirt over a lean, muscular body. Her hair was combed back into a pony tail and her face was freshly scrubbed. He could see now that she was pretty in a wholesome way. She flipped off the blender.

"Joe Difalco," she replied as if the conversation hadn't been interrupted. "Joe hates his guts, and it's pure, simple jealousy.

Joe thinks he's God's gift to women, but he's just a swaggering Latin pig. He's supposed to be Professor Halton's golden boy, but people went to Jonathan when they needed brains. Joe grew up in a sixteen-room mansion in Cedarhill, and his daddy owns five cars, including a Lamborghini, but Jonathan gets invited to 24 Sussex Drive. Joe thinks the world is at his feet because his parents always told him it was, but it was really at Jonathan's feet."

"You don't like this guy much, do you?"

To her credit, she managed a laugh. "When you hold Joe and Jonathan up together, there's no comparison. If someone had to die…" Her voice trailed off as she busied herself setting out glasses. He tried to imagine mentally how yogurt, carrots, club soda and wheat germ would taste.

"Did you ever hear Joe threaten Jonathan or act as if he wanted to harm him?"

"No. Joe's strategy was to pretend Jonathan didn't exist. Joe is a doctoral student in the final stages of his dissertation. He's one of Halton's most senior students. Jonathan's a lowly Masters student. Final year, so higher than me, who's just beginning, but I'm not sure Professor Halton would even have noticed him if his mother wasn't made of money. Jonathan presented a threat, but more for his potential than his present status."

"Does Joe have a temper? Ever seen him angry?"

"I'm sure he does. He can be very intense. Wound up like a spring, impatient, restless." She poured a yellow sludge into each glass. "It suggests inadequate cortical control of the limbic system."

He skirted the editorializing deftly as he took his glass from her. "What does this guy look like?"

"Good-looking, I suppose, if you like the Mediterranean look. Dark, curly hair, big brown eyes. Compact but muscular.

47

I'd say he does weights."

"Mustache?"

She shuddered. "No, at least not that."

"Do you think he is capable of murder?"

"Absolutely."

They returned to the living room and, as casually as he could, he set his drink on the floor by his side, out of sight. Over the next half hour, he probed her knowledge of the routine details of Jonathan Blair's life. Blair enjoyed cycling, boating and skiing, but in recent months had done little but his research.

"Did he enjoy a good read?" Green asked casually. "The classics, for example?"

Her brow furrowed in confusion.

"He was in the literature section."

"Oh." Her brow cleared. "He read constantly, yes, and he did enjoy mysteries as an escape."

Mysteries were hardly Shakespeare, Green observed privately, but he left the topic to probe her views closer to the case, unearthing little of interest. She could think of no one else with the remotest reason for wanting him dead and no situation that might put him in danger.

"He studied the brains of cats, for heaven's sake!" she exclaimed. "Most of his days were spent in the animal room, the EEG lab, or at his computer. He didn't even help to teach a course. So there isn't even the motive of a student driven berserk by a poor mark."

"What did he do with the cats?"

"You don't really want to know." She eyed him balefully. "He drilled holes in their heads and inserted probes to stimulate electrical activity in the hippocampal region. Which is part of the limbic system and crucial for new memory." Seeing his blank look, she waved an impatient hand. "He trains his cats on different listening tasks and measures brain responses."

Green winced. "I get the picture. What about the anti-vivisectionists? That's a pretty fanatical bunch. Did he receive any threats or complaints from them?"

She rolled her eyes. "That's clutching at straws, I'd say. He never mentioned complaints."

"Well, I am clutching at straws," he replied, allowing a plaintive edge in his voice. Appeal to her maternal side; he'd often found that worked with women. "I don't have any real motives for murder here, and everyone I talk to describes him as Mr. Perfect."

"Well, if I were you, I'd check into the dark-haired bitch he's had on his arm for the past two months. Raquel's Arabic, and you know how protective those guys can be about their women."

As a Jew, Green had a finely tuned radar for prejudice and was no longer surprised when it cropped up in the most unexpected places. In some ways, the subtle bigotry of the educated white elite was more deadly than the crude ignorance of the streets. Vanessa Weeks probably didn't even think of her remark as racist, merely factual. But prejudice aside, in this case she had a point, he realized, particularly when he considered the murder weapon MacPhail had described. An eight-inch, smooth-bladed knife. If folklore was to be believed, the weapon of choice among Arab desert tribes.

He excused himself and slipped into the hall to call the station. He reached Sullivan at his own phone.

"Any breaks yet?"

"The guys are collecting a lot of stuff, Mike, but we don't have a clear-cut motive or an obvious suspect yet. No sign of our mystery student in the plaid shirt. Paquette has come up empty on the fingerprint analysis so far. MacPhail says the body has no defensive wounds on it, so Blair didn't try to block the blow. Looks like he was taken by surprise. "

"That suggests somebody smooth and quick with a knife."

"Ruthless, too. The guy couldn't afford to hesitate."

"Did MacPhail speculate on how much strength it would take? Could it have been a woman?"

"It was a hell of a sharp knife. Double edge and pointed tip. A woman could slip it in without trouble."

"Have the guys got anything on the dark-haired girlfriend yet? Her name's Raquel Haddad."

"Yup. Jackson's already heading out to her home as we speak."

*   *   *

The University of Ottawa was scattered through the aging downtown district of Sandy Hill, once the elegant home of the lumber barons, entrepreneurs and founding politicians of the fledgling town. Some of the stately mansions of a hundred years ago were now embassies, but many had been subdivided into cheap tenements filled with immigrants and the transient poor. Green dodged swaddled Somali women pushing strollers as well as the usual throngs of scruffy students as he raced to the university administration building to track down Raquel Haddad before Jackson did. He was fuming. Jackson was supposed to contact him, not blunder off after sensitive witnesses on his own.

Green was glad he knew every pothole and stop sign in the neighbourhood, for he had been born in a dilapidated little house a mere mile away in Lowertown, on the working class side of Rideau Street. After his first brief, but expensive foray into marriage and home-ownership, which had scared him off both for years, he had moved back to the inner city to a run-down brick low-rise in Sandy Hill. He had always referred to it, rather proudly, as "the dump". With each promotion and pay raise, he kept intending to move into larger, sleeker, more modern quarters but always found himself reluctant to part with it. It was in the heart of his daily life, a short drive from the police station, Nate's Delicatessen and his father, who now lived in a seniors' apartment just off Rideau Street.

Green's apartment was cramped and drafty; it had no balcony, only one bedroom, creaky floors, balky plumbing and a shower that never stopped dripping. There was no room large enough for the spectacular, four-speaker sound system he wanted to buy so that he could blast the great rock classics from the four corners of the room. His mother had come from a musical family in Warsaw, before they all perished in Treblinka, and while he was growing up, she had supplemented his father's assistant shipper's salary by giving piano lessons. The children had been excruciating, but his mother's fingers could make the dullest Bach *étude* come alive. His taste ran to a more raucous sound than hers, but even now, fifteen years after her death, music still brought her back to him.

But musical yearnings aside, a single man could live in the "dump" quite nicely, as long as he wasn't picky. Three, however, was a definite crowd. When Sharon had given up her modern high-rise apartment to move in with him, both had understood the accommodations would be temporary. She had grown up in a sprawling suburban bungalow, and she did not share his attachment to noise, car fumes and crumbling corner stores. She had been a good sport, but the arrival of the baby, which had ousted his favourite green lazee-boy from the living room corner to accommodate the crib, had given the matter a new urgency.

Under the guidance of Mary, Brian Sullivan's wife, they had looked at half a dozen houses in the price range they could afford, which wasn't high, because in addition to child support for a daughter he barely knew, Green paid almost all his father's expenses at the seniors' home. But the houses Mary had found had been soulless chunks of vinyl and particle board; none had felt like homes to him.

This was home, he thought, as his car wove in and out between parked cars and potholes on the back streets of Sandy Hill. He covered the six blocks to the administration building with his accelerator foot to the floor. For once he appreciated the spritely little blue Corolla Sharon had insisted he buy last winter. At the time he'd considered it an alien yuppie affectation, but his rusty yellow Pony had been twelve years old by the time Tony was born, and Sharon had refused to allow the baby anywhere near it.

His first impulse had been to buy a Suzuki Swift, which was one step above a moped and the cheapest, most anti-inspectorish vehicle he could find, or, as a concession to his incipient midlife crisis, a used Mustang convertible. But Sharon was pushing for a mini-van. The Corolla was her bottom line, and given that choice, Green considered himself lucky. He'd parted with his Pony reluctantly because, like his apartment, it had sentimental value, but as the Corolla leaped in response to the gas, he realized how loathe he'd been to admit that everything, including himself, was growing old.

His old Pony would have been smoking by the time he pulled into the parking lot of the University of Ottawa administration building. He parked the Corolla in a spot marked "Dean of Arts", slapped a police sticker in his window and headed for the records department. The mention of murder and Professor Myles Halton sent the chief records clerk scurrying for the confidential file on Raquel Haddad.

Raquel was twenty-two, born in Beirut to a Lebanese physician, but she was listed as living with her uncle Pierre Haddad, a Canadian citizen with a local Loretta Street Address. Green jotted it down, then scanned the rest of her file. She appeared to be in the fourth year of an Honours Biology program with a heavy emphasis on physiology, anatomy and biochemistry. Something Vanessa Weeks had said came to mind. Jonathan had told her Raquel was only a research assistant. Did senior Honours students help Masters students with their research?

A visit to the eminent Dr. Myles Halton was certainly in order, but first he had to check out Pierre Haddad. The Loretta Street address proved to be a corner convenience store on the fringe of Little Italy. The front door sagged and the "L" and "Y" on the sign "Loretta Confectionery" had peeled off. Another victim of big box stores, Green thought as he pushed the door open with a screech of rusty hinges and entered a room full of dark, half-empty shelves. No wonder business was bad. Mr. Haddad needed some pointers in presentation.

In response to the screech, a curtain parted at the back of the store and a man emerged. Early forties, swarthy and prematurely gone to fat. He rolled down the aisle to the cash.

"Pierre Haddad?"

The man scowled, drawing his heavy black brows over his eyes. Green produced his badge and kept his voice soothing. Experience had taught him that people from violence-plagued countries were easily alarmed. "I'm Inspector Green of the Ottawa Police. As you probably know, a student at the University of Ottawa named Jonathan Blair was murdered last night. I'm told that Raquel Haddad was one of his research assistants. We are asking everyone who knew him if they know anything that might help us. Raquel listed you as next of kin, and this as her address. I wonder if I could speak to her."

Haddad had betrayed nothing during the entire speech, no doubt a habit learned on the streets of Beirut. But once Green had finished, he arranged an expression of dismay on his face.

"Murdered! No, I did not know that. How terrible."

A foolish error, Green thought; he had passed the newspapers stacked for sale by the door. The news was blazoned across the front in large bold print.

Green let the lie pass. "Yes, it's terrible, and we need all the help we can get. She's your niece, I understand? Living here with you?"

"She is the daughter of my brother in Beirut. But we don't live here. This is my business."

"Did she ever talk about someone named Jonathan Blair?"

He shook his head, then smiled and became effusive. "My brother sent her over here to be safer with me, but Canadian girls, they have much more freedom than Lebanese girls. She doesn't like to talk to me about her school. I try to take care of her—keep an eye, you know, but not too much. I know she studies science, but I don't know who are her friends."

Green knew it was ludicrous to think Haddad knew little of his niece's university life. Mediterranean families brought their traditional values and their protectiveness with them, and it took several generations to wash out. Raquel might have refused to tell him anything, but he would have found out anyway.

But it was not yet time to get tough. "Can you give me the address where I can find her?"

Haddad sighed. "This is too bad, because I just put Raquel on the plane back to Beirut yesterday. Her school was finished, and she had been looking forward to going home."

Green's thoughts raced. The trip to Beirut could easily be verified through the airline records, but he suspected Haddad was not lying. Raquel had suddenly flown halfway around the world to a country where it would be almost impossible to find her. The question was why? And how much did Haddad know behind his impenetrable smile?

Green jotted down the Beirut address Haddad gave him and dashed back to his car to use his cell phone. A quick call confirmed that Raquel had been on the eight p.m. flight from Ottawa to New York the night before. It was interesting, though, that the flight for the long-awaited visit home had been booked only two hours before.

Four

Green arrived back at his office six minutes later, his colour high with excitement.

"We're on the scent! I can feel it!"

Sullivan looked up from Green's desk with relief. His eyes were half-shut with fatigue, and he stretched noisily to get the stiffness out of his joints. "Jeez, Mike, I should be the inspector and you should be the field man. I thought you said you'd be back in an hour. I've been manning the fort for two and a half hours. This Peter Weiss creep has called three times. Jules is circling. There's so much stuff coming in, I can't keep up. So I set a progress meeting for three-thirty. I hope that's okay."

Green glanced at his watch. It gave him barely half an hour, but the meeting was timely. He needed to get an overview of the findings and then focus the investigation to follow the leads he had uncovered.

"That's good. Anything on the student in the red plaid shirt?"

Sullivan shook his head. "But your wife called. She wants you to call, because she's got the long night shift tonight."

He frowned as he calculated his time. Sharon worked as a psychiatric nurse on an inpatient ward at the Royal Ottawa Hospital. The long night shift meant seven p.m. to seven a.m., which gave him barely three hours before he had to be home.

To encourage father-son bonding, and to help them save money for a house, he had agreed to babysit in the evenings and nights if Sharon had to work shift, and they would only pay a sitter if both were working days. But things kept getting in the way, and the old excuses were wearing thin.

"Did you tell her I was on the Jonathan Blair case?"

"I told her you'd call."

Even he wants me to grow up, Green thought with a sigh. He picked up the phone and could tell from Sharon's irritated croak that he had woken her. Oh no, Tony's nap time. When she worked the night shift, she caught sleep whenever she could. How different from four years ago, when he'd first walked onto her ward to investigate the death of a psychologist. He could still remember how her warmth and humour had taken his breath away.

"Will you be home, Mike?"

"Is Mrs. Louks available?" The elderly widow across the hall rarely went out and had often rescued him from a child care crisis.

"I'm sure she is, but I thought Tony might enjoy your company. It's such a rarity."

He winced. "I'll try to get there."

"Try?"

He suppressed a flash of irritation. There was nothing he hated more than being on the moral low ground. "I tell you what. I promise I'll do my best, and if you have to, take him to Mrs. Louks and I'll pick him up as soon as I can."

He felt Sullivan's disapproving eyes on his back when he hung up, but he didn't turn. As if to counterbalance the depravity he confronted every day, Sullivan had dedicated his life to being the perfect father and he set a tough standard, which Green rarely met. Tossing a quick "Back soon" over his shoulder, he headed for the door.

"Mike! Where are you going?"

Green paused on the threshold. "I'll be back for the meeting. I've just got one last thing…" Without waiting for the wrath, he ducked out.

*　　*　　*

The University Sciences building was a squat concrete bunker built in the psychedelic sixties, but more evocative of post-war Moscow. Virtually the entire fourth floor was devoted to the offices, labs and equipment rooms of Myles Halton's research group. Green imagined that normally it was alive with the bustle of students and the hum of equipment, but on the afternoon following Jonathan Blair's murder, everything was hushed. Most of the offices were empty, and only one secretary sat at her desk, staring at her blank computer screen. Somewhere in the background he could hear the murmur of voices, but there was no one to be seen.

The secretary was called back from her trance by his cough. She raised startled gray eyes, which made her look even younger than her probable twenty years. A pretty secretary, he thought. My first clue to Halton's character.

"I'd like to see Professor Halton, please."

"Uh…" she wavered, until he produced his badge. "He spoke to two detectives earlier," she supplied hastily. "After that, he went out."

He took down her name in his notebook. "Could you tell me where the professor went?"

"I didn't ask. We're all upset, sir. Professor Halton told us to take the day off."

"Is there anyone here from his staff?"

"Umm..." Her hands fluttered to her face distractedly. "I could check for you. Mr. Difalco was here earlier, he might still be here. Dr. Miller's in his office, I think."

"Is Raquel Haddad here?" He knew she wasn't—she would be in Beirut by now—but he wanted to see her reaction. For a split second her eyes widened, before she drew her brows down over them in a frown.

"Miss Haddad doesn't really work here. She's only been helping out a bit with the research."

"Helping who?"

The brows drew lower. "I wouldn't know. I'm Dr. Halton's secretary, and I don't keep track of all the projects his students are doing. I only type their research when it's part of the book."

"What book?"

"Dr. Halton's book on language mechanisms in the brain. All the research goes into it."

"So all his students are doing research on his theory?"

"Well..." Her gray eyes roamed up the hall nervously. "I'd prefer you talk to Dr. Halton himself about it."

He raised an innocent eyebrow. "Why?"

"I'm just the secretary. Dr. Halton told us it would be better if he handled all the police and press."

"But he's not here, and I need information. How long did Raquel Haddad work for Jonathan Blair?"

The girl's eyes flitted nervously up and down the corridor. "Maybe you should talk to Dr. Miller."

"Who's he?"

"Dr. Halton's research fellow. I'll get him." She scurried down the hall and disappeared into an office without a backward glance. Curious, he padded down the hall until he could make out what she was saying.

Her voice was breathy, anxious. "Dr. Halton said specifically that people were not to talk to anyone about his or Jonathan's work. He was afraid the press would distort things."

"But this is a policeman, right?" A male voice responded.

"Yes, but you know I don't like to go against what Dr. Halton says. And the detective was asking about Raquel. Oh David, would you talk to him? Please? Dr. Halton wouldn't get mad at you."

"I don't know about that right now." Green heard a scraping sound and a sigh. "Fine, show him in."

David Miller was a paunchy, balding man of medium height with stooped shoulders and pale blue eyes. No thick black hair, no mustache. Not my first choice for killer of the year, Green thought as he introduced himself. Miller gave a nervous laugh as he shuffled forward, head bent and eyes averted.

"An inspector! I guess I'm going up in the world. It was a plain detective this morning."

"I'm just verifying some new information. You're Dr. Miller?"

"Dave. The doctor handle is kind of new, and it still makes me nervous. Besides, for the money I make…"

Green made notes. "What's your position here?"

"I'm a post-doctoral fellow working under Dr. Halton. Which means I'm a highly educated gofer, but I'm so grateful to work with him that the money doesn't matter. Besides," Miller ran his stubby fingers over his bald spot, "I've been penniless for so long, I wouldn't know what to do if I found a real job."

"Halton's a real hotshot, eh?"

Miller hesitated a fraction of a second. "Oh yes. Tops in his field in Canada and doing some fascinating research."

"What can you tell me about Raquel Haddad?"

"Raquel?" Crimson suffused his doughy face. "I—I hardly

know her. She was in my class—I teach one undergraduate course—and she helped out in the labs sometimes."

"Was she friendly with anyone here?"

"I didn't notice. I told you, I hardly know her."

"What was her connection to Jonathan Blair?"

"I believe he hired her to help him with some data collection."

"That's all?"

"That's all I know."

"They weren't involved?"

Miller picked at a brown stain on his jeans. Green saw that his fingers were quivering very slightly. "Some people thought so, but I never saw it. Jonathan was a straight kind of guy. He took his work seriously."

"Do you know if Raquel had any friends or family nearby?"

Miller licked his finger and rubbed at the stain. "I never paid any attention. But Rosalind—Miss Simmons, my associate, might know. Her office is three doors down." He stood up as if to escort Green.

"One last question, Dave. Can you think of anyone who might have wanted Jonathan Blair dead?"

Miller's nostrils flared, and for a fraction of time he seemed to vacillate. But then he shook his head with vigour and certainty.

He makes a lousy liar, Green thought to himself as he left. Not enough practice. He's one of those guilty-conscience types who can't look you in the eye when they're hiding something.

Green was wondering what it might be as he walked back down the hall. Just when he was about to knock on the third door, he was stopped by voices within, the voices he had heard murmuring earlier, only now they were raised in anger.

Quickly he switched on his pocket tape recorder.

"That's a cheap thing to say, Joe!"

"Oh, come on, we all know why he was murdered." The first voice was shrill, the second rich and sensual.

"I know no such thing. Jonathan was still in love with Vanessa."

"This isn't about love, it's about the cock, sweetheart. The cock calls the tune. But you know that, don't you?"

"You're such a pig."

The man laughed, a low, mocking chuckle. He murmured something which Green couldn't hear, and the woman exploded.

"Get out of my office! Or I'll scream. I swear it!"

"What, and you think lover boy will come running?"

"You reduce everything to sex, don't you. Sex and power."

"What else is there?"

"This. Dr. Halton's work."

"Like you said, baby. Sex and power."

"That's your warped view."

"Okay, then why didn't you tell the police what's going on here?"

"Because...because it isn't relevant."

"Bullshit," the man hissed. "It's because you don't want to lose your goddamn job with Halton. And because—" he paused for drama, "you're not sure if Miller did it."

"I am! I am!" she raged. Before Green had a chance to jump away, she threw open the door.

Green found himself face to face with a pair of horrified blue eyes in a tangle of brassy curls. Behind her, a dark-eyed young man leaped to his feet, the last traces of a sardonic smile fleeing from his face. No mustache, but rich black hair.

The man found his voice first. "Who the fuck are you!"

Green pushed past the blonde and strode into the room. "Inspector Green of the Ottawa Police," he said, flipping open his notebook. He left his pocket tape recorder on, which he sometimes used to record interviews secretly, but the notebook was necessary for court. "Your names, please."

"Can you just barge in here and ask us that?" the young man blustered.

"I'm investigating a homicide. You're within your rights to refuse to cooperate, but then, of course, I'd probably wonder why. And I can get pretty nosy."

Green was always amazed how well that subtle threat worked with bullies. He was afraid he'd look ludicrous waving his badge around and sounding like Columbo, but somehow the effect transcended the freckles, the nose and the Zellers attire. Meekly, the two identified themselves. Joseph Difalco and Rosalind Simmons.

Green gestured to Difalco. "You wait here while I take Miss Simmons' statement outside. If you both cooperate, we'll be through in no time."

The two exchanged one long, wordless stare before Rosalind turned and marched out the door. Green chose an empty office next door and gestured her to a seat. She was clearly nervous, but she remained standing and fixed him with a stubborn stare.

"I overheard some interesting things in there," he began softly. "I think you'd better begin by telling me what the hell is going on here."

He could almost see her mind racing backwards over the conversation, trying to recall what she and Difalco had let slip. To buy herself time, she chose to be obtuse.

"Going on? Joe and I were just talking, officer." She widened her eyes. "Not what you think."

"I sure didn't think that," Green replied drily. "Not from what I heard. So don't play me for a fool, Miss Simmons. I haven't the time for it. And don't think that I'm dumb just because I'm a cop. Stop batting the eyelashes, sit down, and tell me straight why you think Miller did it."

"Did what?"

"Murdered Jonathan Blair."

"I don't think that!" she gasped in horror. "Why should you...?"

"Difalco said you weren't sure if Miller did it."

She frowned, and her bewilderment seemed genuine. Then abruptly the memory fell into place. "Oh! No, not the murder. Nothing to do with the murder, just some professional matter. Joe was just taunting me."

"What professional matter?"

"It's...it's a long story and really very trivial."

"Difalco didn't make it sound trivial."

"Joe can't stand the fact that I won't jump into his bed like everyone else. He takes pot shots at me every chance he gets."

Green sat down in the swivel chair opposite her. "I'm waiting."

She studied the floor, gathering her forces. Finally, she took a deep breath. "It's just professional rivalry. Between Joe and Dave. Joe has been Professor Halton's student for six years, and Dave just came last year. But Dave already has his Ph.D. from Stanford." She cast him a look that could have been disdain. "That's a top university in the States. Anyway, Joe couldn't stand that. He said some of his research data disappeared, and he accused Dave of deliberately erasing it from his computer."

"Why?"

She shrugged. "So that Joe wouldn't get finished so soon, I

guess. Joe's problem is that he assumes everyone thinks like him. He thinks Dave would care if he succeeded, that Dave would be jealous of his success. That's nonsense. Dave is a classic scientist—nose in his books, clueless about the world around him. Naïvely thinking everyone is as passionate about truth and discovery as he is. He honestly thinks Joe cares about his research for the light it will cast on the world."

"But he doesn't?"

She snorted. "Joe cares about the three letters after his name and how the name 'Halton' will look on his résumé."

"Does Halton know about the disappearing data?"

"Oh yes. What would be the point of the accusation if Halton didn't know about it? But I don't know what Halton did about it. He kept it under wraps. That's his style. He solved it, I'm sure, and I suspect he read Joe the riot act in private, but no one's ever going to know. No hint of a scandal to threaten his grant money."

"So Halton would believe Dave over Joe?"

She paused, her brows knitted. "I hope so. Joe's been with him for six years, and I think Professor Halton has a soft spot for him, but I don't think he's naïve." She shook her head impatiently. "I don't mean to sound all negative about Joe, officer. He's an obnoxious pig, and he can't handle any woman with an IQ over 90, but he's a bright guy. Quick-witted and charming in a boys' locker room kind of way. Men like him."

"He doesn't sound like the kind of guy you'd find in an Ph.D. program, though," Green observed. "More likely law or MBA."

Surprise flickered briefly in her eyes, and when she spoke, he thought he detected more respect. "I have wondered about that myself. But you don't get a straight answer out of Joe. He says it's because he gets the best pickings of the female undergraduate groupies who cluster around Halton."

"A macho front to hide a serious mind?" Green replied with a laugh. Rosalind laughed too, briefly forgetting why she was there, and some of the wariness left her eyes.

"How did Jonathan Blair fit into this dispute?"

The wariness returned. "Not at all. That's why Halton didn't want the incident mentioned. His reputation is important to him, and Jonathan Blair didn't work with either Joe or Dave."

"Who did he work with?"

"Halton. Dave has a couple of graduate students helping him, but most of us work directly under Halton, doing our own research related to his theory. We sometimes have assistants, usually Honours students. Jonathan had..." She hesitated briefly.

"Raquel Haddad?"

She smiled, but without humour. "Raquel kind of made the rounds, in more ways than one. She was one of those undergraduate groupies I mentioned earlier. For some women, power is a great aphrodisiac."

"And did Professor Halton sample the offerings?"

She eyed him levelly. "I thought we were talking about Jonathan Blair."

"Jonathan Blair always seems to be the least important person in my conversations about him."

Her eyes narrowed intently as she inspected the idea. "What a curious observation," she said. "But you know, it's quite true. When Jonathan first came, he created quite a stir. I mean, he had a lot of star qualities—loads of money, good looks, brains, an impressive integrity. But in a way, drama plays around him. He's always rock stable, calm, unobtrusive."

"Like the eye of a hurricane, maybe?"

She laughed. "My God, you're a great improvement over the detective who was here this morning. So plodding and unimaginative. 'Do you know anyone who had reason to kill him? When did you last see him? Did he ever say anything that led you to think he was in trouble?'"

"And what did you tell him?"

"Nothing useful. I've been wracking my brains. We all have! But it's beyond me. Unless he was murdered because he was too perfect. Kind of like Christ."

"It's been suggested that Difalco might have done it."

She snorted. "Why, because of Raquel Haddad? That's ridiculous. Jonathan wasn't involved with Raquel."

Green remembered a snatch of the conversation between Rosalind and Difalco and took a wild guess. "But Difalco thought he was."

She shook her head. "It still doesn't fit. Maybe Raquel got to Joe more than most, but no woman would ever mean enough that he would kill for her. To him, women are just playthings."

More likely possessions, Green thought, and remembered the grisly aftermath of domestic violence wrought by men who thought like that. But he kept the memories to himself.

"Jonathan's ex-girlfriend thinks Difalco might have been jealous of Jonathan for other reasons."

Rosalind shrugged. "Well, she could be right. Vanessa's even more cynical of people than I am, especially when she's hurting. But I've been burnt trusting people I shouldn't, so who's to say? Certainly of all of us, Joe is the one with the fewest scruples. I'm not sure he's a murderer, but he sure as hell would sell his grandmother for a piece of fame and glory."

Privately Green thought that the crushing indictment of Joe Difalco by Rosalind Simmons and Vanessa Weeks revealed more about the women's own psyches than it did about

Difalco's. There was a hint of fascination in the disgust. It made him very curious to get the man under his own microscope to see what a male's reaction to him would be.

But when he finally dismissed Rosalind Simmons and emerged into the hall, Joe Difalco was nowhere to be found.

Five

The ten detectives had been waiting almost an hour by the time Green burst through the briefing room door, dishevelled and out of breath. Previous experience had prepared Sullivan for this likelihood, however, and he had used the time to get progress reports from the teams and to chart the useful information on the blackboards around the room. By this time he had been awake for twenty-eight hours, aside from catnaps in Green's chair, and he was almost beyond fatigue. Artificially propped up by caffeine, he moved like a well-trained automaton, struggling to remain coherent. It took him more than twenty minutes to summarize for Green all the evidence to date.

Or lack of it, for it was a dismal harvest.

Hundreds of students had volunteered information, but not one could provide useful eyewitness testimony. No one had seen the stabbing, no one had heard it. The killing had been quick and neat, committed without hesitation or warning.

"We should be looking for a goddamn commando," Green muttered grimly; the neatness bothered him. Amateur killers made mistakes. They didn't know where to strike. They hesitated, blundered, panicked. They allowed screams and blows in self-defence. To have foreseen all the problems and taken steps against them, this suggested a professional who had killed before and for whom murder was a practised art. But that meant researching Marianne Blair's possible connections to the underworld, which would not go down well with her pal the Police Chief. Besides, the mob didn't operate this obliquely. If they had a message to deliver, they made it loud and clear. Marianne Blair had received no threats prior to the murder, and no one had come forward to claim responsibility. Thus, there was no evidence to suggest Jonathan was being used as a pawn in a settling of accounts.

There was, however, evidence that something was very wrong in his own life. His friends described him as moody and preoccupied. Usually gentle and agreeable, he had become impatient and irritable. He wouldn't go out with them, he wouldn't join in the laughter and the jokes. He had broken up with his girlfriend without telling anyone why. He had spent hours locked away in his lab, pouring his energies into his dissertation but rebuffing all sympathetic inquiries into how it was going. His friends assumed he had hit a major snag in his research, but Dr. Halton assured the detectives everything had been proceeding normally.

Inquiries into his love life had yielded mixed views. Some friends thought he had been embroiled in a passionate, secret affair with Raquel Haddad, but others stubbornly refused to believe it. He had been seen with her but always at arm's length. No one knew in what capacity she had been helping him with his research, because he avoided talking about the subject altogether.

The search of Jonathan's university office had failed to produce a wallet or a diary, but had yielded an appointment/ address book as well as a bank book. Jonathan Blair had a savings account with a healthy four-figure balance, but there was nothing alarming in the pattern of small withdrawals and deposits which peppered the previous month. If he were into drugs, it was minor league. The toxicology screen which had been rushed through the RCMP forensics lab had revealed no trace of drugs in his body, and MacPhail's conclusion from the autopsy was the same. All Jonathan had in his body were the remains of cola and a grilled cheese sandwich, consumed about three hours before the stabbing.

"All right, that means he ate some supper at about seven o'clock," Green broke in, rescuing Sullivan, whose eyes had begun to close. Green moved to an empty blackboard and turned to look at his teams. "Let's put together his last day. He got up and had breakfast with his mother at seven a.m., then left for the university on his bike at ten to eight. Does anyone know what happened next?"

Laplante flipped open his notebook. "We've tracked most of his day at work. Dr. Halton's secretary said he arrived at his office just before nine o'clock and asked her if Halton was coming in that day. She said he was in Toronto, and he asked when was the earliest time he could see him. She said first thing tomorrow. That's today, of course."

"What was his state of mind at that point?"

"The secretary said he seemed upset that he couldn't see Halton till the next day."

"Upset how? Distraught?"

Laplante shrugged. "She just said upset. She didn't say he freaked out. He thanked her for the appointment and went off down to his office."

"Alone?"

"I guess. His computer shows he was logged on from then till twelve-fifteen. It looks like he worked for three hours straight."

"Doing what?"

"Oh hell, Mike, Jackson and I didn't try to figure that out. There were print-outs of graphs and numbers and tables all over his desk. His walls are covered with diagrams of the brain, and he has a big, multi-coloured plastic model of one sitting on his desk. There's photographs of cats with pink stuff stuck on their head and wires coming out. Gave me the willies."

"What did he do from noon till five?"

"He was in the lab working with the poor suckers. One of the other guys—Dr. Difalco—showed us around the place and it's full of high-tech crap. Computers, scanners, videos, machines that measure eye blinks and foot twitches and brain waves…"

"Hard-ons too, I bet," came a faceless voice from the table, and laughter rippled through the room. Sullivan's eyes fluttered open.

Laplante grinned and livened up for the group. "Shit, Difalco kept rattling off these long names. and he just lost me. All I can tell is everything you want to measure about someone, inside or out, it seems like you can measure nowadays. Different parts of the brain are working during different tasks, and Dr. Difalco said you can see what parts are working with these new machines. Colours in one part, shapes in another, put colours and shapes together and you get another part going."

"Sounds like you got a new career out there when the budget cuts come, Laplante," one of the detectives quipped.

Laplante shook his head. "I'd go squirrelly in one of those little rooms day after day staring at a computer screen. And tempers do get hot. One of the guys told me Difalco and Miller got into a fight one day two or three months ago and nearly killed each other. Broke a computer in the heat of it, and Miller could hardly get out of bed for a week. Difalco's some kind of martial arts pro. They're still not talking to each other."

Green perked up. This incident hadn't been mentioned in the detective's report, because in the average investigator's mind it had no direct relevance to the victim or to the time frame in question. But it was exactly the type of peripheral detail which might open up an entire new line of inquiry. The type of peripheral detail on which Green's mind took wing.

"What was it about?" he demanded.

"It was all hushed up," Laplante said. "Halton's a guy who doesn't stand for nonsense. Difalco's files went missing, and Miller accused him of making them up, so Halton hauled both guys into his office and laid down the law, and I guess nobody else found out the whole story. "

"You've met both men. Who do you think is guilty?"

Laplante glanced across at Jackson for support. Neither seemed to have given the matter much thought. Finally, Laplante gestured lamely. "These guys are a little different from the kind of suspect we usually meet on the street, Mike. This Dr. Difalco acts more like the slime we see, but maybe Miller is just a more sophisticated kind of creep."

"Difalco—who said he was a doctor?"

"Well, he—" Laplante broke off, puzzled. "We just thought...I think he just acted like one. And he never said we were wrong."

I'll just bet he didn't, Green thought. His brief encounter with the man had not left him impressed by his integrity. Difalco remained high on his list of witnesses to be interviewed, along with Myles Halton. But for now he had to focus on the results of the investigation to date so that he could figure out where his men should go from there.

He sat in silence for two minutes, his eyes flitting from one blackboard to another, groping for a toehold. After hours of interviews and mountains of evidence, they had so few usable facts. The killing was perfect—no witness, no sound, no mess, no physical evidence left behind. The victim was perfect, not even his ex-girlfriend hated him. No drugs, no money problems, no hint of scandal. The only glimmer of suspicion was a dark-haired beauty who may have been his mistress and who had abruptly vanished to Beirut only hours before his death. Raquel Haddad was his only toehold, except for the unknown student who had been up in the library at the time of the murder and who had vanished in the confusion following the alarm.

He assigned one team to track down the activities of Raquel and Pierre Haddad and another to continue the search for the red-shirted student. The third team was to pursue the routine inquiry into Blair's known associates and their activities on the day of the murder, while the remaining team was to continue piecing together Blair's final day, in the hopes of finding out what had brought him to the remote medieval literature section of the library.

Ferreting out the intrigue surrounding Difalco, Miller and the missing files, he left for himself. It was past five o'clock, only an hour before Sharon left for work, but he still had two major witnesses to interview before he could even consider calling it a day. Not to mention the phone messages from Peter Weiss and the Deputy Chief, demanding a progress report. If he were lucky—really lucky—he'd get home in time for Tony's bedtime story.

But there was no one else he could trust with the Difalco-Miller mystery except Sullivan, who by now was propped up against the wall in the corner, snoring softly. His face was grey with fatigue, and when Green shook him, he seemed to struggle back to consciousness from very far away. He rubbed his square hand over his face.

"What do you want me to do?" he managed thickly.

"Go home, see your family and sleep till morning."

Sullivan shook his head. "I just need a couple of hours.

Mary's out tonight showing a house for once anyway. First nibble she's had all month. I'll just go home, put the boys to bed, and meet you wherever later."

Green chuckled. "I'm babysitting Tony, remember? Calling it a night early. I thought you'd approve."

"I do, I do. But wait till Tony starts to want hockey camp, and his baby sister needs a costume for her ballet recital. You'll be glad for every overtime hour you can get."

"Brian, you're no good to me asleep on your feet. I only have a couple of small things to do, and the sooner I get on them, the sooner I can get home too."

He pointed Sullivan in the direction of the elevator, watched him weave down the hall, then turned to collect his notes for the interviews. Two hours tops, he thought. But just as he was heading past his office on his way back outside, he was intercepted by the Chief of Detectives.

"Update, Michael."

"Adam, I have to—"

"Two minutes. Your office." Adam Jules steered him towards the door. Once inside, Green glanced at him sharply.

"Is this for your ears or someone else's?"

"Mine. I'll give a one-minute version to Lynch."

Green smiled. "Nothing solid yet, but some leads. It looks personal, probably something to do with his love life. Can you get the Mounties and Immigration to give us all they've got on a Pierre and Raquel Haddad?" He jotted down the addresses.

Jules' eyebrow shot up. "An Arab connection? Political?"

Green shook his head. "I don't think so, but the RCMP can ask around. Then Lynch can bug them for a change." He chuckled. "That ought to keep him busy."

Jules managed his approximation of a smile. "I've had several calls from Marianne Blair's ex, Jonathan's father. He's just arrived in Ottawa. Do you want to see him?"

"Does he know anything useful?"

"He says no. Lives in Vancouver, only sees Jonathan every few months."

"Find out where he's staying and tell him I'll see him there at—" Green glanced at his watch and swore. One hour to see Halton, another to see Difalco, minimum. If he added Mr. Blair Senior to the list, he'd be lucky even to tuck Tony in. Sharon would kill him. "Tell him eight o'clock."

"He won't like that. He's pretty upset. Only learnt the news from the TV."

"Huh. That tells us where Mrs. Blair's priorities lie, doesn't it," Green noted drily. "She gave me the impression she was still fond of the guy, they just couldn't work things out." He shrugged. "Well, you don't get rich by being nice, do you? Tell the guy I'm sorry, but I'll give him a personal report at eight o'clock. By then, once I've seen Professor Halton and his hot-tempered golden boy, I hope I'll have something to report."

Six

Green had intended to pay a surprise visit to Myles Halton at his home, a tactic which he liked because witnesses had no time to mount a defence. But as he steered the Corolla onto the Queensway towards Constance Bay, where the renowned and wealthy professor had his waterfront getaway, an alternative struck him. He could kill two birds with one stone if Halton met him at the University. In order not to lose the element of surprise entirely, he dispatched a police cruiser to pick Halton up.

At seven in the evening, the offices of Halton's team were even more deserted than they had been that morning. The secretary had gone home, and most of the lights in the hall and reception area had been turned off, leaving only hazy yellow splashes at intervals down the hall to guide the cleaning staff. The chatter of Green's police radio was deafening in the silence. He was just reaching for the light switch by the secretary's desk when he heard a distant crash. He paused, straining his eyes to see down the hall. The security guard downstairs had told him everyone from Halton's floor had gone home. All the doors were shut and dark. From down the hall came a screech of metal, like an unoiled wheel. Then a soft rustling, barely audible even in the tomb-like silence of the building.

Green dropped down behind the desk, turned his radio

down and fumbled beneath his jacket for his gun. He hated it. Hated carrying it and hoped he never had to fire it except on the range, but the rule book and every instructor he'd ever had said that one day he'd be grateful he had it. Clairvoyant bastards. Green stared at the gun lying cold and alien in his hand, then cautiously lifted it in front of him. For a moment he crouched behind the desk, his heart thumping and his mind racing as he tried to organize his thoughts. He had always been a lousy policeman. A good detective, but useless on the front lines. If Jules had not yanked him off the street into CID fourteen years ago, he would have been kicked off the Force within a year. He never followed procedure and rarely worked within the team.

Now, as he crouched low and took deep breaths to slow his heart, he tried to remember those basic procedures. He had surprised an intruder in a deserted office complex after hours. An office where a recent murder victim had worked and where a lot of questions remained unanswered. He could not tell from the muffled sounds how many intruders there were nor in which office they were working. Procedure dictated that he call for back-up. Otherwise he would be crucified by the Professional Standards Unit if things went wrong. If he were still alive to be crucified.

On the other hand, the intruder might hear his voice if he used his radio to call for back-up. It was also possible that the intruder was merely a researcher working late, in which case he would be a laughingstock. Among the muffled sounds, he could hear nothing resembling voices, so it was possible there was only one intruder. With only one intruder and the element of surprise on his side, surely he could gain the upper hand in a confrontation.

On the other hand, I don't know where the bastard is, he

thought, so who's going to surprise whom? I could sneak down the hall listening at every door until…but the guy could suddenly decide to come out and…

Jeez, Green, what a cop you make!

Leaning his head against the secretary's desk, he took several slow, deep breaths. Then he rose, gun ready, and began slowly down the hall toward the sounds. Outside Jonathan Blair's office, he stopped. A thin shaft of light leaked under the door and the sounds of rustling were sharp and near. Gingerly, he touched the knob and felt it give beneath his fingers. Levelling his gun, he took a deep breath, flung the door back and leaped into the doorway.

"Police, freeze!"

Difalco dropped the sheaf of papers he was holding and staggered back, jaw gaping.

"What the—! Inspec…what—!" He stammered incoherently.

"Turn around! Hands on the wall!"

"I—I—"

"Against the wall!"

Ashen-faced, Difalco stumbled against the wall and remained immobile while Green frisked him. There were no hidden weapons.

"Sit down." With the gun, Green gestured to the chair in front of the computer. Difalco bent to pick up the scattered files and a handful of CD-ROMs fell out of his jacket pocket.

"Don't touch a fucking thing!"

Difalco scrambled into the chair and stared at him.

"What the hell's going on here?" Green demanded.

"Nothing! My office is next door. I—I was just getting some of my files that were in Jonathan's room."

"What files?"

"Computer print-outs. Just raw data." Some colour was

returning to Difalco's cheeks. "It wouldn't mean anything to you, it's just brain wave patterns and stuff. Jonathan and I were working on similar questions, and we often checked how each other's data were coming along."

"So you're saying these are your files?"

"Well, they're not exactly my—I mean, no, they're Jonathan's files. But—"

"So you were removing Jonathan's files from his office."

"Yes, but he was going to give them to me anyway. We had arranged it a couple of days ago."

"And you figured why let a small thing like his murder interfere with your day's work, right? The same reason you didn't stick around this morning when I asked you to wait."

Difalco scrounged for some bluster. "I did wait! Almost fifteen minutes! But I had things to do—a subject was due to meet me in the lab."

Without a word, Green turned up his radio and paged the Ident Unit at the police station. Lou Paquette was just logging the last of his analyses and was looking forward to a warm meal and bed. He suppressed a groan when he heard Green's request, but he agreed to be there within fifteen minutes.

"Fingerprints!" Difalco sputtered, but Green held up a brusque hand and rang dispatch. This time he ordered a squad car to take Difalco down to the station and hold him for questioning. When he hung up, Difalco was staring at him, ashen again.

"What are you doing?"

"Bringing you down for questioning on break and enter, attempted robbery."

"But I told you—"

"You told me you were removing Jonathan Blair's files from his office!" Green retorted. "That's attempted robbery. The fingerprinting will tell us what else you touched in here. Now let's move!"

Difalco's eyes darted from the gun to the open door, but in the end he seemed to deflate. A sullen look stole over his face as he slumped towards the door. Green herded him briskly; he was anxious to have Difalco out of the building before Halton arrived. He wanted Halton ignorant of Difalco's misdeeds until he himself chose the crucial moment to deliver the news.

Besides, an hour or two sitting alone in an interrogation room might do Difalco some good. Green smiled as he watched the squad car pull away, the handcuffed Difalco scowling in the back seat. Now we're getting somewhere.

The squad car had barely turned the corner, and the smile was still on Green's face when a second squad car pulled up to the curb. A huge, bearded man hauled himself from the back seat, visibly perturbed.

"I hardly think this was necessary, Detective. Having this man pull up in full view of the neighbours! You've embarrassed my wife, you've embarrassed me! I'm not a criminal, I pay plenty of taxes and I think a little consideration is in order."

The devaluation of his rank may not have been intentional, but Green suspected it was. He pretended to be oblivious. "This is common procedure, Professor. No disrespect intended. I need you to help me examine the contents of Jonathan Blair's office, and I was anxious to expedite matters as much as I could. Homicide trails grow stale very quickly."

Ice blue eyes appraised him from behind shaggy white brows, then Halton bobbed his massive head. "Very well, let's get on with it. I want to visit Marianne Blair tonight."

It was very smoothly done, the delivery beyond reproach, but this time the message was unequivocal: "I move in the same circles as the country's elite, sonny, you remember that."

I'll be the picture of respect, asshole, Green replied inwardly and put on his breeziest smile. "I shouldn't keep you more than an hour, sir. Shall we start in your office?"

Inside his office, Halton chose to sit behind his mammoth mahogany desk, flanked by his degrees, which left Green the hard-backed student's chair opposite. Looking up at the icy eyes across the desk, Green realized he had made a tactical error. To regain control of the interview, he had to alter the power balance. Rising, he walked to the window to study the view of the canal and the Château Laurier which glistened in the rain-slicked evening light. Halton was forced to swivel his chair and look up at him.

From his vantage point, Green tried for the grave and humble look. "To minimize the inconvenience to you, sir, I won't go over the routine ground which my detectives covered earlier. Instead, I'd like to clarify some inconsistencies which have emerged in the investigation. First of all, what was Jonathan Blair working on?"

"It's highly technical, Detective. And hardly relevant, I can assure you."

The grave and humble tone never wavered. "I'm sure you're right, but I'm trying to fill in his last few weeks. He seemed to be working very hard, and a few people thought he had run into a snag in his research."

"Snags are commonplace in technical research. In fact, ironing out the kinks in the methodology is often the major part of original research. Jonathan was a hard worker, and when it came to problems he was like a dog with a bone. He would forget all else."

"Did he seem upset or preoccupied to you?"

"I hadn't seen him in a few days, and I don't babysit my graduate students."

"He tried to make an appointment with you yesterday morning. He seemed upset then."

Halton shrugged. "Then you know more than me, Detective. I wish I could be of more help."

Green pretended to study his notes while he let the silence lengthen. "Was he working with cats or humans?"

"Cats."

"What were Joe Difalco and Dave Miller working with? Animals or humans?"

Halton seemed to pause, and a frown flickered across his face. "Humans."

"Did their research have anything to do with Blair's?"

"Well, it all fit together. We were all checking out facets of language or auditory processing."

"Would Blair have reason to share his data with the other two? Would his data on cats be of any use to—say, Difalco?"

Halton scrutinized Green with a long, level gaze. "What are you getting at, detective?"

Green left the window to return to his student's chair. The power shift had been achieved, and now it was time to enlist the professor's help. He spoke softly.

"Professor, I don't mean to imply one of your students killed Jonathan Blair, but I believe something unusual was going on. I know police investigations are very intrusive, and it's uncomfortable to have your whole operation under a microscope. But everything I learn will go no further than my own notebook, not into the file or into my reports to superiors, unless it is relevant to the murder. And I will never be able to distinguish what is relevant from what isn't if I don't have the whole picture. So please bear with me on this."

Halton had been watching him carefully, but now he lowered his gaze. "What have you been told so far?"

"That Difalco's data disappeared. Difalco accused Miller of erasing it from the computer and Miller accused Difalco of falsifying his results. At one point, it came to blows."

Halton nodded, his gaze still lowered. "That is the official version. I'm going to hold you to your word, detective. Not one word of what I'm about to tell you must leak beyond these walls, or the cause of my brain research will be set back years."

Green said nothing. From his desk, Halton picked up a polished wooden brain that resembled a shelled walnut, stained different hues. He cradled it in his large hands reverently. "Back in the 60's, this was called the black box. After centuries of ludicrous theories trying to guess its inner workings, behavioural psychologists said 'Don't even try'. Concentrate on what goes in and what comes out. Stimulus and response. But that's like buying a twelve-cylinder Lamborghini and never looking under the hood. From medical and biological research, we knew the basics of how functions are located in the brain." He turned the brain and pointed as he talked. "Visual cortex in the back here, motor cortex, language in the left temporal lobe. We knew if the occipital lobe was damaged the person wouldn't be able to see. Cut out his prefrontal lobe—like in a lobotomy—and you not only disconnect his emotions but he can't plan or organize."

Halton split the wooden sphere in two and held each out dramatically. "There are two to three billion brain cells in here in the cortex alone. At least some are firing all the time, reacting to all the sights and sounds in this room, to the feel of my own body and the smell of the stale air conditioning. Put electrodes all over the scalp to record this electrical activity and they generate brain wave tracings called an EEG. Put enough electrodes, make them sensitive enough, filter the waves through the proper computer program and you can detect the activity of a very small group of neurons. If you say a word, a tiny EEG spike shows up in this little section of the temporal lobe. That tiny spike is called an event-related potential, and it's how we can map the functions of any part of the brain we want. We can see what parts of the brain become engaged when we ask it to do a particular task.

"We used to think every function had its own special corner of the brain, but we know now that's it's much more collaborative than that. Yes, there are specialized centres for different things, but there are also more neural connections from one to another than can be imagined." Halton wrote something on a notepad and held it up. "Read this."

It was the word "cat", and Green smiled in spite of himself. In his work, he'd seen more brains than he cared to, splattered on the floor beneath a corpse or laid bare by the pathologist's saw. He found this abstract insight intriguing but sensed that the professor had lost his rare moment of humility and was settling back into his favourite role of Grand Poobah. To forestall this, even more than to hasten the interview, Green shook his head.

"Professor, I don't—"

Halton held up his hand sharply. "Now you bear with me, Detective. If you're going to be running roughshod through the intricacies of my students' work, I want you to understand the complexity of this organ, and the daunting challenge we face. Besides, you'll never understand what you're investigating without a bit of background."

Dutifully, Green said "cat" and Halton grinned. "Now, in your brain, the following probably just happened, all within two or three hundred milliseconds. The visual cortex deciphered the shapes, said oh, letters, and pulled in the left temporal lobe to get the sounds to match the letters, then the millisecond you got the word 'cat', a big chain of neurons all over your brain went off—in your visual cortex to activate the picture of a cat, in the temporal lobe because cats meow, maybe in the parietal lobe because they feel furry. All those ideas are part of your image of a cat, and it takes the whole brain to remind you what a cat is. And if you're afraid of cats, the amygdala, which is the emotional control centre deep down inside here, might kick in its two-cents worth too." He set the brain down again in the corner of his desk and took a deep breath, as if he were finally nearing the crucial point.

"For the past twenty-five years, I've been chipping away at the black box using this EEG technology to study language processing, especially in people with language impairment. But every day, expensive new technology is developed, and if I want to stay on the cutting edge, I have to keep up, or give up. Without money, I can't buy equipment, without equipment, I can't attract top students and researchers, without them, I can't build a credible program to attract grant money."

"Ring around the rosy."

Halton looked up with a grim smile. "Exactly. In Canada especially, it's a constant struggle to stay competitive with the Americans. High-resolution EEG is a wonderful tool for tracking a chain of events that all occur in less than half a second, but EEGs are not good at pinpointing the exact location in the brain. We can calculate a rough idea from electrode placements on the scalp. But brain imaging techniques that measure blood flow inside the brain can give us three-D pictures of exactly where the activity is occurring. They're slower, so they can't measure changes in tenths of a second, like an EEG, but the latest ones can tell us exact locations. So, put the EEG and the imager together, and you've got dynamite. And that's exactly my next step."

Halton leaned forward with his shaggy brows drawn, and Green could feel the drama. "At this very moment, I'm in the midst of negotiations to team up with some medical researchers from Yale and combine resources to buy the most state-of-the-art, high-resolution functional magnetic resonance imager."

"You mean an MRI? Like the ones in the hospital?"

"Yes, but one designed to study not just abnormalities in the brain but specific areas of the brain as we stimulate it in different ways. We could map the brain on a far more detailed and complex level than was ever possible before. There are only a few of these units around for research purposes, because they are prohibitively expensive. Over three million dollars each. I have spent years building up the necessary financial backing to make this deal, and I now have the reputation I need to get the backing. But one hint that my results might be fraudulent, and the reputation, the backing, and the deal will collapse in moments. And with it, all hope of making the breakthroughs in learning that I know are just around the corner. Breakthroughs that will help the learning disabled, the retarded, the brain damaged. You cannot let that happen, Detective. And I can assure you Jonathan Blair would not have wanted himself to be the cause."

Finally, we're back to the crux of the case, Green thought. "What do you want to tell me, Professor?"

"I have wrestled with this all day. Believe me, Detective, I do not want to obstruct a police investigation. I have searched my soul to decide whether it was relevant. I honestly don't know. The implications horrify me, but I can't ignore the possibility that they are true." Professor Halton took a deep breath. His humility had returned; he looked pale, even small, behind his desk. Green waited out the silence patiently until Halton resumed.

"David Miller is a rare find in the highly technical field of brain research today. He's a first-rate mathematician and statistician, a master at computer programming and simulation, and he has solid knowledge of brain research. For his Ph.D. dissertation, he developed an algorithm for analyzing multiple event-related potentials that is nothing short of genius. But half the people in the field can't understand his work. They think it's obscure, hopelessly complex and theoretical. And Dave can't sell himself. He comes across like a bumbling, absent-minded, half-mad scientist. You can't be like that anymore. The days of the creative genius left alone in his lab to make discoveries are long gone. Dave had trouble finding a university willing to continue his research once he got his doctorate. When I read his thesis, I thought he was on to something, and I offered him a post-doc. I hoped eventually to persuade the university to give him a proper professorship once he'd established his name with me."

Halton stood and began to pace. "Joe Difalco has been with me since his undergraduate years. He's my most senior doctoral student, and he has spent years piecing together a theory of word processing deficits using EEG data. When we know where the deficits are—what part of that 'cat' chain doesn't work right, for example—then we can begin to study how to fix them. Joe is a bright boy, and he has a wonderful intuitive intelligence. He makes creative leaps and as a result he's always been a useful addition to my group. He can critique others' work as well, and it helps to advance our thinking." Halton paused at the window, tracing a drop of rain down the glass. "I've kept Joe on for another reason too. This may sound crass, and it's not my favourite aspect of university life, but Joe is my salesman. He can be smooth, charming and persuasive, unlike Dave, who stands head and shoulders above him intellectually but can't sell himself to save his soul."

"Does Difalco know he's mainly window dressing?"

Halton hesitated but did not contradict his appraisal. "The two of them are both working on word processing, but their theories are different, and Dave's means of analyzing the brain waves is much more complex than Joe's."

"So suddenly the golden boy is dethroned."

Halton nodded grimly. "I don't tolerate rivalry in my department, and I will not permit personal animosities to come before the advancement of science. Joe is a bright boy, but he's lazy and he's a sloppy researcher. Intuitive people often are; they haven't the patience to plod through all the steps. I've always had to watch him to make sure no corners had been cut. I thought I had done that, but between teaching responsibilities and travelling to present papers, trying to get my book together, negotiating this new joint project with Yale and arguing with granting agencies..." He sighed as if the mere thought of his obligations exhausted him. "I may have lost track of things a bit right here in the lab. I have twenty students working for me here at one level or another. I've been running things on my own this year; I have an associate, but he's on sabbatical, and I've been trying to take on another associate as well, but with the budget cuts to the university...well, my students have been left to fend for themselves more than they should. Joe Difalco was working hard on his research, he was wrapping up the final data analysis on the last phase of his dissertation, and the results looked impressive. It was an almost complete confirmation of his approach. Then Dave Miller came to me and told me he thought Joe's data were fudged. He said he had run part of Joe's research through a computer simulation, and it was impossible for Joe to have gotten the results he did. So Dave went further. All the analyses and the original raw data—the EEG tracings themselves—are stored on our main computer in the central lab. Dave went into Joe's computer database and looked at his raw data, and he said they weren't anything like those Joe had reported."

Green looked up from his notes. "What did you do?"

"I hauled Joe in. I will not tolerate anyone interfering with science. I didn't tell him what Dave had claimed. I merely asked to look over his raw data. To double-check, I said. I told him I had questions about the algorithm he'd used to transform the data for statistical purposes..." Seeing Green's eyes glaze, he waved a hand in dismissal. "Never mind. Just number crunching. Anyway, Joe came back and said someone had wiped out his data banks. The raw data was lost. He went further. He accused Dave of doing it to prevent him from proving the validity of his model over Dave's."

Halton stared out the window at the gold-lit city. Outrage battled sorrow on his face. "Who was I to believe? Dave had admitted he went into Joe's databank. Both men knew the outcome of their studies was important to their futures. Yale wants one of my researchers to work at their end of things, and there is nothing more unwanted in science than negative results, no greater blow to your stature than to be wrong. Although, of course, negative results are essential to the progress of knowledge. If Joe's model was right, then Dave's was wrong. But if Joe, after years of work, found out he was wrong, well...Joe hates to lose, to come in second. I could see him erasing the raw data so I'd never know. A perfect whodunit, actually, Detective. You probably run into this quite often. Two suspects, two perfect motives, two perfect explanations. Who's lying?" Halton turned from the window to face Green. "Tell me, detective. What would you do?"

"I'd look for independent corroboration, first of all. Did anyone else see the data? If not, I'd see if I could get some new data, to see which way it leans."

Halton's eyes lit up. "And that's exactly what I did."

Suddenly the pieces fell into place. Green's pulse leaped. "You asked Jonathan Blair to check into the research."

The professor nodded. "In strictest confidence. I asked him to examine the rest of Joe's computer files to see if he could glean any useful information. If he had to, he was to run a few subjects for us to see whether they supported Joe's conclusions."

"Did Miller and Difalco know he was doing this?"

Halton met his questioning gaze levelly. "That, of course, is the question. That is why I've been soul-searching today. Is it possible they knew, and if so, did one of them kill him? I didn't tell them, that's for sure. I indicated to them only that I would be investigating the matter. I suppose I should have—" He broke off, his jaw working. He was a big man, barrel-chested and ramrod-straight, and he was obviously used to being in command. Self-doubt and regret probably did not come easily, and he struggled a moment to resume control.

Green trod carefully. "How might Miller and Difalco have found out? Who else knew?"

"No one. At least, I told no one."

"Not even your secretary?"

"Not even her. It was a completely private matter. Jonathan was given access to Joe's files, but he was very careful."

"Could Difalco tell from his computer records—by dates or something—that someone had been in his files?"

"The computer only registers something if there has been a change in the file. Jonathan never changed any data, he merely looked at them or printed them out."

"What about Jonathan himself? Would he have told anyone else?"

Halton shook his head. "Oh no. Jonathan was very private, very honest. It's the reason I chose him, besides his intelligence and his knowledge."

"If he did tell anyone, who would it probably be?"

Only the faint hum of the building's air conditioning punctuated the silence as Halton pondered the question. Finally he shrugged. "Perhaps his girlfriend, Vanessa Weeks, one of my Masters students. But she works under Dave, so I doubt he'd tell her."

"What about Raquel Haddad?"

"Raquel!" The professor looked astonished. "Certainly not her! That would be tantamount to shouting it from the rooftops. Besides, Raquel was Joe's special number, if I recall."

"She didn't go out with Jonathan?"

"Oh, she may have tried, but Jonathan was not that great a fool."

Green grinned. "'*Ven der putz shteit, hob der seicle in dreird*', my father used to say. Yiddish, which roughly translated is 'When the penis stands, the brain goes in the ground.'"

Halton laughed, a little too heartily, Green thought. "You've got a point. But even if Jonathan did bed her, he wouldn't confide in her."

"What was Raquel's role around here?"

"Flirt, basically," Halton replied without hesitation. "She's an undergrad taking some psych courses. I think it started when she took the physiological psychology course Joe teaches. He has an eye for an attractive woman, and Raquel certainly is that. They were involved for some time, and he brought her around to help him. Dazzle her with all the technology is more likely. She became friendly with the other students on the floor."

"So she helped Joe with his research. When was this?"

"Oh, within the past…maybe six months. She turned it into her Honours thesis."

"Would Joe have confided in her?"

"He might have told her all sorts of things in order to impress her, but probably not the truth. I wouldn't regard her as a credible witness, Detective."

"Did Raquel also help Jonathan with his research?"

Halton frowned. "Not that I'm aware of. I hope not. But your father's old saying has got me thinking. I did see her with him, just recently. They looked…definitely friendly. And he did take her into his office for quite some time." He sucked in his breath, his eyes narrowing intently behind the bristly brows. "But he wouldn't have told her anything about the investigation. No." His voice grew more certain. "No, not Jonathan. Too level-headed. Joe, now. Joe is a hothead. Joe might have complained to her about Dave's accusation, but she wouldn't know about Jonathan."

"Could either of them, Raquel or Joe, find out by searching Jonathan's office?"

He looked alarmed. "I insist that all my students keep their offices and cabinets locked. With all the expensive equipment and the irreplaceable nature of some of the files…"

"Did they have keys to each other's offices?"

Halton shook his head. "Certainly not to the filing cabinets and desk drawers. And Jonathan would not be so stupid as to leave his files out."

"Even if he planned to return? Just going for supper, say?"

Halton's voice wavered. "I don't know. I tell them not to, but they can be pretty casual about these things."

Green stood up abruptly. "I want you to come down to Jonathan's office with me. I need to know if anything's been tampered with."

Seven

As if by prearrangement, Halton and Green were just going down the hall when Lou Paquette emerged from Jonathan Blair's office. He sighed sourly as he peeled his latex gloves off his hands.

"More fingerprints, Green. Hundreds of them. What do you want me to do with them?"

"Fingerprints!" Halton began to splutter. "What the hell is going on!" He tried to push past to see into Blair's office, but Green blocked his way.

"Someone broke into Blair's office, Professor. I want to know everyone who's been in here." Cutting off Halton's attempts to protest, he turned to Paquette. "Get the prints of all the people on this floor and run a check."

"All the people—" Paquette gaped. "There must be fifty!"

"Twenty," Green replied.

Halton burst in impatiently. "This is absurd! Most of my students had nothing whatsoever to do with Jonathan. Their paths hardly crossed. All the Honours students and the first year post-grads—they're down on the other wing. They never even saw him. I won't have you upsetting them."

Paquette ran a weary hand over the beginnings of stubble on his chin. Like Sullivan, he was a policeman who put in all the overtime a case required, but, unlike Sullivan, his wife had left him because of it years ago. He had little reason to go home any more and often fell asleep over his microscope. Green took pity on him.

"Okay, just do the people on this wing. They work the most closely with him. Oh, and there's one other person I'd like you to check, but I'll have to get you her prints off something in her house. She's flown the coop."

Paquette's bleak face brightened. "Are we getting hot?"

"Definitely," Green replied. "You find anything else interesting in here? Any signs of forced entry? Tampering?"

Paquette nodded. "Not the office door, but the top drawer to this filing cabinet. Someone picked the lock—not very expertly." He led the way back inside, stepping over the files which still lay scattered on the floor where Difalco had dropped them. Green and Halton followed him into the room. Halton stopped short, staring at the mess.

"What the hell happened here?"

"Someone was curious about his files, apparently."

"Who?"

Green shrugged. "I'm not at liberty to say, sir."

"These people work for me!" Halton cried, his voice rising. "I must know—"

"Rumours, Dr. Halton," Green snapped. "Remember what you said about rumours? This investigation must be kept strictly confidential, for everyone's protection, including yours. Now would you please tell me what those files contain?"

Halton glowered at him briefly, then barrelled his way across the office. He scanned the files and his eyebrows shot up.

"They're computer print-outs of statistical analyses. On the data Jonathan had collected to replicate Difalco's research."

Green knew enough about scientific research to grasp the significance of the material. In research, the subjects are tested first, then at the end the scores are subjected to statistical analysis to determine if there were differences, patterns or trends in the scores which supported or contradicted the original theory.

"Are you saying Blair was at the point of proving or disproving Difalco's hypothesis?"

"Apparently. These analyses were dated Monday." Halton had been scanning the pages avidly, but now he raised his eyes in dismay. "The day before he died."

"What did he find?"

Halton wrestled his emotions back. "I don't know yet. It will take me some time to study them."

"How much time?"

"I don't know. Ah, tomorrow morning. I'll take them with me tonight."

Green shook his head. "I can't allow them to be out of police custody. You can look at them here tonight. I'll post a police guard in the room with you."

"But I have a meeting with Marianne Blair—"

"I'm sure she would not want the police investigation slowed down in any way." Ignoring Halton's reddening face, Green called dispatch and requested a police guard. Then he nodded to Paquette, who stood fidgeting at the door. "That filing cabinet. Was it open like that when you found it?"

Paquette nodded. "Open and empty. Looks like those files on the floor came from there."

"Interesting. Thanks, Lou. I should be down at the station in ten minutes."

"You going to sleep tonight?"

Green grinned. "Only if I run out of things to do."

*　　*　　*

That seemed an unlikely prospect as Green returned to the station and made his way to the interview room where Difalco had been detained. The young man had pushed a chair into a corner and was sprawled with his legs outstretched, pretending to be asleep. He jerked upright when Green appeared, accompanied by a constable who settled unobtrusively in the corner with his notebook. Difalco barely gave him a second look.

"Two hours, Detective," he snarled at Green, glancing at his watch. "Two hours you left me sitting in this dump. I know my rights. You've got to book me and let me see my lawyer, or you've got to let me go."

"Paperwork, Mr. Difalco," Green mimicked, swinging a chair into place beside the table. It was a barren room, small, airless and painted institutional beige. "It takes us ages sometimes. And you're quite right. I have to caution you— you don't have to say anything, you have a right to speak to a lawyer, and a right to free legal advice. But if you really weren't doing anything wrong, you can save both of us all the trouble and paperwork if you tell me what you were doing in Jonathan Blair's office tonight."

"I told you. Getting some data of his that fit with my own study."

"He was working with cats. You're working with humans."

"It's called comparative psychology, Officer," Difalco sneered. "You've probably never heard of it, but much of our knowledge about human learning comes from animals. A brain is a brain—although some less so than others." Difalco had sprawled back in his chair again, arms folded, head propped against the wall. His dark eyes simmered with disdain.

Green held his gaze and leaned forward intently. "Don't be too glib. Myles Halton is going over those files right now, and he'll be able to tell me exactly what relevance they have to your work."

Very briefly, Green detected a flare of alarm in the dark eyes before the smile widened. "You're barking up the wrong tree, Officer. You think just because I'm a rich Italian brat I'm automatically more guilty than that fumbling limpdick, Miller."

"You're the one who skipped out on my interview this morning. And you're the one I found stealing files from Blair's private office. Miller's done bugger-all."

"Still waters run deep, Mr. Detective," Difalco replied darkly. "And you never know what's hidden in their depths."

His equanimity was maddening. He was far too complacent for someone who had spent two hours awaiting interrogation in a murder investigation. Difalco was fencing with him, switching images and styles faster than Green could keep up. One minute a street tough, the next a petulant child, still the next a serious scientist. He was probably used to running circles around everyone else, and he had made the mistake of assuming Green was just another dumb cop. Perhaps that vanity could be used.

Green abandoned the bullying approach and sat back with a sigh. "Then why don't you enlighten me?"

Difalco sat forward with a smile and pulled his chair up to the table. "I'm not fooled by that righteous 'research-is-my-life' routine of his. He's got as many desires as the rest of us, but he's just no good at getting them fulfilled, so he pretends they're not there. But don't believe it for a moment! I've seen how he looks at Rosalind Simmons—she's the cheap piece with the peroxide hair you met this morning—and he'd fling her down on the office floor and rape her in a second if he thought he could get away with it. But he can't, so he's sneaky and secretive. He makes out like he's interested in her work, in her mind." Difalco threw his head back with a laugh. "Oldest line in the book. God, some women are dumb!"

"Including Rosalind Simmons?"

"When it comes to men, yeah. They believe what they want to believe, and who am I to disillusion them? Rosalind bought Miller's act, she might even have let him between her legs, although I can't imagine what he'd do there, but it's Halton she really wants. And poor old Miller hasn't a hope in hell against the big man."

"What makes you think Rosalind wants Halton?"

"Because every chick in the place wants Halton! You got to see how she looks at him in our research seminars. Her tongue hangs out, she lives for his every word. Miller doesn't exist any more."

"Does Halton respond?"

Difalco's handsome face grimaced in disgust. "Rosalind's not his type. Too old and tough. He likes them young, tender and adoring."

"Like Raquel Haddad?"

A shadow flitted across his face, marring the studied smile. "Where'd you hear about her?"

"She was your research assistant. I heard she kind of hung around the floor, and I wondered if Halton had noticed her."

Difalco flicked a piece of lint off his black Polo shirt as he worked to repair the smile. "He noticed her, sure. We're talking a ten here, Officer, and there's no way she could parade around the place unnoticed even if she wanted to, which she didn't. But you don't mess with Raquel. Lebanese women are worse than Italians. You get their whole goddamn family on your back."

"Is that what happened to you?"

"No, but that's what happened to Jonathan Blair, I'll bet you any money. And isn't that why we're here? I mean, you want to learn who killed him, right? Not why I was poking around in Blair's office or what lurks beneath Miller's choir boy smile."

"All right, what do you think happened to him?"

Difalco seemed to sense the sarcasm in his voice, because he pouted theatrically. "Oh, but you've got to take me seriously, man. Don't play me along like some dumb Eye-talian from the street."

"I don't think you're dumb, believe me, Mr. Difalco. I'm just getting tired of the fancy footwork."

Difalco sighed like a child deprived of his game. "Everyone else thinks Blair is another dickless wonder like Miller, but I know Raquel had the same effect on him as she had on every other red-blooded male in the place. He got her into his lab, then he fucked her, and before he knew it, he had the entire Canadian contingent of the Lebanese Christian Militia on his ass. They're not subtle, those guys. The honour of their women is a sacred thing."

"Do you have any evidence to support your theory?

"Oh sure. I'm sitting here with a signed confession which I forgot to give you because I'm enjoying this so much."

Green grinned at him patiently. He had learned the art of silence from Sharon, who used it as a therapy tool to get people to open up. Green had found it equally effective with suspects. Most people couldn't stand silence, and Difalco was no exception.

"No, I don't have any proof," he snapped peevishly. "Raquel never said to me 'my uncle is going to kill Jonathan Blair' or anything. But she talked about her uncle always interfering in her life, trying to fix her up with nice Lebanese men, screening her phone calls, threatening to send her back to Beirut if she didn't shape up. Not that I blame the guy, actually! Raquel was wild. If my sister did half of what she did, I'd be packing her off to a convent so fast her head would spin."

"Did Raquel seem afraid of him?"

"Afraid, but defiant—that was the way she was. She wasn't going to let that fat old blow-bag push her around."

"Do you have any proof Raquel was sexually involved with Blair?"

"Sexually involved?" Difalco repeated the phrase as if it were in a foreign tongue. "God, you cops. How about the sated look in Raquel's eye, does that qualify? She draped herself all over him, whispered in his ear, stuck her tits in his face. It didn't take an Einstein to figure out what was up."

"But did you ever see Blair reciprocate?"

"Blair was one of those Upper Canada College types, smooth and unreadable. Not like me. I like a girl, I let her know. But I can tell you this: he never pushed her hand away. Once, I surprised them in the elevator, and their tongues were halfway down each other's throats. When he saw me he broke away, and that's the only time I ever saw him unglued. He was all red in the face and breathing like he'd climbed Mount Everest."

"When was this?"

"About two weeks ago."

"Did they say anything to you?"

He laughed at the memory. "Blair looked like he wanted the earth to swallow him up. Raquel winked at me."

"Did she seem serious about him?"

A faraway light glinted in Difalco's eyes. "For that week, yeah, maybe. Raquel's like a summer storm. She blows into your life all wild and full of passion, turns it upside down, and then—" He broke off, casting Green a startled glance that revealed yet another of his personae, one that was almost wistful. Then he restored his languid smile. "But you should be asking her all these questions, Officer, not me. See for yourself. It'll make your day, and your night too, I bet."

"Joe," Green began, deliberately choosing a more intimate

address, "there is something that doesn't add up here, and I wonder if you can help me out…"

Difalco frowned at him warily.

"I've been a criminal investigator for over fourteen years, and I've seen a lot of street toughs in my day. I've seen Native Indian stoic, Irish and French Canadian bully, English boor, Italian macho…you're trying to fit, but it just doesn't sit right. I get your message loud and clear—you think you're hot stuff, you like sex, you like women—their bodies, anyway. But I also see someone else sitting in front of me. We're all alone here, Joe." He gestured around the room expressively. "Just you, me and the constable taking notes, and he's heard it all, believe me. So drop the macho stuff for me. You can put it back on when you leave here if it makes you feel better."

Difalco came alive. "Are you trying to psychoanalyze me, Detective? You implying deep down I'm afraid my dick's not big enough—"

"This has nothing to do with your dick. Your dick is fine. It's just not all you've got."

Difalco laughed, but a faint dull red spread up his neck. A lock of curly black hair fell over his brow, giving him the vulnerable look Green had glimpsed earlier. "I hope not. Sex is fine, but even I can't do it twenty-four hours a day."

"Right. So the other twenty-three hours or so, you spend closeted with computer blips and pages of numbers trying to understand how people speak. That's the part that doesn't fit, Joe. Where's the glory in that, where's the power and the big bucks that a real macho guy would need to keep going? Studs aren't interested in brain theory."

"Something wrong with brain theory? You saying I'm a wimp?"

"Cut the bluster, Joe. You know exactly what I'm saying.

Will the real Joe Difalco please talk to me?"

Difalco studied him, his eyes narrowed and the lazy smile quite gone. "Did you really think I was that shallow? That to me being a man just means fucking all day and riding around in a white Cadillac with gold chains around my neck? I want to be somebody. Those gold-chained Romeos, they're a dime a dozen on the street, but a doctor or a professor, they have respect. I was going into med school, you know. I was going to be 'il Dottore', but I couldn't hack the bullshit. In med school they tell you where to piss and when. That's not my style. Then I took Halton's undergraduate physiology course and I met 'il Professore', and I said to myself 'This is it!' Nobody pushes you around, you call your own shots. Halton goes to conferences all over the world and rubs shoulders with the best. In August he's presenting our work in Stockholm, and if I play my cards right, I get to go." Difalco rolled his eyes knowingly. "Stockholm. You know, in Europe they have great respect for university professors. Much more than they have here. There, learning and wisdom count more than money. That's my kind of power and glory, Officer. Hell, I already have all the money I need anyway. My old man swims in it. There's no mystery to me, no deep dark secrets. Sorry to fuck up your amateur analysis."

"Respect," Green remarked, undaunted. "Respect is important to you?"

"Isn't it to you? Would you be doing this job if you weren't good at it and other people didn't think you were good at it?"

"I do this job because I enjoy it and because I like the feeling of solving a case."

Difalco snorted, flashing his white teeth. "Another dickless wonder. A 'research-is-my-life' type like Miller and Blair. Bullshit. Human nature isn't like that. I'm just more honest about it than the rest of you."

Green let the silence hang as he collected his impressions. He still felt he was grappling with illusions and contradictions that bore little resemblance to the real Joseph Difalco. Halton had said Difalco was bright and intuitive, and the last hour spent dodging each other had certainly proved that. Green had made very little headway in shaking Difalco's story or breaking down his façade, but a few chinks had shown through. The young man had feigned disdain for women and for the gentler subtleties of romance, yet Raquel Haddad had certainly shaken him. Like a summer storm, he had said—a curiously poetic phrase for a macho stud. And more importantly, Difalco was a man who craved recognition, for whom belittlement or failure would be tantamount to emasculation. Such a man might do anything to ensure his success. Falsifying his research would be as natural as breathing...

But two minutes later, when Myles Halton called his office and a constable came down to tap on the interrogation room door, he found himself back at square one. The analysis Jonathan Blair had conducted unequivocally supported Difalco's claim, Halton said. There had been no fraud, no attempt to mislead.

Except, perhaps, by David Miller.

* * *

Pointing his Corolla gratefully towards home, Green slipped a Sting CD into the player. Mellow rock to soothe the frazzled spirit. He was just beginning to unwind when his cell phone rang. It was Superintendent Jules himself, reminding him that he was over two hours late for his appointment with Jonathan Blair's father, who by this time probably had a blister on his right index finger from phoning.

Swearing, Green glanced at his watch. His son would be asleep by now anyway, and any chance for a goodnight tuck-in was long gone. It didn't matter what time he got home now, as long as he retrieved the baby from the sitter's before Sharon got home at seven in the morning. Promising himself he'd read two bedtime stories tomorrow, he turned the car around and headed up Elgin Street towards the Château Laurier Hotel, which presided like a Disneyland castle over the downtown core. The neo-gothic stone spires gave way inside to carved oak, marble, and muted oriental carpeting. Henry Blair's suite was on the fourth floor, and when Green knocked, the door was flung back immediately as if Blair had been pacing just inside.

In the doorway stood a handsome, well-preserved man in his late fifties, his silver hair on end and his tie askew. He seized Green's hand and literally pulled him into the room.

"You have no idea how difficult it is, Inspector, to be trapped in this room with nothing to do but think about your dead son."

"I'm sorry, Mr. Blair. I was delayed interrogating a witness."

Blair had paced half way across the room, light and restless on his feet, and he swung back sharply.

"Any luck? Do you know who did it?"

Green could see the desperation in the man's eyes and understood his need for answers, but he had handled enough grieving relatives over the years to know that false or premature answers, and the brief comfort they offered, were worse than no answers. And with all the people clamouring for answers in this case, he had to choose his confidants carefully. So with reluctance and regret, he trotted out his standard line. "My investigation reveals several leads. We're pursuing them, I assure you."

"When will you have a solution?"

"At this stage it's too early to tell. It's a very complex case."

Blair had paused by a silver tray on which stood a bottle of Rémi Martin and two cognac glasses. "I'm finally going to allow myself one of these. I didn't want to be incoherent by the time you arrived, but by God! if ever I needed a drink! Will you join me?"

When Green demurred, Blair poured himself a healthy dose of the amber liquid and picked up the glass in shaking hands. Green pictured the man under ordinary circumstances swirling the glass in his elegant, fine-boned hand, inhaling the vapours and only then taking a slow, appreciative sip. But tonight he clutched the glass and gulped at the cognac like a man just out of the desert. Green gave him a few seconds.

"When was the last time you saw or heard from your son, Mr. Blair?"

Blair slumped into a chair. "He was coming home to visit me for Father's Day. Next Saturday, he would have arrived. He was going this weekend to buy the plane ticket. Said he'd been working too hard, wanted a break to get away from it all. University life can be claustrophobic, I know; too much inbreeding and jealousy. He sounded worn out and disillusioned, said he was thinking of transferring to the University of British Columbia. Myles Halton had been Marianne's idea. She'd known him from her undergraduate days—we both had, actually, we were at Simon Fraser together—and she never could resist using her influence. Not that Halton needed much persuading. He was delighted to have Jonathan. Bright, articulate, hard-working and the son of an influential heiress who runs a granting agency. And to show her gratitude, Marianne is already underwriting half the cost of some new equipment he wants. I'd rather hoped Jonathan would come to graduate school in Vancouver and give just the two of us a chance for once. But who am I, after all?" He smiled wanly and rose to replenish his cognac glass.

Green watched him splash half the cognac on the table trying to get it into the glass, but he resisted the urge to help. He knew that nothing he could do would ease the pain, and he had learned to watch and wait. Brian Sullivan had a strength and presence that was somehow comforting, but despite all the compassion Green felt, he'd never learned that skill. The best way he could help was to find the loved one's killer, and he hoped that he could glean all the important information he needed before the poor man was reduced to incoherence.

As he had hoped, after a few gulps Blair returned to his seat and picked up the thread. "I'm not going to get cynical. I'm not a cynic. Some maniac comes out of the darkness and wipes out my only child, but I'm not going to be a cynic. My son was finally coming home to me, was talking of living with me, and..." Blair broke off, pressing his eyes shut. For a long moment he breathed raggedly, and Green prayed he would recover. Finally he placed the brandy shakily on the table beside him. "I'd better not have any more of that for a bit."

"When did Jonathan tell you about his plans to come home?"

"Last Sunday." Blair dried his eyes with a deep, shuddering sigh. "He always calls Sunday. He said he was almost finished a portion of his research, only a week or so to go. I'd even got as far as planning some of his favourite meals. Damn!" Blair clenched his fists. "This is so hard! Have you any leads, Inspector? Oh yes, you told me you had. But who would want to do this to Jonathan? Jonathan wasn't like his mother, always centre stage and stirring up trouble. He didn't make enemies. Do you have any idea why he was killed?"

"I'm afraid I can't say at this time, sir."

"But I suppose you'll tell Marianne. I understand within the hour she had the three heads of the police department at her fingertips, whereas I had to wait eight hours to get an interview with one inspector."

"I have revealed nothing to Mrs. Blair either, sir."

The distraught man ran his hand over his face. "I'm sorry. I'm sounding petty and God knows, I'm way beyond petty. I don't begrudge Marianne her influence; I just feel so damn impotent! I don't know what I'm supposed to do while you people figure out what happened, and Marianne runs around pretending to be in charge."

"I'd be happy to give you the same briefings I give her."

"Oh!" Blair looked at Green, and his expression grew rueful. "That isn't what I meant, but thank you. I appreciate that. I'm sorry, Inspector. I know I keep saying that, but I can't seem to keep my thoughts in order. I hope you'll treat our conversation tonight as confidential. I wouldn't want Marianne to know what a mess I am."

"I don't think she's feeling all that different from you at this moment. The murder of one's child is probably the worst trauma a person ever has to survive." Green winced even as he said the words. Sullivan would have managed to make them sound human. "I think you might find it helps to talk to her."

"I called while I was waiting for you. I asked if she wanted to come here to meet you with me. She said she was expecting Myles Halton to come over." His face twisted, and Green watched with alarm as he paced around the oriental carpet. Anxious to fend off an emotional scene, Green flipped quickly back through his notes. Blair seemed a sensitive and intelligent man, bound to his son by similar temperament as well as by blood. Beneath the scattered thoughts, he perhaps had some intuitive grasp of his son's recent distress.

"You said Jonathan sounded disillusioned. Did he say with what?"

"He didn't. He's a private person, as I normally am, present circumstances excepted. But I had the impression it might have been with Myles Halton."

"Halton?" Green kept his voice carefully neutral. "Can you recall exactly what he said?"

"It wasn't anything he said—about Halton, that is. He said he'd been working really hard on this project but wasn't sure he liked the way it was turning out. I said something about all scholarly work having its setbacks, and he said he wished that was all it was. I asked him what he meant, and he said he thought he needed to get away for a bit to get some perspective. Then he commented that while he was out in Vancouver, he might look up Professor George Lester at UBC. I took that to mean that perhaps everything wasn't as rosy as when he had started with Halton. He began with such high hopes. I'd had my doubts from the beginning, but of course I kept them to myself. Marianne would not have regarded them as credible."

"What doubts?"

"That working for Halton would prove to be the edifying experience everyone expected."

"Why?"

Blair had returned to his armchair and had been quietly controlled as he reported his son's conversation. Now he fidgeted and reached for his cognac. "I'm not sure any of this is relevant, and I'm also not sure I can be objective about Halton—" he stopped abruptly "—but I knew him at Simon Fraser, even before Marianne did, and I know his flaws go deeper than Marianne thinks they do. I was in my fourth year of economics, and Halton was a freshman trying to get into our fraternity. He was brilliant and ambitious, but he was also an opinionated, loud-mouthed bully. He wanted in, and he didn't care who he stepped on to get in. He's acquired some social finesse since then and is probably more circumspect, but I imagine that ambitious bully is never far below the surface. I suspect he wouldn't let too much stand in his way."

Green let the man ramble on until the brandy and exhaustion had taken firm hold, and then he slipped quietly away. Driving back to the apartment to the soothing strains of Sting, he pondered what Henry Blair had said. The man was under extreme stress, his thoughts fragmented by shock and grief, and his judgment marred by resentment and envy. It was hard to know how much truth there was in his suspicions about Halton and about Jonathan's disillusionment, and how much wishful thinking. Blair had lost his only son, and he was entitled to a lapse in realism. Green remembered how he had felt years ago when he came home to find his house empty and nothing but a cold note from his first wife: "I've taken Hannah. We've gone to Fred in Vancouver". His daughter hadn't died, just left his life, and yet the pain had been excruciating.

He shuddered as he entered the empty, too-quiet apartment, and he felt a powerful urge to go across and fetch Tony. But reason soon prevailed. Tony and Mrs. Louks were probably both fast asleep, and he was too exhausted to face night bottles and diapers. Self-preservation won and instead, he set the alarm for six-thirty and fell into bed. A night's sleep would restore his equilibrium and as long as he picked up the baby before Sharon got home from the hospital at seven, he would be safe from her censure.

But when Sharon came home the next morning to find Tony in his high chair and pablum all over his face, she gave the baby a warm, knowing smile.

"So, pumpkin, did you have a good time sleeping over at Mrs. Louks?"

Green thought of protesting but decided against it. Somehow, she knew. The truth, humble and apologetic, was the wiser course.

"This case will take a lot of my time, Sharon. I can't help that."

Sharon kicked her shoes off, poured herself a cup of coffee, and reached over to wipe Tony's chin. The baby responded by pounding his table with his spoon and laughing in delight.

Oh great, thought Green, the famous Levy silent treatment. He gritted his teeth. "It's a mess, and there's big pressure from on high."

Sharon chucked the baby under the chin, picked up her coffee, and headed towards the bedroom, unbuttoning her cotton dress. Tony's face fell as he stared at her retreating back, and in the next instant, he began to wail.

"Fuck it," Green muttered and pulled him out of the high chair. He found her sitting on the bed in her underwear, massaging her swollen feet, and he sat the baby down beside her.

"I gotta go. Nice talking to you."

He fumed all the way to the university. Maybe he was wrong, but she was barely cutting him any slack. Relationships were hard work, but you had to be willing to do the work. All right, he knew that she had a demanding job too, that wrestling with psychotics and talking down suicides could leave a person drained at the end of the day. But when would she understand that his wasn't a job like any other, that he couldn't just leave it behind at the end of an eight-hour shift? People's futures, their freedom, sometimes their very lives depended on his being right. In his job, one slip-up could shatter a life.

He was acutely aware of this when he arrived at Halton's laboratories to check further into Jonathan's data and found David Miller already summoned to the great man's office. The secretary had no idea how long he might be there, but Green had only waited five minutes before Halton's door flung back and Miller blundered past him unseeing, his skin the colour of parchment.

Green sprang forward. "Dr. Miller, a word in your office, please."

Trancelike, Miller turned towards the sound of his voice and stared uncomprehendingly.

"Inspector Green of the Ottawa Police. We spoke yesterday."

"Oh…" Miller passed a hand over his eyes as if to clear them. "Ah…now is not a good time, Inspector."

"This can't wait, I'm afraid." Green took his elbow and steered him bodily down the hall into his office. Once inside, Miller collapsed onto the swivel chair in front of his computer and plunged his head into his hands.

"What did Halton say?" Green began carefully.

Miller rocked his head back and forth. "I'm ruined. He cut off my fellowship, he's throwing me out of the university. All my work, all my hopes…"

"Did he say why?"

"He says I sabotaged Joe's work. I can't believe it! He believes that putz over me! He thinks so little of me that he'd believe… Shit!" Miller broke off, sobbing. "Shit! Shit! Shit! It's not fair! That guy has been out to get me ever since I got here and finally he's succeeded. But how? That's what doesn't make any sense!"

"Did Halton tell you how he came to this conclusion?"

Miller wiped tears from his eyes and tried for a deep, steadying breath. "I'm sorry. I'm not up to this right now. I can't think straight. I need to get out of here and clear my head."

113

Green rose to his feet. "I'll buy you a coffee somewhere."

Five minutes later, they were settled over coffee at a little sidewalk café across from the library. Although it was just after nine o'clock, the sun was harsh and the air already soggy. Traffic crawled by in front of them, exhaust fumes mingling with the heat off the asphalt, and Green felt sweat trickling down his back. He studied Miller surreptitiously. Something in the man's initial raw shock touched a chord. It was hard to imagine that the anguish had been faked, and that the man was capable of the calculated betrayal of which he'd been accused.

The hot, bitter coffee seemed to steady Miller, drawing colour to his cheeks. Green took up the thread obliquely.

"This place hasn't changed at all since I came here eight years ago. There's still only one outdoor café on the whole campus."

Miller frowned. "You went to university?"

"Masters in Criminology, piece by painful piece. Evenings, nights, weekends. Took forever!" He grinned. "You look surprised."

"I am. I mean—a cop. I never expected..."

"I did research, I did a thesis. I know how you get to live the stuff day and night, how important it becomes to you."

Miller shook his head. "Not enough to sabotage somebody else, if that's what you're suggesting. You see, I don't view Joe's work as competition. Joe does. His mind is full of dreams of a post-doc at Yale, and he thinks he has to be right. But that's not how research works. I was really interested in whether his model would work. That's what's important, finding theories that work, building on them and chipping away bit by bit at the mystery of the brain. All our theories are wrong, Inspector. Mine is wrong, Joe's is wrong. We're still light years away from the truth. All we can do is find which is a little less wrong, so we can keep expanding. Ten or twenty years down the road, scientists will look back on our work and shake their heads at the simple-mindedness of it all. Where would we be if Best had sabotaged Banting's work? I thought Halton knew how I felt. I thought that's one reason he took me on. I can't believe Joe pulled it off."

"Did Halton tell you why he believed Joe and not you?"

Miller gestured vaguely. "He said something about independent data corroborating Joe's. I was so upset I couldn't take it all in. But it doesn't make sense. You can't get the data Joe says he got. Vanessa and I ran simulations. Simulations aren't perfect, and maybe mine were way off base, but I couldn't get them to give figures anything like those Joe reported. And Joe's scores were faked. I saw it with my own two eyes. The numbers didn't match!"

"You're absolutely positive? You weren't looking at the wrong data?"

"Oh, no." Miller took a big bite of muffin and shook his head vigorously, sending crumbs flying. He was quite in control now that outrage was taking hold. "After I ran the simulations, I broke right into his raw data. I know I was out of line to break into his files, but I wasn't going to go to Halton with an accusation about a fellow student until I had proof. Joe's raw data bore absolutely no resemblance to the figures he used in his analyses. But I never dreamed the slippery bastard would turn the tables on me. In one fell swoop he wipes out his raw data and blames it on me."

Green studied him carefully. He had seen a lot of liars in his day and had learnt to be suspicious. Still waters run deep, Difalco had warned him, but Green could not sense even a hint of deception in the man before him. Something did not add up. Blair's own research supported Difalco's claims, and yet Miller argued just as convincingly that it was impossible.

"Do you know where the independent corroborating data came from?" Green asked quietly.

There was no hint of deception in Miller's reaction either. His bewildered shrug seemed genuine. "I have no idea. Halton himself, I guess. Unless…" His colour fled. "My God, Jonathan Blair!"

"What about Jonathan Blair?"

Miller covered his mouth in horror. "No! Could it be? That's impossible!" He looked up with stricken eyes. "Inspector, this is awful!"

"What are you thinking?"

"I can't believe I'm thinking it. I know Joe really wanted that Yale appointment, but I didn't think he'd go as far as murder!"

"How do you figure that?" Green demanded. "Joe's claims have been substantiated."

"Not necessarily." David Miller was already rising from his chair, stumbling as he groped around the table.

"Where are you going?"

"To check Jonathan's files for myself," Miller shot back.

"No you don't! Miller! Wait!" Green watched the balding man blunder through the maze of tables toward the street. "Damn!" He threw a couple of loonies on the table and headed in pursuit. As he ran, he groped at his belt for his radio.

"Get me a twenty-four hour police guard on Jonathan Blair's office. ASAP!"

Eight

Once the uniformed officer was installed outside Blair's office, Green felt it safe to return to his own. He needed more hard facts so that he could make sense of the conflicting stories he was hearing about Halton's research team. But when he arrived back at the station, he was assailed by half-a-dozen detectives clamouring to give him their reports and demanding their next assignment. I can't operate this way, he thought. I'm a solo performer, not an orchestra conductor. I need an accompanist, maybe two, and occasional guidance from a music critic, but this cacophony of sound just blows my mind.

Backing into his office doorway, he held up his hands. "Give me all you've got on the university colleagues, and leave everything else with Sullivan. Then if you've got nothing to follow up on from yesterday, go back to your regular duties. I'll call you if I need you. And don't anybody—anybody—disturb me for an hour."

Once the last of the reports had been handed to him, he shut his office door and took a deep breath. Peace. Swiftly he cleared the clutter from his desk and piled it on the floor, then spread the reports out on the desk. During the next half-hour he pored over every page, and gradually the community of scientists began to unfold. A diverse group drawn together only by their mutual fascination with the brain. And by the magnetism of Myles Halton.

Myles Halton was born forty-eight years earlier in Vancouver, the son of a wealthy logging magnate. He spent his winters in the genteel, well-manicured Vancouver suburb of British Properties and his summers among the lumberjacks in the bush. He attended an elite private school, where he was always something of an outsider among the bankers' and lawyers' sons, then went on to Simon Fraser University and Berkeley for his Ph.D. in the fledgling field of neuropsychology. In the years since, he had earned a reputation as a rigorous scientist and a demanding professor who used his own personal charisma to keep colleagues, critics and students in line.

At the same time, he liked high living and enjoyed the company of powerful friends. He married the daughter of a Toronto millionaire and sent his two daughters to boarding school in Toronto. It was rumoured that his wife spent most of her time in Europe, and that he had a girlfriend in nearly every major Canadian city. He owned a house in Rockcliffe Park, home of Ottawa's moneyed and diplomatic elite, as well as a large summer house on the Ottawa River near Constance Bay, where he moored his single-engine Cessna seaplane. The bush was in his blood, and every summer he took two weeks off to fly north into the wilderness to fish.

A man of contradictions, Green thought as he pictured the bearded giant wrestling with timber deep in the B.C. interior, learning the violence of nature and the supremacy of might. Halton had the capacity for murder, he decided. But unless a large piece of the puzzle was missing, he had no motive. And, Green discovered when he read the next report, he had an ironclad alibi.

On the night of the murder, Halton had been in Toronto dining at the Whaler's Wharf with a colleague from York University. He had driven down the previous evening, spent the day sailing Lake Ontario on the colleague's fifty-foot yacht and driven back to Ottawa after dinner late Tuesday evening.

Joe Difalco's alibi was less ironclad but still impressive. He had spent the evening carousing with friends at the Royal Oak Pub on campus, and at least half a dozen fellow students recalled seeing him at one point or another. No one was very clear on the times, but he had certainly been there to close the place down at two in the morning. Everyone who knew Joe agreed that once he arrived at a watering hole, he rarely left before closing.

Unlike his rugged mentor, Joe Difalco was a pampered city boy, the only son of a successful Italian restauranteur who had started as a dishwasher in a back street café and now owned four restaurants and a catering business. The family lived in a multi-turreted mansion on a rolling half-acre in the wealthy suburb of Cedarhill, and Joe drove a Jaguar to the university. In his undergraduate years he had earned a reputation as an amateur boxer. It was in this capacity, rather than through any academic distinction, that he first caught the attention of Myles Halton. Halton was a fan of the sport, which married agility, cunning and brute force, and had dabbled in it himself as a youth. People who knew him theorized that he always regretted not having a son and that he took Joe under his wing to fill that void.

Joe's lack of discipline and his love of wine, women and late nights proved to be his downfall, however, and he gave up serious boxing in his first post-graduate year. By that time he had already found a comfortable niche among Halton's favoured few, and he had stayed there ever since. There had been no major concerns or complaints from his professors over the years, but most regarded him as flighty and self-indulgent. Hardly the blueprint for a cold-blooded killer, Green thought.

For that, David Miller's profile held more promise.

David Miller's life was in some ways the mirror opposite of Difalco's. He was the eldest of five children and had grown up in the tough blue-collar Montreal district of Park Extension. His grandfather had immigrated to Montreal from Russia in the wave of Jewish immigrants escaping the pogroms in the early part of the century. The grandfather had peddled rags, and the father had become a butcher. While his neighbourhood friends dropped out of school and squired girls around in stolen cars, David swept factory floors on evenings and weekends to earn enough money for the tuition. At McGill University he had no friends, played no sports, and belonged to no clubs. All he had were his books.

"Dave Miller couldn't sell himself to save his soul," Halton had said. In his final undergraduate year, he had suffered a nervous breakdown and apparently required two more psychiatric hospitalizations at Stanford, where he had spent over ten years completing his Ph.D.

But it was after graduation that his real troubles began. The job market was tight, and he returned to his family in Montreal penniless and depressed until Myles Halton tracked him down almost two years ago.

A history of mental instability, Green thought. He flung open his door and spotted Sullivan hunched over his desk, talking on the phone. As Green approached, Sullivan caught his eye, finished his conversation quickly and hung up. Freshly shaved and wearing a crisp white shirt, he looked revived, but the worry lines were still there. Green eyed the phone.

"I didn't mean to interrupt you."

Sullivan shrugged. "It's just as well. I was about to lose my temper."

Green frowned. His quick eye had noticed a letter from the

Toronto Dominion Bank on the desk before Sullivan shoved it into a drawer. "Problems?"

"Just the little guy against the system," Sullivan replied with a grin. "It amazes me how the system always wins."

"Yeah, well, the rules are fixed, aren't they? Sharon and I figure that even if we do manage to find a house we can both stand, after twenty-five years we'll have paid the bank four times what it's worth. Talk about indentured service!"

"Why do you think Mary can't sell any houses? Welcome to family life, buddy." Sullivan shook his head wryly and nodded at the report Green held in his hand. "You want something, or are you just trying to depress me?"

It was Sullivan's way of drawing the curtain, closing his personal life off from his professional, and Green followed suit. "I want you to dig around in Miller's medical history. Especially the Allan Memorial in Montreal and the Royal Ottawa here."

Sullivan's eyebrows shot up. "Is he a psycho?"

"He's done some stints. Find out why. Anything that looks like paranoia or violent outbursts, let me know."

"Is he our best bet?"

Green hesitated. Miller's anguish had seemed so raw and his protestations of innocence so genuine, that it was hard to see him as a killer. But if Jonathan Blair's research was correct, he was the one with the strongest motive.

"I'm still going through the reports," Green replied. "Miller told Jackson he was working on his computer all evening when Blair was killed, but Jackson thought he seemed nervous. He was sure Miller was hiding something."

Jackson had drawn the same conclusion about Miller's friend, Rosalind Simmons, Green discovered when he returned to the reports in his office. Before leaving the university that evening, she said she'd dropped in to see if

Miller was hungry, because when he became absorbed in his work he forgot to eat and on several occasions had nearly passed out from hypoglycemia. But on the night in question, she found Miller sitting at his terminal with a coke and a half-eaten hamburger at his elbow, intent on his work. She had gone straight home, making no stops and seeing no one who could confirm the time she arrived at her apartment. Rosalind Simmons lived alone, and Jackson's inquiries into her background had met with limited success.

Her friends and colleagues knew surprisingly little about her. She was raised in Toronto by a single mother, attended local public schools and completed her undergraduate work at York University. She had been working on her Ph.D. with Myles Halton for two years, and Halton reported that her progress was so slow that he was considering dropping her from the program. Other professors recalled that she was not a memorable student; she lacked dynamism and insight, but she had a slow, plodding perseverance that kept her on track. They had no concerns about her ethics, however, and could not even remotely imagine her capable of murder. Socially, no one knew much about her, except that she kept to herself. She had no known friends or boyfriends, and some of her colleagues speculated that she might be gay.

Green mulled that idea over. He remembered the fierceness with which she had defended Miller and the glow in her cheeks when she spoke of him. No, he thought, she's not gay. Joe Difalco is right about one thing—she's in love with David Miller. However, given Miller's social ineptitude and her instinct for self-protection, it was questionable whether the two were actually involved. Green had known lots of street girls like her, who wanted closeness yet didn't trust. Someone had probably hurt her badly once, and she was reluctant to give anyone a second chance. She would not wear her heart on her sleeve, but beneath the surface…

Jonathan's former girlfriend, on the other hand, had worn her heart on her sleeve and had suffered the consequences. Everyone had expected wedding bells before the year was out, but then suddenly, with the appearance of Raquel Haddad, the romance was over. Vanessa Weeks had presented a brave front, saying both of them needed to focus on their studies at the moment, but privately her friends thought she was heartbroken. All the more so because her parents had regarded her choice to study at Ottawa University under Halton as misguided rebellion, the one redeeming feature of which had been her alliance with Jonathan Blair. Her father was an ex-chief of surgery at Harvard Medical School who had treated presidents, and her mother was on staff at Massachusetts General Hospital, where she was slated to be the next chief of psychiatry. They had been adding the MD to Vanessa's name ever since she was old enough to talk, and up to the age of twenty her academic and athletic accomplishments had fuelled their hopes. High School graduation at age sixteen, straight A's at Radcliffe and a bronze medal at the National Women's Singles Tennis Championships. But then a broken wrist and the death of her Olympic dreams had prompted her to re-evaluate her direction and to choose a new course. She had been studying under Halton for a year, and he had given her glowing reports. She was one of the few students who could understand David Miller's work and that, coupled with her self-discipline and drive, was raising her quickly through the Halton ranks.

She had begun dating Jonathan Blair nine months earlier, and through most of the winter, the two had been inseparable. She shared his enthusiasm for skating and cross-country skiing, and they had spent much of their free time together. In temperament too, they had seemed well-suited. Both quiet, private people, they were discreet in their passion, but no one doubted they were deeply attached. There were no fights, no scenes.

Unlike Sharon and me, thought Green wryly, recalling the numerous times Sharon had walked out on him amid screaming and tears in the three years of their marriage. Only to find that being apart was worse than being together.

On the evening of Jonathan Blair's murder, Vanessa Weeks had been at the university gym, working off her bitterness with laps in the indoor pool. Following a sauna and a shower, she had been seen leaving the facility by the pool attendant at closing a few minutes after eleven. She was a regular evening swimmer, and the attendants knew her by sight.

Green sat back, scanning the reports spread out on his desk. Somewhere in this compilation of facts lay the key to the killer. Rarely had he encountered a killer so subtle and elusive. Not everyone had those qualities, and this murderer, by the very method he had chosen, had left a unique signature on the crime. Match the signature, and the murderer's identity might leap out at him.

Taking a fresh white pad of paper, he pushed the reports aside and began to write.

Profile of the killer:
—Clever, some knowledge of forensics
—Thorough and prepared, careful with planning
—Quick and agile, maybe some training in fighting?
—Cold-blooded, nerves of steel, capable of close-range killing without panicking
—Passionate about work? Or psychopathic—kill those who get in way?

He studied his suspects. All of them were clever, and all had enough scientific background to be a quick study in forensics. Hell, the books they would need were probably right in the library where Blair was killed! All were thorough and capable of planning—scientific research demanded it. Perhaps Difalco was less so, but Green was not about to underestimate him. He suspected Difalco let people see what he wanted them to see but kept a large part of himself under wraps.

Agile. Now here…

His phone buzzed at his elbow, startling him. Swearing, he pounced on it, and Jules' dry voice came through.

"Michael, Peter Weiss is in my office."

"Lucky you."

Silence greeted him through the wires. It's that bad, he thought. "Adam, I'm up to my ears in reports. I've got to have some time to piece things together."

"I need something he can take back to Marianne Blair."

"And then Marianne Blair will take it back to Myles Halton. Absolutely no way."

He could almost hear Jules processing the implications. Finally, he spoke. "I'm coming down."

Green hung up, fuming. Why couldn't everyone just leave him alone to do his job? Now, with Jules' deadline hanging over his head, he'd never be able to free his mind for thought. On impulse. he scooped up his reports and headed for the door, catching sight of Sullivan still on the phone. He approached and lowered his voice.

"I'm going home to work and don't tell a damn soul where I am."

Over the years, Green had often retreated to the peace and solitude of his own apartment when he needed to think. The drive home took five minutes but he was already beginning to unwind by the time he unlocked the door to his apartment. Until he heard the all-too-familiar sound of the baby whining. He had forgotten all about them! How much simpler life had been before…

He stomped into the kitchen to find Tony banging pots together and Sharon on her knees, wiping up the puréed peas beneath the high chair. Seeing him, Tony crowed in delight. Green gave him a distracted pat on the head and tossed his reports on the kitchen table.

"Sharon, could you take the baby for a walk? I've got to have some peace and quiet."

She rose slowly to her feet, pushing her black curls out of her eyes with the back of her hand. She was dressed in her usual baggy shorts and shapeless T-shirt, and she fixed him with a cold, level glare.

"Excuse me? You have an office to work in."

"And a million people on my ass. Honey, I haven't got time to explain. Just please bear with me, okay?"

"If we'd bought that house in Barrhaven, there'd be room for all of us, you know. But no, Barrhaven didn't have enough character. It had plumbing that worked, nice quiet streets, but God forbid you should join the grey suits in suburbia."

It was a refrain she dredged up every time they felt the pressure of their tiny home, and his own response had become automatic. "Barrhaven isn't suburbia, it's the end of the earth."

She set her jaw as if preparing to defend the sprawling suburb that had sprung up in the cow pastures southwest of the city, but then seemed to sense the futility of it. She tossed the sponge into the sink, scooped up the baby and stalked by him out of the room. "I'll take your son out for a walk, Green, but don't be surprised if we're mowed down in the streets the minute we step out the door."

Fuck, he thought. Just what I need. I've got two hours—tops—before Jules tracks me down, even if I take the phone off the hook, and I've got so much adrenaline coursing through me I'll never be able to think. Why can't she realize that the murder of Jonathan Blair is not just another day at the office? It's always her and her needs! Hers, and now the baby's. She has a new weapon to brandish over me now. Tony needs a father, Green. Tony needs a home. Get your priorities straight, Green. Green, Green, Green... Whatever happened to Mike? Or darling? What happened to the tender look in those sparkling black eyes? What happened to the wide, sexy smile?

He heard the front door slam behind her, and he plunged his face into his hands wearily. I'm getting nowhere this way, he thought. I can't deal with this now. I can't afford to wonder if my marriage is falling apart.

Clear your mind, Green. Focus on Jonathan Blair and on the facts of this case. Logic, Green. Means, motive and opportunity—focus on these, and the answer will come.

He fixed himself an ice cold coke and slipped a CD of instrumental blues into his player. Music to think by. Clearing the kitchen table of all its debris, he put his pad of paper in the centre. In a column down the left-hand side, he listed the major players in the drama. Using the basics tenets of police deduction, he began to fill in the right side of the page.

—Joe Defalco: Motive: *jealousy or cover-up of fraud*
Pro: *fits personality type, hates to lose.*
Con: *crime too neatly planned for this kind of rage.*
Also, Blair's research supports his.
Alibi: *campus pub, several witnesses.*

—Vanessa Weeks	Motive: *punish him for jilting her.* Pro: *appears to have loved him a lot.* Con: *seems like fairly together girl* Alibi: *at university pool, seen by pool attendants.*
—David Miller:	Motive: *cover-up of fraud* Pro: *personality unstable, paranoia or hidden rage? Research is his life. If taken away, might erupt.* Con: *gut feeling not the type* Alibi: *none*
—Rosalind Simmons:	Motive: *protect Miller from Blair's exposure* Pro: *fiercely protective* Con: *far-fetched, Green.* Alibi: *none*

Of these four, Difalco had the most promising behavioural profile for the killing, but he had a strong alibi and a weak motive. David Miller had no alibi and the strongest motive, but...quick and agile?

There was, however, one more name. Thoughtfully, Green put it down.

Myles Halton: Motive...

At this point, Green laid down his pen. Heat was seeping into the airless little room, and he wiped a trickle of sweat from his temple. Taking a sip of lukewarm cola, he pondered the character of Myles Halton. Halton was a brilliant scientist, no one disputed that, and no one seemed to question the integrity of his rise to prominence. In the interview, Halton

128

had come across as an intense, no-nonsense, ambitious man committed to the pursuit of his research. He had not seemed self-serving or unethical, and if he was determined to protect his research effort, it was only because he had fought so hard for it, and it was just beginning to pay dividends.

Green felt his antennae quiver. How hard had the man fought, and just what was he willing to sacrifice in order to preserve his status? He was uncompromising. Was he also ruthless? He was ambitious. Was he also unethical? Henry Blair had said Halton didn't care whom he stepped on to achieve his goal. And one of his goals right now was a three million dollar magnetic resonance imager and the competitive research it promised.

Powerful men were rarely lily-white, but would Halton go as far as murder? Particularly the murder of a wealthy scion, which he knew would make his operation the focus of an intense, highly publicized police investigation? He would only have done so if he had no choice. What possible scenario would give him no choice?

Normally, the power balance between a graduate student and a prominent professor is highly weighted in the latter's favour. If conflicts arose, the student would simply be failed. This would be more difficult in the case of a potential backer's son, but the alternative, killing the student, hardly seemed designed to maintain friends in high places.

The balance of power shifts in the student's favour only if the student has some leverage, perhaps something on the professor that could destroy his career. A politician had once said that only two things could ruin his reputation—being caught in bed with a live boy or a dead girl. What could ruin Halton's reputation? A sex-related charge? Fairly iffy. Professors were not politicians. Universities and granting agencies were probably much more tolerant of the sexual perversities of their errant geniuses than the general public was of its elected officials. If Halton had been accused of sleeping with a student, particularly the likes of Raquel Haddad, he would have endured a slap on the wrist, some unpleasant publicity, some hisses and boos from the feminist community, and then it would be business as usual. A sex scandal involving a male student might prove stickier and more humiliating, but was it worth the risk of murder?

It was possible that an old skeleton, which Halton thought safely buried in his closet, had come to light and was threatening his career. An old research fraud, a suspicious death, a serious crime. If Jonathan had unearthed it, what would he do with it? He was not the blackmailing kind. Everyone said his moral standards were unassailable. He would not use information against his professor for personal gain. But those same standards would not allow him to turn a blind eye to a crime. If he had uncovered a major breach of ethics or law on Halton's part, he would have agonized, but he would have turned him in.

Yes, Green thought, in this remote scenario the dynamics for murder were there. The personalities fit—Halton's ambition pitted against Blair's moral rectitude. Now it was time to speculate on what might have happened.

The timing of Blair's murder was crucial. He had been murdered just as he completed his investigation into the research fraud. The statistical analysis was done. On the morning of his murder, in fact, he had asked for an urgent appointment with Halton, probably to discuss those very results. But Blair had not been relieved or triumphant, he had been upset, as if he had uncovered something unexpected in his study of Difalco's work. Yet the activities of Miller and

Difalco, no matter how nefarious, would hardly have upset him that much. He had been disillusioned to the point of considering a transfer to another university. Disillusioned with Halton? What might he have discovered? That Halton had been party to the fraud? If so, why ask Blair to investigate in the first place?

Green stood up, stretched his stiff legs and unglued his sweaty shirt from his back. Leaning on the kitchen counter, he frowned down at his notes. Was he clutching at straws? Winging out into the wild blue yonder, as Sullivan called it when his deductive fantasies took flight? Possibly, but over the years he had learned to trust his fantasies. Halton, with his ambition and his reputation to protect, was as good a murder suspect as the rest. Maybe even better.

But to uncover the motive, Green had to put Halton's research, and that of Miller, Difalco and Blair, under a microscope to determine who was lying. He had only Halton's word that Blair's results supported Difalco. He needed an impartial expert in neuropsychology and a search warrant to seize all the files in the four offices. A sense of urgency gripped him; search warrants took hours to write up, but if he didn't act fast, Halton and the others might get to the files first.

*   *   *

Several hours later, Green arrived back at the squad room with the signed search warrant triumphantly in hand. He was high with energy, no longer impatient and irritable as he rounded up the only two detectives still at their desks.

"Watts and Charbonneau, I want you to get over to the university. I have a warrant to seize all the files, computers, disks and any other paper or electronic data belonging to Miller, Difalco, Blair and Halton. Load every last piece of paper in their four offices into boxes. Make sure you label each box carefully so none of the files gets mixed up, and put them all in Halton's main computer lab. Then seal the offices and post a twenty-four hour guard so no one can tamper with anything until we can get an outside expert in there to look at this stuff. I hope to have someone lined up to start tomorrow. Okay, guys, go!"

Without waiting for the two detectives to get out the door, Green entered his office, pushed the stack of phone messages out of the way and pulled out his phone book. It took him almost an hour of phone calls to four different universities before he located an expert in neuropsychology who was not only familiar with Halton's work but also willing to drop everything to spend several days holed up in a computer lab going over files. Dr. Stanley Baker, professor of physiological psychology at McGill University, was less than gracious but grudgingly agreed. For a fee.

After Green hung up the phone, feeling very pleased with himself, he wondered fleetingly if he ought to have cleared the expense with Jules first. He was just steeling himself to go upstairs to discuss it when his door swung open and Superintendent Jules strode in, gray eyes as narrow as pinpricks. He shut the door behind him and stood ramrod straight, his arms crossed over his chest.

"Michael, what the hell is going on?"

Green was taken aback. Jules was always polished, precise and understated. In a station full of obscenities, he never swore. "I was just coming up, Adam."

"How nice. Then you can tell me what the hell I'm supposed to say to the Deputy Chief that he can explain to

132

Marianne Blair that she can explain to Myles Halton about why the hell all his university files are being carted off by the police."

Green burst out laughing. He knew it was unwise, but it was irrepressible. "Poor Adam. Superiors are such a pain in the ass, aren't they?"

For an instant he thought Jules was going to erupt. Never had he seen him quite that shade of fuchsia. But then, in spite of himself, Jules broke into a real smile. This is a day for firsts, thought Green.

Jules pulled back the guest chair and sat down. "Michael, there must be at least the appearance that I control you."

"I know. So Halton is pissed, is he?"

Jules nodded. "I think he expected something slightly better from his friendship with Mrs. Blair than the appearance of two non-ranking detectives. No me, no you."

"No brass band." Green shook his head dolefully. "I would have gone, but I had other arrangements to make, and we had to move very fast. As it is, the horse has probably already left the barn."

"Enlighten me."

Green took twenty minutes to summarize the progress of the investigation to date and to outline his next moves. He was about to broach the subject of expenses when there was a sharp knock at the door, and Sullivan flung it open. He was so excited that the sight of Jules barely gave him pause.

"A suspect! Maybe two or three. The Raquel Haddad connection."

Jules glanced at Green, eyebrows high. "You didn't mention a Raquel Haddad connection."

"That's just another avenue we're pursuing," Green replied irritably. "On the back-burner right now."

Sullivan flourished a report. "Not any more! Some heavy-duty stuff was going on between Raquel, her uncle and Blair on the day he was killed."

Green perked up. "Tell me!"

"First, you know that Blair and Raquel were likely an item. Well, a student saw Blair in the student coffee shop eating supper with a black-haired woman. The student phoned our hotline once she saw Blair's picture in the paper. Anyway," Sullivan flipped open his notebook, "the witness said they were sitting very close, whispering. The black-haired girl was crying, and then this student overheard Blair say to her 'But he'd never really do it!' and Raquel said 'You don't know him! You don't know my family!' A few minutes later these two tough-looking guys come along and they tell her to come with them. She starts to get up and Jonathan Blair tells them to lay off, it's a free country. And she shouts 'Jonathan, don't!' They grab her arm. Jonathan steps between them, and they punch him. He falls over the table. They're hauling Raquel along, Jonathan starts after them, and she yells at him to go away. Then they all get out of view, and our witness didn't see what else happened."

"What time was this?"

"About six-thirty."

"These tough-looking guys, what did they look like?"

Sullivan glanced through his notebook. "Twentyish. Medium height and weight, thick dark hair, brown eyes, heavy eyebrows. One had a mustache. Dressed in casual summer clothes. One had on a light T-shirt and jeans, the other a black Metallica T-shirt and black jeans. No distinguishing marks."

"Twentyish?" Green frowned. "Raquel's uncle is in his forties and fat."

Sullivan shrugged. "Henchmen, probably. An older, heavy-set, dark guy was seen arguing with Raquel outside Halton's building earlier that afternoon."

Green sat up sharply. "Seen by whom?"

"David Miller."

"Why the hell didn't anyone tell me!"

"I'm telling you now. I just saw the report."

Green frowned in thought, tapping his pencil against his desk. "Might be just a coincidence. Okay, this has to be low key. Get a photo of Pierre Haddad and show a photo line-up to Miller. See if he can make a positive ID on the guy arguing with Raquel."

Sullivan's eyes flitted from Green to Jules. "Low-key?"

Green shrugged. "Just don't spook him. The guy's paranoid about cops. Tell him it's routine, standard operating procedure—improvise. Just don't mention the fight in the coffee shop. If this is our guy, I don't want to tip him off, or he'll send those young thugs underground."

Even before the door had closed on Sullivan, Green was riffling through the files on the floor. He had glimpsed the background check on Pierre Haddad earlier in passing, but had discarded it as irrelevant to the mystery of the research data. Now he pounced on it.

The team investigating the background of the Haddad family had come up with precious little. From the tone of the report it sounded as if the entire Lebanese community had shut down tight at the first sight of the police. Official records provided a skeleton of information but little insight into the family. Pierre Haddad, a Christian, had immigrated from Beirut in 1978 through regular immigration channels, not as a refugee. Initially, he had worked as a taxi driver, but in 1984, he had purchased the corner confectionary store in Little Italy. His payments to the Toronto Dominion Bank were regular and reliable, and his business dealings seemed completely above board.

A search of police and motor vehicle records had revealed the same wholesome picture. Haddad had no record of criminal activity and only a handful of traffic tickets to his name. He owned two cars, a Taurus family sedan and a four-wheel drive pick-up. Expensive, but not outrageous. Since 1988 Haddad had lived with his family in a modest bungalow in the older Ottawa suburb of Elmvale Acres. His wife was also a Lebanese Christian and the couple had made a strict, traditional Lebanese home for their two sons, who were now young men. The neighbours reported that the Haddads were a quiet, courteous family who kept to themselves but were happy to lend a hand in an emergency. The father in particular was popular with the neighbourhood children, because he sometimes gave out free candy.

Another Mr. Perfect, thought Green grimly as he saw his theory gradually turn to dust. No temper, no history of violence or intimidation.

As he was scanning, he had forgotten Jules, who was reading over his shoulder, until Jules' quiet voice cut in. "Michael, this could be sticky."

Green cocked his head, puzzled. Jules waved a manicured hand. "The Middle East, you know. Things can be ...misconstrued."

"Adam, so far I have a fight and a tyrannical uncle, not an international plot. There's nothing here to suggest anything political."

"What about the young men who assaulted Blair in the coffee shop?"

"They could be just sons of friends. Did CSIS or the RCMP turn up any connection to political groups? Terrorists, organized crime?"

Jules shook his head. "But ethnic groups usually stick together. If one person is in trouble, the others pitch in, like one big happy family—"

Green broke in abruptly, his eyes widening. "Family!" He dived for the report he had tossed aside and scanned it, reaching for the phone. "Pierre Haddad has two sons who might be twentyish."

"Michael, please. Remember the rule book."

Green paused, his hand on the receiver. "I'm just going to tell Sullivan to get pictures of the two sons and show them to our coffee shop witness. If she can ID either of them as being involved in the fight, we'll take it from there. Is that 'by the book' enough for you?"

Jules paused on his way out the door. "Keep me informed."

Once he had relayed the added requests to Sullivan, Green sat in his office, feeling restless and ill at ease. Had he forgotten anything? The Halton files had been seized and an expert lined up to review them the next day. Alibis had been obtained on all Blair's known colleagues, and background checks had been done on Pierre Haddad. Blair's activities had been traced on the day he died and arrangements made to identify the suspects who had assaulted him shortly before his death. Nothing tied in directly to the murder, but it was the best he could do. For now, it was a waiting game.

He glanced at his watch. Past five o'clock. He looked at the phone, thinking of Sharon and remembering the bitterness in her eyes when he had thrown her out. He should send her some flowers. A dozen red roses with a note saying "I'm sorry". She was his wife, after all. She put up with a lot, and she was entitled to better.

Entitled, he thought with dismay. Is that the word that comes to mind when I think of her? Not love, not passion—

but entitlement? He put his face in his hands with a groan. This relationship was not going to go the way of all his previous ones, three or four years and off to greener pastures. He tried to picture Sharon as she had been in the beginning, when he had fallen so hard. Fresh, wise-cracking and sexy, with a sly smile that drove him crazy and a tender wisdom that brought a lump to his throat.

But instead, his mind conjured up honey-blond hair, tight jeans and a full, pouting mouth.

He jerked his head up, the memory chasing out all else. There *was* a stone unturned! There was someone who might be able to tie the Haddads directly to the murder.

Nine

Carrie MacDonald answered her apartment bell on the second ring, at first peering out warily, then flinging the door wide at the sight of Green.

"I thought you had forgotten all about me!" she cried, eyes shining, and he was grateful she could not read his mind. Forgotten like hell! "Come on in. I've been getting so many nuisance callers that I'm almost thinking of moving."

The policeman in him reacted. "What kind of nuisance callers?" he demanded sharply.

"Oh, reporters, nosy neighbours. I just slam the door in their faces." Seeing his worried look, she smiled. "I can take care of myself, have since I was nine. It's my daughter. If they start bugging her…"

"Get a good dead bolt installed, and a chain and peephole."

She pranced after him as he made his way into the living room. "Aye, aye, sir. Want some tea? Coffee? You look tired."

He rubbed his eyes as he sank down on the sofa. Toys were strewn all over the floor, reminding him of home. And Sharon. He still hadn't called her, hadn't sent her flowers. He banished the guilt with an effort. "Long hours. Tea would be nice."

"How's it coming?" she called over her shoulder from her tiny kitchen.

"It's coming. That's why I'm here. I want you to look at some photos."

139

She came back into the room and leaned against the doorframe. Her smile scattered his thoughts. With an effort he took out the envelope he had just obtained from Sullivan and laid eight scanned photographs out on the cluttered coffee table, among them Pierre Haddad and his two sons. She came to sit at his side on the sofa, her thigh brushing his.

His voice sounded hoarse when he spoke. "Did you see any of these men on the fourth floor of the library at any time on the evening of the stabbing?"

Honey-coloured hair cascaded over her face as she bent close to study the line-up. The urge to brush it aside for her was almost irresistible. He locked his hands in his lap. She took the task seriously, and her eyes probed each picture in turn before she finally looked up at him, curls falling in her eyes. She pushed them aside as she shook her head.

"I feel bad. I'd like to help, but none of these guys looks familiar."

The kettle began to whistle, and she sprang to her feet. For a moment he was left to slow his breathing and wrestle his desires under control. This time it's bad, he thought to himself. But it's purely physical, something to do with coming home every night to find your wife on her knees mopping up pablum and smelling of milk.

He could hear the soft tinkle of spoons, and even that sounded seductive. When she came back into the room balancing two mugs in her hands, he thought she too looked flushed. She held out his tea and his fingers brushed hers, sending a jolt of electricity through him. He realized she was talking, and he forced himself to focus on her words.

"I do have the drawings you asked me to do, though. Maybe they will help."

She disappeared and reappeared seconds later with a large

sketch pad. Eagerly, she sat at his side again and leaned forward to spread out her drawings. Her loose fitting plaid shirt gaped open at the neck. Green wrenched his eyes from her cleavage to the table. Arranged before him were four pencil drawings of faces gazing out at him. There was a fat John Candy look-alike, a skinny horse-faced youth with acne and a dark, liquid-eyed man with wavy hair and a mustache. The fourth was a woman, staring out hard-eyed through a cloud of frizz. The drawings were exquisite and almost seemed to breathe as he looked at them. He sensed something strangely familiar about them, but the more he stared the more elusive the feeling became. He had seen someone like this, he knew it. Perhaps, when his body was calmer and his thoughts more collected, he would be able to remember.

*　　*　　*

Green pulled back into the police station parking lot just as Sullivan slewed his unmarked Taurus around the corner and screeched to a halt. The big man leaped out, eyes dancing.

Green waited for him. "Good news?"

"A double-hitter!"

"What!"

Sullivan slapped Green on the back. "Come on, I'm starved. Buy me a steak at the Crown and Castle and I'll fill you in."

"Me buy you? Since when?"

"Who's the one with the inspector's salary? And who wants to know the good news?"

Green knew Sullivan was teasing him, but since he had forgotten lunch and it was now past dinnertime, a steak and a draft was not a bad price to pay for Sullivan's report. He thought briefly of Sharon, who was probably wondering if she should leave some dinner for him before she left for work. But Sullivan's dancing eyes got the better of him. Besides, through trial and error, surely Sharon had learned to let him fend for himself. I hope, he thought as he scrambled after Sullivan's retreating back. The two men covered the three blocks up Elgin Street in two minutes. The sun had mercifully sunk behind the tall buildings, but its heat hung on, and Green felt sweat break out on his back.

"I had a bit of trouble with Raquel's Uncle Pierre," Sullivan chatted as he strode, seemingly oblivious to the heat. "He wanted a lawyer's opinion. I said we were just tracing Blair's activities and wanted to be able to rule out people who weren't involved. Eventually, he agreed. Gave me a picture of Raquel too." He pulled a photo from his pocket and held it out. "Gorgeous piece, eh?"

Green glanced at the picture of a dark-eyed beauty with a wide, sexy smile and sparkling eyes. Like Sharon's. He pushed it away with a grimace. "Don't talk to me about gorgeous pieces."

Sullivan shot him a brief, quizzical glance as they turned to enter the cool, dark interior of the pub. Sullivan was greeted by off-duty policemen and other regulars and stopped to exchange jokes on his way to the table, leaving Green to stand by, impatient and left out. Despite his dedication to his family and his strict one-drink limit, Sullivan could always be one of the boys, whereas Green remained an outsider. As they sat, he frowned at Sullivan irritably.

"So? What did you find?"

"First let me get a beer." He signalled the waiter. "Brian!"

Sullivan laughed. "Okay. I showed a photo line-up to David Miller, and without hesitation, he picked out Pierre

Haddad as the guy he saw arguing with Raquel outside Halton's building Tuesday afternoon. Then I tracked down the student who reported the fight in the coffee shop, and I showed her a line-up with all the Haddads in it—I stuck Miller and Difalco in there too—"

He broke off as the waiter brought them two foaming mugs of draft beer. Eyes alight, he reached for his.

"Goddamn it, Brian! And?"

Sullivan took a long, deep swallow. "Ah-h! And? Guess what, Mike. She took one look at the two Haddad boys and bingo!"

"Bingo? No hesitation?"

"None at all."

"Hah!" Green pounded the table. "All right! The trap is closing."

"So what's next? Haul them in for questioning?"

Green shook his head, his mind racing. "We don't have enough on them yet."

"What are you talking about! We have an assault against the victim three hours before his death."

"But we still can't place them at the scene."

"We could lean on them. The two kids'd probably crumble."

"Maybe, maybe not. But we couldn't make it stick, and their old man would be screaming police harassment and racial discrimination before the ink was dry."

"So what?" Sullivan stared at Green in surprise. "Since when do you care?"

"I don't," Green snapped, wondering why he was hesitating. Was it because of Jules' warning or something else? "I just don't want these guys spooked and covering their tracks. Carrie MacDonald can't place them at the library that night. That's a big hole. Without more evidence to tie them to the scene, we'll lose this one."

Sullivan sighed and shook his head, deflated. "Oh well, I promised Danny and Mark a Blue Jays game this month. Kind of a Father's Day treat. Maybe this way I'll even be able to afford it, if the overtime doesn't kill me first."

Father's Day. Green had a flash of himself with his own son ten years from now. Father-son sports games, especially hockey, were a Canadian rite of passage. He could even remember his own father, with his post-Holocaust fears of crowds and noise, trying to leave *shtetl* Poland behind him and packing them both onto the bus to see the Montreal Canadians play the Toronto Maple Leafs at the Montreal Forum. Once. *Mechugas*, his father had proclaimed after watching fans scream drunkenly at the little black disc being whacked around the rink. Craziness. And since then, at any sports game he had ever tried to attend, Green could still hear that word ringing in his head.

But that was a father-son sports memory in itself, he thought. As sappy as any once-in-a-lifetime trek down to the Toronto skydome. And now that Ottawa had its own hockey team as well as baseball, he had no excuse for not giving his own son something to remember him by.

He wanted to ask Sullivan how old a child had to be to enjoy a ball game, but he was afraid Sullivan would have the tickets bought and a picnic lunch packed for them all before he even turned around. Despite twenty years of friendship on the job, he wasn't ready for that. Instead, he picked up the earlier thread.

"No overtime," he replied, then had a sinking sensation. "At least not for you. I have to get a search warrant for the Haddad house. We have enough evidence for that. And tomorrow we'll go in mid-morning when the men are likely to be out."

"And we're looking for?"

"Three things. Bloody clothes, Blair's wallet, or a six-inch, double-bladed knife. If we get any of those, then we pick the bastards up."

*　　*　　*

Two search warrants in one day, Green thought as he finally arrived at his apartment door. I should get a medal for devotion to paper pushing. It was past midnight, but he found himself reluctant to go in. He leaned against the door, steeling himself for a confrontation. He had never sent the roses, never even called to apologize or warn her about dinner. He didn't even know if she was home or still working the night shift, and he realized with a pang how distant they had become. Memories of Carrie MacDonald wafted in uninvited. Of her tumbling blonde curls and her rising breasts. He remembered his arousal, the feeling of freshness and adventure.

"Oh God," he groaned, shutting his eyes against the images. Taking a deep breath, he opened the door. The apartment was dark and stifling, and the fridge hummed in the distance. The acrid smell of diapers assailed him as he moved down the hall towards the kitchen. With the narrow old windows and boxy rooms, the fetid summer air never seemed to move.

"Sharon?" he called, heading into the kitchen. Alone in the middle of the table stood a pair of brass candlesticks, a wedding gift from his in-laws, who lived in eternal hope that somewhere deep inside him, there was a good Jewish boy to be salvaged. Celebration of the Sabbath had not been part of the family ritual during his childhood, and when Sharon had first set the candles out on Friday night, he'd felt oddly alien, like an actor in a foreign play. When she had invited his father over for Shabbat dinner and lit the candles, however, Sid Green's eyes had welled with silent tears. Sharon had understood, and the candles had been set out ever since.

Tonight the kitchen was neatly cleared. Too neat. There were no signs of dinner, no notes or instructions for him. Only the white candles standing unlit in readiness for tomorrow night. A clear and eloquent message to him, with no need for words.

He checked the baby's crib, which was empty. Even the blanket was gone. Irrational fear seized him, like a sense of *déjà vu*. Had it happened again? He hurried into the bathroom and found her toothbrush still in its puddle by the sink. It was then that he saw the note, taped to the toilet—another eloquent message, if he cared to dwell on it: "If you're interested in knowing, your son is across the hall with Mrs. Louks."

Relief brought anger and a renewal of his discontent. He left Tony where he was and crawled naked into bed, grateful for the prospect of an uninterrupted night's sleep. Uninterrupted, as it turned out, except for erotic dreams of tawny curls and velvet thighs...

And the crash of the front door at seven a.m.

He lay in bed expectantly, listening as she tossed her purse on the shelf, kicked her shoes into the closet, and padded shoeless down the hall to the kitchen. She opened the fridge, unwrapped something crinkly and gave a deep sigh. She'll come in here in a moment, he thought, and I'll have to fight with her.

But five minutes later, she still had not budged from the kitchen, and he heard no sound but the rattling of paper. He could delay the confrontation no further. He had to get up and shower to get to a briefing he had called at eight. He wanted to get his men started on background checks of the Haddad sons while he and Sullivan went out to search the house.

With a sigh he climbed out of bed, gritted his teeth and headed toward the kitchen. Sharon was slumped over their little table, a glass of juice and a hunk of stale gruyère in front of her. She held her head in her hands and did not even look up as he entered.

"Get out of here, Mike," she muttered. "I don't have the energy to deal with you."

Shaken, he withdrew. Standing under the hot shower, he berated himself. He should have spoken to her. She had worked a twelve-hour graveyard shift the last three nights in a row. He should have made some gesture of support, but he couldn't face her. A simple caress, a simple "Hard night, sweetheart?" would not have been enough for her. It would have unleashed a torrent of rebuke, and he didn't have time for that. He was grateful when he emerged from the bathroom to find she had gone across the hall to fetch Tony. He would be able to slip into the kitchen for some juice and cereal before she returned. Then maybe a quick kiss and a "Sorry, darling" before he dashed from the house.

But before he had even poured his juice, his attention was drawn to the morning newspaper which lay scattered over the table. Right in the centre of the front page, smiling out at him, was Carrie MacDonald and across the page above ran the headline: "Librarian Key Witness in Murder Hunt".

Goddamn it! He scanned the article to see how bad it was. There was the usual human interest detail: Carrie MacDonald, 28-year-old single mother...worked at the library to pay her way through university...no stranger to violence, grew up in a neighbourhood where drunks beat down doors at two a.m. and women locked themselves in the bathroom...

Interspersed with these tidbits from her private life was the real meat of the story, however. About her habit of observing and recording interesting faces, about the sketches of possible suspects. Enough to make her a threat.

Cursing, he abandoned his juice, grabbed his suit jacket and dashed out the door.

* * *

Carrie stood wide-eyed in her doorway. "But Mike, I didn't tell them anything secret!" she cried. "It's just background. I mean, you've told me nothing. I don't even know who those guys were that you showed me last night."

He pushed past her into the apartment and shut the door. "You shouldn't have even told them your name."

"They wouldn't settle for that." She flushed as she followed him into the living room. "They knew I was at the library, they knew you'd been to see me. I had to tell them something."

"Why?"

"Because…" Her gaze shifted as she pondered the question. Slowly, a rueful smile spread over her face. "I guess I found it kind of fun being the centre of attention like that, my name in the newspapers. Even my picture."

"Did it ever occur to you that the killer might not be amused?"

She waved her hand in dismissal. "Oh, phooey. I didn't say I knew anything."

"The paper makes it sound like you did." He held out the article, and she read it in silence. Curled up on the sofa, she gradually sobered. At last, she looked up in dismay.

"I didn't say half these things, Mike. It's all out of context!"

"I know," he replied grimly. "A reporter's modus operandi."

"What do I do now? Should I write a letter to the editor?"

"You keep your mouth shut and you lie low. Have you got some place you can stay for a few days?"

She frowned in thought, her fingers idly twirling her golden hair. Finally she bit her lip. "I have no family. It was just my mother and me when I was growing up, but she's dead. And I haven't any real friends. I've always been too busy for a social life." She cocked her head. "Do you think it's that serious?"

He hesitated between reassuring her and scaring her into greater caution. Why was even the simplest of professional decisions so complicated with her? "I don't know," he equivocated. "But I think I'll send a female officer over here to stay with you till you're set up in a hotel."

"A hotel! I don't have money—"

"Departmental expense. Just for a few days, for your safety."

She smiled, a little wryly. "I've handled worse than this, you know. But it's kind of nice having you worry over me. Can I repay you with some coffee?"

He glanced at his watch. The neuropsychology professor from McGill was due within the hour, and Sullivan would be waiting to begin the search of the Haddad house. I really have no time, he thought, watching the blonde curls bounce as she walked down the hall towards the kitchen.

"Sure, just a quick one."

Her kitchen was so small that when she turned to hand him his coffee, her shoulder brushed his. She looked up into his eyes. "Sorry I was bad," she murmured.

He thought he was melting, so great was the heat. He didn't trust his voice not to betray him, so he merely shook his head. She smiled.

"We should go sit down." But she didn't move. Her eyes held his, intensely blue. He burned beneath her gaze. When she set her coffee down and touched his arm, all willpower vanished. He pulled her into his arms. Wedged between the counter and the fridge, they grappled like a fire out of control. Her mouth bruised his, her breasts filled his hands. Lilac scent rushed to his head, and dimly through the haze of arousal, he felt her hands upon his groin. She had his clothes half-off before he wrenched free.

"No," he gasped, pushing her away.

She reached for him. "Why not?"

He kept her at bay, shaking his head.

"You want to."

His denial stuck in his throat. His heart hammered, and his hands shook as he pulled his pants back up. "I'm a police officer. You're a witness."

She gripped his shirt, pulled him to her and kissed him. "When the case is over, then. You're the sexiest man to come into my life in a long time!"

He felt her thigh on his, her warm breath on his cheek. Not daring to answer, he seized his jacket and fled.

*   *   *

He was still shaking when he arrived at his office, and he was sure his guilt was written all over his face. But the receptionist, upon seeing him, held up her hand as if nothing had changed.

"Oh, Inspector Green! A Mr. Peter Weiss is on the line."

"Mike," a detective called from across the room. "Sullivan gave up and went without you for the Haddad search. Took Watts and Charbonneau."

Shaking his head towards the receptionist, he crossed the squad room, reaching to smooth his hair and straighten his tie. His hands closed on nothing. His tie was gone! Vaguely he remembered her yanking it off and tossing it on the floor before reaching for his belt. Shit, he thought, as he realized that unless he wanted to write the tie off, he would have to return to her apartment to retrieve it. Oh God!

He was so shaken that he almost tripped over a roly-poly man in a black T-shirt and purple shorts sitting in a chair outside his office. Beside him was a leggy brunette in a flowing cotton dress. Beautiful women everywhere, he thought.

"What the hell do you want?" he snapped, more peevishly than necessary.

The man flushed. "I want nothing. You want me."

Green hesitated, scrambling to reassemble his thoughts. The neuropsychology professor from McGill. "Dr. Baker?"

"Stan Baker. And this is my graduate student, Melanie Legault. I assume you're Inspector Green?"

It was Green's turn to redden. He shook their hands and ushered them into his office. "My apologies, Doctor. Things are moving very fast in this case, and I appreciate your agreeing to help us."

"For a thousand dollars a day," Baker reminded him. "Therefore, I suggest we get started, since having me wait half the day outside your office is hardly a good use of the law enforcement budget."

"The computers and files are over at the university in a sealed room. For evidentiary purposes there must be an officer present at all times, but he won't disturb you. Do you need anything? A secretary...?"

Baker was shaking his round head impatiently. "We need a ten-cup pot of black coffee, four cheese Danish and six hours of uninterrupted peace and quiet."

When the little professor laid eyes on the massive computers and stacks of boxes which ringed Halton's lab, Green felt a twinge of satisfaction. That ought to shut the pompous twerp up for a day or two, he thought. Although perhaps being holed up with the luscious, long-limbed Melanie was just what the professor had hoped for. Such sweet distraction... Making his way back to the station, he tried to turn his mind to what he should do next. He needed to arrange protection for Carrie and then get to work putting Halton's empire under a magnifying glass.

The sexiest man to come into her life in a long time, she had said! Me—skinny, freckled, big nose and all! He felt a new rush of desire at the heady thought of it and had to lean against the elevator wall. For some reason, women often found policemen attractive, and all his male colleagues had been targets of aggressive admirers, but such attention was rare for Green. Sometimes his boyish charm and air of vulnerability had worked, when that curious mix of sexual attraction and maternal instinct made them want to take care of him. But it usually took time and persistence, of which he used to have plenty, and he had never known it to happen without his trying.

Had maturity, fatherhood or four years with Sharon given him an extra edge? A confidence or authority? A certain mystique or unattainability? Had he been too anxious and eager before? He had succumbed to every shapely curve and sexy smile that came his way in the ten years between his marriages, and had become the laughingstock and the secret envy of half the Force. He was searching, he had told himself; he would know when he found her. And he thought he had, until now.

Goddamn it, enough of this, he thought, pushing himself off the elevator wall. The necktie had to stay where it was, and his mind had to stay on the job. When the door opened, he strode into the squad room prepared to order Carrie's

152

protection and then get his mind firmly back on Halton's past. But no sooner had he entered than all that was forgotten. The squad room buzzed with excitement, and at the centre was Brian Sullivan, triumphantly returned from his search.

"Mike! Paydirt! An absolute goddamn goldmine! In Pierre Haddad's garage, stuffed in with a bunch of car cleaning equipment, we found a knife and a shirt. Jonathan Blair's blood type is on both of them!"

*   *   *

"You've got to understand, Mike," the serologist lectured. He was used to working with Green and was immune to his impatience. This cluttered, fluorescent-lit laboratory, lined with computers, scanners, microscopes and coloured bottles, was his turf. "You're lucky I can give you anything from what I had to work with. It was hot in the garage. The knife was washed clean, and so was the shirt. If it weren't for the engraving on the knife handle and the lousy job the guy did washing the shirt, I'd have nothing but blood, period. As it is, I can give you A positive. The victim's blood type. As for more detailed subgrouping, forget it. The sample's too broken down."

Green picked up the clear plastic evidence bag containing the knife. It was a dagger with an eight-inch, double-edged steel blade and an ornate, jewel-encrusted silver handle. He turned it over in his hands. "Looks Arabic."

"Certainly not your average Canadian hunting knife."

"Anything on the shirt?"

The serologist shrugged. "Hair and Fibre's got it now. Maybe they can tell you more."

The technician from the Hair and Fibre Division of the RCMP Forensics Sciences Lab was just sealing a little box of slides and labelling it when Green walked into the lab. He removed his thick bifocals to rub his eyes then gave Green a doleful smile.

"Fastest job I've ever done. Got a call from the Director himself telling me to move it."

"What did you find out?"

"The shirt was spot-washed with Ivory bar soap. It left a lot of soap residue and didn't get all the blood out. I'd say it was someone who didn't know much about washing."

"Like a man?"

Winkler shrugged. "Speak for yourself, Green. I'm a bachelor myself. To get blood out, you use cold water, not hot. Heat sets it, and that's what happened here."

"Well, that's a big help. Odds are already 99 out of 100 it's a man anyway."

The elderly technician put his glasses back on, scratched his nose and fidgeted with his box of slides. "I do have something else."

"What!"

"A hair, thick and wavy, dark brown. Found it stuck in the neckline of the shirt. I've sent it to DNA."

Green searched through his memory of the photos. All three Haddads had dark hair, but the father's was stranded with silver. The younger son Paul had black hair cropped close to his head, but Edward had a thick head of rich black curls.

"How curly? Like a black?"

Winkler shook his head. "Oh no. Caucasian—Italian, Greek maybe."

"Lebanese?"

"Sure, any person with dark brown hair. The gene pool is all mixed up among those Mediterranean peoples anyway. The Greeks and Romans invaded the Arab peninsula, then—"

Green raised a hand to interrupt the history lesson. "Anything else you can tell me about our man from the hair? Is it enough to give us a match?"

"You bring me a suspect, and we'll see."

"I think it's time to do just that." Green picked up the phone, relieved to find Sullivan at the station. "Brian, get three teams together. I want all three Haddads picked up for questioning simultaneously, Pierre and his two sons. And don't tell them a goddamn thing. I want them good and spooked."

Ten

Two hours later, Green found himself in a small beige interview room face to face with Pierre Haddad. Sullivan sat in the corner, discreetly taking notes. The fat man was stolidly planted at the table, and despite the icy climate control of the windowless room, he was sweating profusely.

"My apologies for keeping you waiting, Mr. Haddad, but this is a very complex case. I'm pursuing a lot of leads, and there's only one of me. I think you can appreciate that, because of the sensitive nature of the case, I'm conducting all the interviews personally. I hope my men have made you comfortable. Would you like a drink or a snack?"

"Nothing," Haddad snapped. He was trying to sound outraged, but Green sensed panic. He sat down across the table, set a brown paper bag unobtrusively at his feet, and calmly recited the caution. Sometimes that was enough to shake a blustering witness, but Haddad listened poker-faced and then declined a lawyer, saying that he'd done nothing wrong.

Green acknowledged the denial with a slight nod of the head. "Now, Mr. Haddad, in our first discussion yesterday, you indicated that you didn't know the murdered man, Jonathan Blair, and that you knew little about your niece's activities at university. I have evidence to the contrary." Slowly, Green flipped open a thick notebook, one of his favourite dramatic props. "Is there anything you'd like to add now, before I question you about that evidence?"

Haddad wiped the sweat which was trickling down his temples. "What evidence are you talking about?"

"Evidence that Raquel's ticket to Beirut was booked at six o'clock on the evening Blair was murdered, not several weeks in advance, as holidays usually are."

Haddad snorted. "So what?"

"Evidence that Raquel was Blair's girlfriend and his lover for at least two weeks before his death."

"I told you I never knew—"

"Evidence that you had an argument with Raquel on the steps of the science building at four o'clock, just hours before Blair was murdered. An eyewitness identified you both."

For the first time, Haddad's bluster faded. He glared at Green mutely.

Green flipped a page. "Evidence that your sons Edward and Paul forcibly took Raquel away from Jonathan at six-thirty, half an hour after you'd booked her plane ticket. They were in the student coffee shop, your sons argued with Blair, and when he tried to help Raquel, they assaulted him. Another student witnessed the whole thing."

Haddad had turned from flushed to ashen. He seemed about to deny everything but checked himself. The silence lengthened, and Green let him stew. Finally, Haddad glowered.

"Is it against the law to talk to your niece? For her family to take her away from a boy they do not like?"

"Then you're saying you knew about Jonathan Blair?"

Haddad nodded impatiently. "Yes, all right! I knew about him. Raquel is young. Canadian girls—they have more freedom than Lebanese girls. They don't listen to their family. Raquel wanted to be like a Canadian girl, too wild. It's no good."

"So you forced her to go back to Lebanon?"

"Forced? No. She listened to her family. She knows it is best for her."

"Mr. Haddad, she was screaming and crying. Your sons had to drag her away."

"It was because of him! Because he was trying to control her mind. Later, after she talked to me, she knew I was right. I don't care if you don't understand this, sir. Or if you agree or not. Your way is for you. For me and my family, this way is right."

"As simple as that? You talk to her and she forgets all about Jonathan Blair, her freedom, her future, her dreams?"

"She remembered our ways."

"And just by chance, Jonathan Blair is stabbed to death a couple of hours later."

"That has nothing to do with it! I took Raquel away from him. End of story!"

"We have a witness who saw your sons assault him. How do you know they didn't return to finish the job?"

"Because they are good boys! They go to college, Eddie is going to be a lawyer."

Reaching into the bag at his feet, Green withdrew the plastic bag containing a black shirt and laid it on the table between them. "Do you recognize this shirt, Mr. Haddad?"

Haddad began to shake his head.

"Check it very carefully, sir."

Haddad turned the bag over, held it up and checked the label. Again he shook his head. "Not my size or my taste."

"Your sons', maybe?"

A veil of inscrutability descended, and Haddad said nothing for several seconds. Green waited patiently.

"My sons don't wear such clothes."

Green laid down the bag with the knife. In the silence,

Haddad sucked in his breath.

"Do you recognize this knife?"

"I saw knives like it, but not that one."

"Where did you see them?"

Haddad recovered enough to snort with derision. "These knives are sold by the hundreds in the tourist shops in Beirut. Even here in Canada, in a Middle East bazaar."

"So it's a Middle Eastern knife?"

"Bedouin. Not real, of course. For show."

"Do you own one?"

Haddad's eyes met his coldly. "I do not own that one or any other one. What is this about?"

"Your sons? Surely one of you owns one if they're so common."

"Not in my family."

"This knife was found hidden in your garage. It has Jonathan Blair's blood on it."

The fat man wheezed. "That...that's not possible!"

Green shook his head. "We searched your house this morning. These are what we found."

Haddad's eyes darted back and forth between the knife and Green's face. Green saw in them the dawning of panic.

"It's a trick!" Haddad hissed. "You put them there!"

"Why would I do that?"

"Because you need somebody to arrest. Why not a Lebanese?"

Green leaned back in his chair, quiet and firm. "I operate on facts, Mr. Haddad. Other people may get emotional and jump to conclusions, but I wait till all the facts are in. That's what I'm doing here." He held up his hand and began to check off on his fingers. "Fact one: this knife is the murder weapon. Fact two: it was found in your garage. I need an explanation."

Haddad ran his tongue over his trembling lips. "I don't have to talk to you!"

"That's right, you don't. However, if you're innocent as you claim, what do you have to lose by explaining things? On the other hand, if you are not innocent, then I suggest you terminate this discussion right now and get yourself a good lawyer."

"You're twisting things!" Haddad bellowed. "I'm a good Canadian! I obey the law, I teach my sons to obey the law. If the knife was in my house, someone put it there!"

* * *

The sons displayed none of the initial cool of their more worldly father. They had grown up soft and safe on Canadian soil, used to nothing more violent than the everyday rivalries of the schoolyard. Paul, the twenty-year old, made an initial stab at bravado, accusing Green of harassment and threatening the entire police force with a lawsuit. Green rolled his eyes.

"Aw, shut up, Paulie. Do I look scared? We're talking about a serious crime here."

"I don't know anything, man!" Paul protested. "I don't even know why you got me here."

"Well, I'm thinking of charging you with assault. You and Eddie. That charge is as good as in the bag. I've got witnesses, you've been ID'd. Six-thirty, student coffee shop. But I'm working on a bigger charge. Murder. And I don't give a damn if you talk to me or not. I'm just being polite, giving you a chance to tell me your side of the story."

Paul was staring at him, jaw agape. His olive complexion lent a greenish tinge to his pallor and one eye twitched spasmodically. Green could almost see his thoughts racing for cover.

"I—I demand to see a lawyer or talk to my father. You can't

160

do this. I don't have to tell you anything!"

"That's right, you don't. As I said, I'm just being polite. I mean, if you didn't kill him, you might want to tell me about it."

"Tell you about what?"

"About your shirt." Green laid the black shirt on the table. "Funny place for it, hidden in the garage."

"That's not my shirt!"

"What do you take me for, stupid? Of course it's yours. Just your size. Your taste, too."

"I never saw that shirt."

"So it's your brother Eddie's? Is that your story?"

"No—no! Nobody has a shirt like that."

"You check everything your brother buys?"

"Of course not! But black...I mean, Eddie would have a fight with mom over that. She wants us to look, like, geeky at college. To impress the profs."

"You were ID'd at the coffee shop wearing a Metallica T-shirt, so I guess you buy them anyway."

Paul's face fell as he saw the trap. "Well, yeah, sometimes. We put them on when she's not around."

"So Eddie might sneak it off before he gets home and hide it in the garage?"

"Naw, naw! Are you kidding? Eddie's not a wimp, he wouldn't give a fuck what Mom thinks."

"You own a knife, Paulie?"

The youth blinked in surprise. "Yeah?" he ventured warily.

"What type?"

"Swiss army knife. Got it a couple of years back."

"What for?"

Paul shrugged. "Nothing! For fun. Just to have a knife, you know."

"Your parents know about it?"

"Naw. Dad would freak. Dad's into all this non-violence shit."

"Eddie own a knife?"

"I don't know."

"Sure you do. Every guy likes to boast. That's why you got yours. Now what does Eddie's look like?"

Paul grew sulky. "He used to own a hunting knife, in a leather holster. But I don't know if he's still got it."

"What about an Arab knife? They're beautiful and part of your heritage."

"Yeah." Paul's expression darkened. "Eddie had one of those once, and Dad took it away. Threw an absolute shit fit." He shook his head as if at the folly of the older generation.

Green laid the bagged knife on the table. "This it?"

Paul turned the knife over in his hand curiously. "Looks a bit like it. I can't remember. Where'd this come from?"

"It was hidden in the garage along with the shirt."

"Well then, maybe Eddie—" He froze. The knife fell with a clatter.

"Maybe Eddie what?"

"Nothing! You're trying to trick me! You want me to finger my own brother! I'm not saying one more fucking word and if you—" He had turned purple, and tears threatened. "You can't prove a fucking thing!"

*   *   *

Eddie, the older son, was a law student. From that, as well as from Paul's account of him, Green expected a fight. Eddie was the last one to be picked up, because the police had trouble finding him. He did not show up for the afternoon shift at the construction site where he had a summer job, and the police had to stake it out. Eddie arrived late, dishevelled and out of breath, and nearly panicked at the sight of the squad car. Now he was falling all over himself to be helpful.

"You guys have a tough job, I know that, sir," he gushed even before Green had finished his caution. "Your hands are tied, the criminals get all the breaks. I really wanted to be a cop when I was a kid, but my father wanted me to go to college. He thinks I'm going to be a corporate lawyer and make lots of money, but actually I'm going to be a prosecutor. You guys work closely with the Crowns, right? Is it a good job? I mean, do they feel like they're doing any good?"

"It's a busy job," Green replied. "And so's mine. Maybe when the case is over, you can come down, and I'll introduce you to one of the Crown Attorneys. But for now, let's try to get home some time today, okay? I'll cut to the chase and save us some time. Tuesday evening, June 10. I know you and Paul had a fight with Jonathan Blair over your cousin Raquel. I know you assaulted him, I know you dragged your cousin away under protest. That was six-thirty. Can you give me an account of your actions from then on?"

Eddie Haddad had grown ashen. His enthusiasm had fled along with his rosy vision of the future. He sat quite still as he regrouped his forces. Finally, he wet his lips. "Paul and I took Raquel to the house, then Dad drove us all to the airport. Afterwards, we went back home."

"How did Raquel react?"

Eddie shook his head. "Mad. I was scared she'd cause a scene—she usually does—but she didn't. Too scared of Dad, I guess. Of what he'd tell her father back in Beirut."

"Did you agree with sending her away to Beirut?"

The young man looked up at him, the conflict between old and new clearly reflected in his face. He was the handsomer of the sons, with thick wavy black hair, rich eyes and a luxuriant mustache. He was recovering his composure and with it his charm. He'll make a good lawyer, thought Green. Thinks on his feet.

"Raquel was wild. Some things are good about the West, but not the freedom. It's just an excuse to do whatever you want without caring about others or about the future. There has to be rules. There has to be respect. Everyone thinks Lebanon is just a crazy place where everyone kills each other, but even after all the civil war it's still a beautiful country, the most progressive in all the Arabic world. We have universities and museums, the people are educated. And we have our values—family, loyalty, respect for your parents, respect for tradition. Raquel should have stayed in Beirut, but my Dad thought it was less dangerous over here. But he couldn't make Canada like Lebanon. She was losing her Lebanese traditions and values. And once a woman starts losing her values, you can't ever get her back."

Green leaned back in his chair. "You really believe that stuff?"

"Absolutely," Eddie replied. "Call me old-fashioned, but look where things are going. There can be only one boss in the family, and that's the man. If the woman disagrees with the man, then pretty soon the kids don't listen to him either and everybody fights and goes in different directions. There are divorces, the kids suffer, they grow up wild. It doesn't work, you'll see." Eddie pointed to Green's left hand. "You're married. Does your wife do what you want?"

Green smiled, deciding to play along. As in fishing, there were times to let the suspect run. "Not usually."

"You fight a lot?"

"I guess so. But we usually reach a compromise."

"Compromise? What's a compromise? Where neither of

you gets what you want, right?"

Green remembered Sharon's face when he'd asked her to leave the house the day before. To be the boss, to be obeyed unquestioningly—how seductive! Yet how wrong!

"But your way, Raquel doesn't ever get what she wants."

Eddie grinned. "You think Lebanese women don't know how to get what they want out of their husbands? Or any woman? They're all the same, they all learn to play the game. And in return they get protection, security, the status of their husband."

"But Raquel obviously wanted something very different— a career, the right to make her own decisions."

"She could have a career. Lebanese women have good careers, the best in all the Arabic world." Eddie shook his head in exasperation. "We don't hide them behind veils in Lebanon, sir. At least not the Christians."

Watching the young man flush with excitement and pride, it occurred to Green that if Eddie Haddad had driven a stiletto into Blair's ribs two days earlier, it was highly unlikely that he would be sitting in the interrogation room today debating the philosophical rights of women. Can anybody be that smooth? That much in control? And if so, how was he going to break him?

"I don't claim to be an expert, believe me," Green began chattily. "But one thing I've learned about Middle Eastern traditions is that honour is very important."

"What's wrong with that?"

"The honour of the family has to be protected, and if damaged, it must be restored." Green avoided the word "avenged". He wanted to tiptoe quietly.

"The honour of the family is what keeps society in check. Everybody belongs, everybody follows the rules. It stops law-breaking, treachery, sexual promiscuity and other ills that would make society fall apart. So it must be upheld. It is just another way of enforcing the law." Eddie waved an expansive hand. "In the United States, everyone is talking about the breakdown of the family and the spread of violence. Drugs, murder—they're everywhere in the ghettoes."

"I know," Green smiled sympathetically. "But don't Middle Eastern cultures believe that if someone dishonours your family—kills one of you or even seduces your women—they must pay? And until they pay, the family lives in shame. Surely that encourages violence."

Eddie's eyes flashed. "It also encourages women not to stray and men not to fool with them. It makes a man think twice before killing you."

"Ah yes, the deterrent factor." Green smiled. "Doesn't work very well. Humans are weak beings, prone to temptation. In the heat of passion, rules are hard to remember."

"You remember well enough if you're going to get a knife in your gut!" Abruptly, Eddie paled. For a moment he cast about, trying to recover his voice, then he forced a laugh. "You got me, Inspector. Just a philosophical debate, of course. In Canada we trust our laws, and we leave our knives on the shelf."

"Do you own a knife?"

Again a forced laugh. "Just an expression. No, I don't own a knife."

"Your brother said you had a Bedouin knife."

Eddie frowned. "My brother's an idiot. I haven't had that thing in years."

"What did it look like?"

"I hardly remember. Silver, covered in fake jewels. Really gaudy. I bought it from a bazaar here in Ottawa, and Dad confiscated it."

Green laid the knife on the table. "Is this it?"

Eddie was startled. He stared at it. "My God, is that the

one—the murder…?"

"Is that your knife?"

"No." Eddie pushed it away hastily. "I'm sure it's not. Those tourist knives all look alike."

"It was found in your garage."

"Well I don't—I didn't—I don't know what it was doing there. I haven't seen mine in years!"

"It was hidden along with your shirt." Green laid the shirt on the table.

"That's not my shirt! Who the hell said it was my shirt!"

"Are you denying it's your shirt? Remember, all this is going down in your sworn statement, and I'll find out the truth anyway. The lab is already running tests on the traces found on the shirt. We can determine incredible things these days. You've heard of DNA testing?"

The charm had all but vanished behind the glassy eyes and ashen skin. The thick mustache he had probably grown to make himself look older quivered at the ends.

"It's not my shirt! I didn't buy it, I didn't hide it. I don't know anything about the knife. I was at home when Blair was killed, and someone is trying to frame me!"

"Who?"

"I don't know." He was near panic. "I don't know! That's your job, not mine. Find out!"

*　　*　　*

Reviewing the interviews with Green afterwards, Sullivan chuckled. "You had fun."

"Yeah, I opened up some chinks in their armour, but we still can't place any of them at the scene. Besides, I'm not sure who to arrest."

"Me neither. Got a favourite?"

Green drained the last of the tepid cola from his glass. It was the middle of the afternoon, and they were almost alone in the police cafeteria. Green had tried to eat a tuna sandwich, but his stomach was in knots. Phone messages from Jules, Weiss, the deputy police chief and Marianne Blair herself lay on his desk downstairs.

"Of the three, I'm less inclined to suspect the father. He has the family honour to protect, of course, and I'm sure he can be ruthless, but I don't think he's the type. If this is a revenge killing, then it needs a hot-head. It's premeditated but fanatical, and it needs someone with a passionate allegiance to a cause. The father strikes me as a pragmatist, not a fanatic."

"One of the sons?"

Green shrugged. "Ideals certainly burn more purely and fanatically in the young. On that basis, Eddie is the more likely. Paul is a typical sulky Canadian teenager. He's rejected his parents' values, and like most North American kids, he thinks his parents are in the stone age. Besides, he's not smart enough. But Eddie seems to have bought that 'honour in the family' code. He's a deeper thinker, worried about the state of the world. He wants to be a crown attorney to uphold the law. Yeah, he suits the profile."

"But?"

Green toyed with his spoon, making slow spirals in the plastic tabletop. He grinned wryly. "Yeah. But. I'm not sure he has the nerve. He's all talk. Could he walk right up to a man, face him square and drive a knife through his ribs, all because the guy is screwing his cousin?" Green shook his head. "These are scared kids. Both of them denied the shirt was theirs."

"Come on, you can't expect them to admit—"

"I know. I didn't expect anybody to break down and

confess, but it would have been nice if I'd gotten just an inkling. Enough of a fumble that we had something concrete to go forward on. But they all acted so bewildered, each hinting it must have been the other. It was either very clever, or true." He sighed again. "We'll have to let all three of them go, Brian. We haven't got enough to hold them on. Their lawyers would walk all over us."

"We'd have the support of the guys upstairs here."

"Fair weather friends, believe me." He sat back, tossing the spoon aside in disgust. "Fuck it. Tell the Haddads not to leave town, and check their alibis. Get as many men on this as you need. Check the airport, phone records, neighbours, friends. They're protecting each other, but someone has to know something. And check the activities of Eddie and Paul. If either has militant connections, I want to know." He sighed. "What else should we do?"

"I ordered a trace on the knife," Sullivan said. "Maybe they're not that common over here."

"Good thinking. Who'd you put on it?"

"Gibbs. You know how he loves shopping through the yellow pages."

They both laughed. Shy, diligent Constable Gibbs gave new meaning to the word "thorough".

"While he's hunting, make sure he finds out when the shops are open so—"

The intercom interrupted them, paging Inspector Green. Green slid down in his chair, hoping to escape notice.

"That will be Adam Jules, wondering why I haven't answered anyone's calls. Answer for me, will you, and tell them I'm out on the road."

But when Sullivan returned from the phone some minutes later, he was tight-lipped and pale.

"Carrie MacDonald's place was hit a couple of hours ago. Turned upside down."

Horror slammed him. He had forgotten all about her police protection! He forced his lips around the words. "And Carrie?"

"Dead."

Eleven

Carrie MacDonald's apartment building was ringed with squad cars by the time Green and Sullivan arrived. Revolving splashes of red flashed off the yellow plastic tape stretched all around the front yard and lobby. Curious neighbours and passers-by had already begun to gather. Green barrelled through the crowd to the policeman at the door.

"What the hell happened?" he roared.

"Dispatch got a 911 at two forty-six from the occupant of 106, sir," the officer replied. "She reported a break-in—"

"What about Carrie! Oh, goddamn it, I'll see for myself!" Green rushed down the hall, ducked under the tape at the entrance to her apartment and started across the living room.

"Hold it, Mike!"

He swung around, startled. Lou Paquette from the Ident Unit was standing in the corner of the room, sketchbook in hand. He stared at Green incredulously.

"Do you mind? Look at this place! You kick one paper out of the way and I might as well kiss the scene good-bye. Check with me, for fuck's sake."

Green paused in his tracks, breathing deeply to restore calm. It would do no good to show his feelings. Glancing around, he realized the enormity of his error. The room was in chaos. Papers and clothing littered the carpet. Cushions had been tossed from the couch and chairs overturned. Seeing

Green's expression, Paquette nodded.

"It was either one hell of a fight or someone was looking for something."

"Where?" Green croaked.

"In her bedroom. MacPhail's been called. Mike—" he called as Green turned gingerly to continue on his way, "my men aren't done in there either."

Green paused in the doorway to the bedroom, shut his eyes and took three deep gulps of air. Through them he heard Paquette's team muttering. There were two men in the room, one taking pictures, the other doing an initial search for physical evidence. With one final gulp of air, he opened his eyes. Carrie lay sprawled naked on her back across the bed, her head flung back and her expression frozen in surprise. Blood covered her forehead and settled in crusting pools beneath her head.

"Oh, oh," he heard someone say. "Green's about to do his passing-out routine."

"I am not," he replied, stepping over to the bedside. "What have we got? Gunshot wound?"

"Yup," said the Ident officer. "One shot between the eyes. But this time I think we got lucky. Look in her hand." He pointed. Following his finger, Green forced himself to look back at the body. Past her long, blood-soaked locks, past her vacant blue eyes, down her outflung arm to her hand. There, clutched in her death grip, was his own necktie.

*   *   *

Green was sitting by the toilet bowl resting his head in his hand when Sullivan found him. They were in the apartment next door, temporarily commandeered as a field command post. Teams from forensics and pathology buzzed about in the outer living room, and now and then shouts punctuated the hum.

"Jeez, Mike, get a grip!" exclaimed Sullivan, leaning against the bathroom door. "Information is coming in fast and furious. We need to stay on top of it."

With an effort, Green rallied his professional front and pulled himself to his feet. "What have we got so far?"

"MacPhail's made a preliminary ETD between eleven a.m. and one p.m. He thinks she was dead three or four hours before she was found, shot from probably five to six feet away with a small caliber gun. Killer probably surprised her in bed. There are no defensive wounds and no sign of a struggle, just one neat, clean bullet to the head."

Green swallowed and groped for strength. "Any sign of sexual…?"

"Assault?" Sullivan shook his head. "No obvious bruising or tearing, although of course MacPhail will have to check for semen. But I don't think the motive for this was sex."

"No. This has to do with Jonathan Blair."

"Yeah, the mess was probably made after the murder. The killer was looking for something."

Green gripped the edge of the sink, swaying as a fresh wave of nausea swept over him. "I should have prevented this. Goddamn it, I told her I'd get her protection!"

"Mike, who could have known—"

"She left a ten-year old kid behind." Green stiffened. "Fuck, the kid!"

"We got the Children's Aid to intercept her at the school bus, so she wouldn't come home to this."

"Yeah, but her mother's dead, her grandmother's dead. She's got nobody, all because I…" Green couldn't finish.

Sullivan sobered. "I know. It stinks. But she's the one who talked to the press, not us."

"And that makes this her fault? I forgot! I forgot to arrange the protection."

"It probably wouldn't have been approved anyway."

"I would have paid for the hotel out of my own pocket!"

Sullivan touched his shoulder, frowning. "Hey buddy, it's done. Don't beat yourself up. The hit was fast, probably too fast to get protection in place anyway. The best we can do for her now is find her killer. At least now we have loads more forensic evidence to sift through. And—we have the tie! That's something we didn't have before. Forensics will put it through every test ever invented. We'll get sweat, we'll get skin cells, and they just might help us nail him!"

Green stared at the faded tiles at his feet. "The tie's mine."

"What?"

He cleared his throat. "I said the tie's mine."

"What the fuck is it doing here?"

"I—I was here this morning to warn her about talking to the press. To tell her to move out for a few days, actually."

"But how—" Sullivan broke off, comprehension dawning. Green felt his cheeks flush hot. He felt Sullivan's eyes upon him, disbelief gradually growing cold. "You stupid sonofabitch," Sullivan muttered. "Never could keep it in your pants, could you? When are you going to grow up, Green?"

"Sh-h!" Green swung the bathroom door shut. Anger, slow in coming, began to take hold. "For your information, nothing happened! I stopped it. But in trying to get away with my marriage vows intact, I forgot my tie. She must have brought it into her bedroom." A deep flush crept up his neck as a thought occurred to him. Her eyes, when he left her that morning, had been hot with need.

In spite of himself, Sullivan began to laugh. "This will look good in the headlines."

Green winced. "Could you maybe talk to Paquette? Keep a lid on this thing?"

"Oh no, you can do your own clean-up. I wish you luck. There's a dozen guys out there, and in half an hour they'll all know Mike Green left his tie behind. You think they'll sit on that? This is the best dirt they've had since you got married. We may be able to keep it out of the media, but sure as hell not out of the locker room."

Green leaned his head back against the bathroom wall. "Shit. If Sharon finds out…"

"Hey, if nothing happened…"

"The way things are right now, I'm not sure she'll believe it."

"Maybe the gossip won't reach her. She's not exactly on the officers' wives hotline." Sullivan clapped him on the shoulder. "Come on, we've got a case to solve."

Reluctantly Green followed Sullivan back into Carrie MacDonald's apartment. The bedroom door was closed, for which he was grateful. It allowed him to keep his detachment. Paquette and his men were covering the living room in a grid inch by inch, photographing, sketching, scraping and dusting. When he spotted them in the doorway, Paquette got up from his knees to join them, mopping sweat from his brow.

"Any clue why he trashed the place?" he wheezed, coughing. "What was he looking for?"

Green nodded. "She had drawn four sketches of people in the library at the time of the murder. I meant to bring them to the station, but unfortunately…" He trailed off, remembering how his hormones had chased all rational thought from his mind. "The killer was probably after them, or something else he thought incriminated him. If we can figure out what he took, we may have him."

It was four hours before the Ident Unit had worked its way

through all Carrie's papers and had handed them over to Green. He took five minutes to flip through them all before he looked up at Sullivan with a puzzled frown.

"That's funny. He's taken two of the sketches. The dark-haired man with the mustache—our mystery student at the elevator."

"So? That's good. The Haddads are dark-haired."

"But he also took the sketch of Jonathan Blair. What possible use is that?"

All the way back to the police station, Green wrestled with that curious twist. Nothing fit together. Violence was no stranger to the man who had killed Blair and Carrie. He knew exactly when and where to strike, so his victims never had a chance. The knife and shirt had been found in Haddad's garage, but Eddie and Paul Haddad were too fresh and guileless, too sheltered to be that deadly. It also bothered him that the sketch of Jonathan had been taken and that Jonathan's wallet had never been found.

But when he and Sullivan arrived back at his office to check field reports, he learned three facts which made him rethink his opinion.

First, a preliminary memo from the officer looking into the Haddad sons' background reported that Eddie belonged to the Arab League, a student group composed mainly of Muslim exchange students from Arab countries. Within the Arab League was a militant core which was anti-Western in its bias and highly inflammatory in its rhetoric. Eddie was not one of this inner circle—as a Canadian and a Christian he was excluded from full acceptance—but he hung around on the fringes eagerly soaking up the zeal.

Secondly, on the night of Blair's murder, a neighbour across the street from the Haddad house had been out walking his dog and had seen a dark silhouette slip out the side door of the Haddad house, climb on a bicycle and pedal away into the dark. The neighbour had been uncertain about the time, but guessed it was about ten.

The third fact was almost icing on the cake. When Green checked the times at which the three Haddads had been brought in for questioning that day, he found the father and the younger son could not have killed Carrie. The father had been picked up at the store about eleven o'clock and Paul from a friend's house in the south end of the city at eleven twenty-five. But Eddie had not been found until one-ten. He had skipped his morning shift at work and had arrived for the afternoon dishevelled and out of breath.

And of course, Eddie had a mustache.

*   *   *

"Jesus, why don't we arrest him?" Sullivan exclaimed.

Green sighed and rubbed his eyes. They were hunched over two Harvey's All-dressed burgers, taking stock of the case. The sun was setting, and the Friday night tattoo-and-leather crowd was just emerging on Rideau Street, but both men barely noticed them. They had been at work for over twelve hours. Sullivan was anxious for some closure, but Green just couldn't face going home.

"The noose isn't tight enough yet," he replied doggedly. "We've got to substantiate the neighbour's report that someone sneaked out that night. The family swears they were all home together. Eddie's not going anywhere. When I've broken his alibi, we'll pick him up."

"What are you talking about! He could skip to Lebanon on the very next plane."

Green fell silent. Sullivan was right. One person was already dead because of his failure to act. And if Eddie did skip, it would be the end of both their careers. Great, he thought, marriage and career both dead in one fell swoop.

"I'll tell you what. I'll put a surveillance team on him to make sure he doesn't skip. If I can prove it was him who sneaked out that night, we'll go straight out to pick him up. For now, go home and get some sleep."

"What about you?"

"I..." Green wavered. The time for Shabbat dinner had come and gone. Sharon would have waited a while, then lit the candles, sung the prayers and gone on without him. He felt a twinge of regret. Shabbat was supposed to be about sharing. But he didn't even know whether Sharon had begun her shift early or late tonight, or indeed at all.

Sullivan had always been a fierce believer in marriage, both Green's and his own. How could he tell him what was happening? Sullivan would see it as all his fault. You have to put your family first, he'd lectured after Green's first wife left. Sullivan played hockey with his boys on the front drive, sat in the front row at his daughter's dance recitals and got sappy poems from his kids on Father's Day. Green wondered what his own first real Father's Day would be like this year, with Sharon not speaking to him and his son barely knowing who he was.

And whose fault is that? a small voice said. If you hurry, you can still catch the candles before they burn down completely.

"I'm going to shake the tree a little first," he replied.

* * *

The Haddads lived in a small post-war bungalow in a modest

178

suburb. Moonlight tipped the white blossoms of the bridal wreath spirea dwarfing the front walk, and a wispy breeze stirred the humid air. As Green approached the front walk, he heard voices raised in anger. A moment later, the front door flung back, and Paul stormed out, hurling obscenities in his wake.

"Fuck you! Fuck all of you! Maybe I'll let the goddamn cops know what kind of family we really are!"

"Paulie!" came two male shouts from within, but he had slammed the door.

He stomped down the cracked cement walk, head down and cursing, until he literally collided with Green. He recoiled, eyes wide with fright. "What the fuck!"

Green placed his fingers to his lips and steered him adroitly down the path. "Just a few questions."

Paul jerked his arm loose. "If you think I'm talking to you, you're out of your mind!"

"You got to talk to somebody sometime, Paul. You can't keep it inside forever."

"I'm not talking to *you!*"

"They want you to lie for them, don't they?"

Paul turned ghostly in the moonlight. "What are you talking about?"

"Say you were all home all night Tuesday."

"It's true!"

"No, it's not. One of you sneaked out. Neighbours have eyes, you know. I'm betting it was you."

Paul backed up, shaking his head. "It wasn't me!"

"You're blaming Eddie again?"

"No! I'm not blaming Eddie."

"Let me see your bicycle."

"Why?"

"Because the neighbour saw the bicycle."

"I don't have to show you anything!"

Green shook his head with a sigh. "Tough guy. Okay, Paulie, get in my car. We'll go downtown."

"Eddie rides my bike! All the time, without asking me!"

"So it was Eddie?"

Paul turned in a circle like a caged animal, swearing softly. "It's always Eddie. Goddamn prick, you'd think he was a saint the way they act. It's always me that catches the shit!"

Green let Paul continue on his way, humbled and scared, and turned his attention back to the house. It was silent now, and the grey light of the television flickered on the drapes. He was all set to ring the bell and confront Eddie when he heard a low whistle from across the street. Inside a dark brown Taurus parked at the curb, he could just make out a figure beckoning to him. It proved to be Constable Wicks, who had been assigned to surveillance.

"Do you want me to stay, sir, or are you handling things from here on?"

Green vacillated then climbed in the car. "Let's watch them a bit, see if we learn anything interesting. This family is beginning to crack apart at the seams."

Over the next hour they shared a thermos of coffee and a doughnut. As it passed eleven, the lights gradually began to go out in the house.

Beside him, the officer yawned. "They're not cracking apart very fast, sir, that's for sure."

Green held up his hand. A shadow of movement had caught his eye. Straining to see through the darkness, he made out a stealthy figure slipping past the overgrown lilacs at the side of the house. The figure emerged onto the driveway, wheeling a bike, and coasted down the drive towards them. By the time he hit the street he was pedalling hard. As he swung left in front of them, Green caught a glimpse of a mustache.

"Follow him! Carefully!"

Eddie pedalled at a steady thirty kilometres an hour, a fast, experienced cyclist familiar with his route. They trailed him for fifteen minutes through the looping suburban crescents and out onto Alta Vista Drive, but at the busy intersection of Riverside and Industrial Avenue, they lost him. Sitting at the traffic light, they watched helplessly as he turned off onto a bicycle path and vanished into the trees.

Constable Wicks broke in on Green's cursing. "We could go ahead and try to catch him at the other end."

Green shook his head. "There are too many exits. He's going downtown, but where?"

"At this hour, a bar in the market, maybe?"

Green smacked the dashboard. "Let's go back to his house and wait for him to come home. Then he'll bloody well tell me."

It was five a.m., however, before Eddie Haddad pedalled wearily back up the street. Sunrise cast shafts of lemony light between the houses. Constable Wicks was fast asleep behind the wheel, and Green had spent the last few hours trying to keep his mind on the case and off the wreckage of his life. Carrie MacDonald kept floating into view, luscious, playful and despite all she had been through, so fatally naïve. How had the killer got in? Why had she been naked? Why so unsuspecting while the killer aimed the deadly bullet at her head? Had she been asleep, maybe dreaming of him? Why hadn't he sent someone to protect her? Why hadn't he stayed with her himself? She had needed him. He could hear her cries ringing in his ears.

He shut his eyes, trying to escape. Only to see Sharon slumped at the kitchen table, her head in her hands, her voice too weary for a fight. She would be at work right now, in this god-forsaken dead of night, probably holding some insomniac's shaky hand and scrounging within herself for the strength to comfort.

He forced his eyes open again. Come home, Eddie, he entreated silently, before I crack up. But it was another two hours before he drifted off into a twilight sleep. The ticking of bicycle gears jolted him awake. He leaped out of the car just as the youth pedalled past. Startled, Eddie nearly fell off his bike.

"Into the car!" Green grabbed him by the scruff of the neck. Eddie was so panic-stricken that he obeyed without question. Only when they were both seated in the back seat did he recover some bluster.

"What the hell are you doing? Spying on me?"

"Exactly. And you've got a lot to explain. Where did you go tonight?"

"None of your goddamn business!"

Green held his thumb and forefinger an inch apart in front of Eddie's face. "Listen, Eddie, you're about this far away from a double murder charge, so you better start talking. Your alibi's blown. A neighbour saw you sneak out of the house at ten p.m. on the night Blair died. I've seen the speed you ride that bike. For you it would be a piece of cake to make it down to the library for ten forty-five. So if you didn't murder Jonathan Blair, you better tell me where the hell you went!"

Constable Wicks had been rudely awakened by the scuffle and now twisted around so that he could watch them. Listening to Green, Eddie's eyes darted first to the door handle and then back to the two men. Seeing himself outnumbered, he deflated.

"I didn't kill Blair!" he whined. "I wasn't anywhere near there. I just went out."

"Where?"

"Nowhere. Just…to hang out with a friend."

"What friend?"

"A…a friend, that's all. They're not part of this."

"You think I'll just take your word for it? Name!"

Eddie hung his head. "Just…just a girl. I—I don't even know her name."

Green raised an eyebrow. "A girl? You spent the night with a girl?"

"Hey, listen, a guy's got to—"

"Where?"

Eddie licked his lips. "Ah…her house. Her parents' house."

Green snorted. "So you sneaked out of your house, sneaked into hers, into her room, slept with her and sneaked out again before morning. All without her parents knowing?"

Eddie attempted a laugh. Colour was returning to his cheeks. "Yeah. You never been young?"

"Oh, I remember vividly. I still need a name or an address. Something I can verify."

The colour faded again. "I—I don't remember."

"Bullshit! I remember every girl I laid when I was your age. You dream about it for weeks. Now, name and address."

"I can't tell you. I can't."

"What? You think you'll get in trouble?"

"No." Almost inaudibly. "She will."

Green hesitated. He sensed fear, but not of him. "Look Eddie, I can be subtle when it's not five a.m. I'll talk to her quietly, without tipping off her family. But I have to verify your story."

Eddie twisted around to look directly at him. "And if I don't tell you, you'll charge me with murder."

"It's a strong possibility."

"Then charge me. Because you won't get her name out of me." His voice quivered with passion. "I won't betray her like that."

God, the purity of first love, Green thought as he dragged himself up the stairs towards his apartment. The flame so unwavering, the truth so clear. Not like his own murky mess. God knows what lay in store for him when he opened his door. Sharon would be just home from her night shift, drained and full of recriminations. What would he say? What could he say?

He found her sitting at the kitchen table, still dressed in her work clothes and sipping a cup of tea. The empty candlesticks had been pushed aside, and the morning newspaper was spread out on the table, headlining the news of Carrie's murder. She raised her head as he appeared.

"Oh honey," she murmured, "this must be awful for you."

There was a softness in her eyes and a warmth in her voice that he had almost forgotten. Without warning, tears scalded his eyes and he turned away to hide them.

She stood up and moved to the stove. "Come, Mike. You'll feel better with some tea."

On rubber legs he eased himself into the chair opposite hers and watched her blurrily as she worked at the counter. He ached for the old days, when she would have taken him into her arms without hesitation. "I…I'm sorry I've been—" he tried when he could trust himself.

"I know." She turned to put his cup in front of him. "Mike, some day we have to talk, but now is not the time. Not after the day you've had."

"I don't deserve this," he murmured, resting his head in his hands. Grief, guilt and gratitude welled inside. He felt her fingers stroke his hair and he longed to wrap his arms around her waist. But all too soon, she withdrew and sat back down across from him.

"It's okay, honey," she said. "You're exhausted. Drink your tea, and then go to bed. I'll leave Tony at Mrs. Louks so nothing will disturb you."

* * *

He awoke with a start to a loud hammering at the door. Shaking the fog from his head, he peered at the night table clock. One-fifteen. One-fifteen! Sunlight poured through a crack in the drapes. He bolted out of bed, groping for the pair of trousers that lay crumpled by the bed.

The hammering grew louder, and when he opened the front door, Jules strode past him into the hall. He was purple as he seized the phone lying disconnected on the hall table.

"How dare you unplug your phone in the middle of so important a case! You've left a half-dozen men milling aimlessly around downtown, a psychology professor without any direction, a stack of unanswered calls from the Deputy Chief, and these—" he flung a fistful of reports down on the hall table "—accumulating unnoticed on your desk."

Green struggled to collect his wits. "My wife must have disconnected the phone to let me sleep. I only got in at seven-thirty this morning, Adam. I was on a stake-out all night."

"You're an inspector. I don't need you on stake-outs, I need you in your office, providing direction."

"I have to know where I'm going before I can do that," Green retorted. "I'm coming in. Tell everyone to keep their pants on. I'll just grab a coffee and a bagel—"

"No time!"

"Adam, I haven't eaten in over fifteen hours! Do you want me to have any functioning brain cells left?" He met Jules' steely eyes. "Tell Dr. Baker I'll be there in twenty minutes."

When his coffee, juice and bagel were ready, he turned his mind to the reports. He quickly discovered that, contrary to Jules' belief, he had read most of them already. I *am* on top of this case, he thought with annoyance. Every conceivable lead is being followed up.

Two reports were new to him, however, and since they pertained to the Haddad family's activities just prior to Blair's death, he bent over them eagerly as he gulped his coffee. A ticket agent at the Air Canada check-in counter remembered a very excited Lebanese family who had arrived to check a female relative onto a flight for New York. He had noticed the woman first of all because she was beautiful and secondly because she was crying. The men had argued among themselves in a mixture of Lebanese and English, so that the agent had only a partial grasp of the content. They seemed to be arguing about what to do next and how much they should tell the family in Beirut.

A girl who had been on the cash at the gift shop near the observation deck on Tuesday remembered three men who had stood at the observation window for about half an hour, arguing loudly in a combination of languages. After watching a jet take off, they had left together, sullen and subdued, at about eight-thirty.

Telephone records indicated that the elder Haddad had made half-a-dozen long-distance phone calls to Beirut between Sunday, June 8 and Tuesday, June 9, the last recorded at six forty-five p.m. Monday. No doubt to inform Raquel's father in Beirut of the flight number and arrival time of her flight home.

Green studied the phone records curiously. There had been a tremendous flurry of activity in the two days preceding her departure to Beirut. What had happened to cause the sudden panic? Phone calls between Beirut and Ottawa prior to June 8 had averaged about two a month, always at the Sunday discount rates.

All these bits of evidence lent credence to the Haddads' version of events. Somehow they had discovered Raquel was too involved with a Canadian boy and they had taken immediate, concrete action to end it. Emergency arrangements had been coordinated by phone with relatives in Lebanon, plane tickets booked, and the rebellious young woman personally escorted onto the aircraft. Archaic, perhaps, but perfectly above board. No outcry for vengeance and murder.

Only Eddie, full of youthful ideals, might have thought differently. Even worse, his alibi had been proven false; he had sneaked out of the house shortly before the murder and refused to give verifiable details about where he had gone. Still, it was much easier to picture Eddie swinging up a flower trellis to his lover's window than driving a knife through another man's ribs.

But if Eddie didn't do it, what was the explanation for the knife and shirt found in the garage? The Haddad family said they must have been planted, an excuse he had heard a hundred times before. But what if this time it was true? Who would have framed them? Someone else with a motive for murder.

That idea brought him full circle back to the research data. To David Miller, Joe Difalco, Rosalind Simmons and even Myles Halton himself. Which one had wanted Blair silenced, and, more importantly, which one had the capacity to do it? The answers to these questions, he hoped, lay with Dr. Stan Baker and the computer files.

Aware of the tenuous thread by which his marriage hung, he searched about for some paper on which to leave Sharon a note of thanks. Earlier, she had reached out to him, however tentatively, and now it was his turn to reciprocate. It was then that he noticed the local tabloid crammed into the garbage can in the corner. He fished it out, curious that Sharon would have allowed the sensationalist rag to cross the threshold and wondering if she had noticed more news about the murders. Worse, he discovered. The headline was sprawled across the front page: "No Progress in Blair Case."

And underneath was a picture of himself with the caption: "Investigator's tie found in nude victim's hand."

"Fuck," he muttered, a sick feeling settling in the pit of his stomach. It grew as the story, upon reading, proved even worse than the headline. One of Carrie's neighbours had spotted Green buttoning his shirt as he ran from the apartment, and the reporter had somehow managed to hint, while deftly skirting the libel laws, that he'd been having an affair with Carrie MacDonald and was now stalling the investigation to prevent this from coming to light.

"Fuck. Fuck," he repeated, his head in his hands. What had Sharon thought? What had she done?

It took him thirty seconds to check through the apartment and confirm his fears. Tony's favourite blanket and toys were gone from his crib, Sharon's toothbrush was gone from its puddle, and her car was not in its parking space below.

"Bloody hell!" he exclaimed and headed across the hall to Mrs. Louks. But Tony was not there. Sharon had picked him up in a great hurry two hours earlier, and although she had not said where she was going, she had been juggling a suitcase and Tony's baby seat.

Green took a deep breath to calm himself as he returned to the apartment. It could be nothing, he tried to tell himself. She had said earlier that she wanted to let him sleep in peace. It was a beautiful sunny day; maybe she had taken the baby to the beach or on a picnic, and she would be back in a few hours, teasing him about his panic. In the meantime, worrying was not going to get Jules and Lynch and the whole damn press corps off his back. Solving the case would.

Trying to be an optimist, he wrote her a big note: "Darling, I'm at work. Please call me. Thanks and love always", and left for the university to meet Dr. Baker, bypassing the police station and the clamour of the squad room. If no one saw him, no one could demand an explanation for the tie.

He found the little round professor hunched over a computer staring at an array of columns on the screen. His assistant Melanie sat cross-legged on the floor, poring over numbers. Baker's eyes were bloodshot and his thinning hair stood on end. He gazed at Green as if he were an apparition from another galaxy.

"What have you got for us, professor?"

Baker shook his head slowly back and forth. "These numbers. It's the damnedest thing."

"Well, that's your ballpark, not mine. Are you ready to give me a report?"

Baker stared at the screen, then flipped through a stack of computer print-outs, pausing now and then to peer at something. For a long while he said nothing. Green was beginning to think the man had forgotten his presence, when he suddenly slammed his books shut and stood up.

"Yes. Let's get a cup of coffee."

Leaving Melanie to her perusal of the numbers, they went down to the little sidewalk café.

"We'll have to talk fast," Green began. "The brass is hounding me."

"Do you want the long answer or the short answer?" Baker asked, a large muffin poised at his lips.

"The short one for now."

"David Miller is your culprit."

Green whistled. "So the data does support Difalco's work?"

Baker put the muffin down. "You want the long answer now?"

"Isn't there a simple yes or no to that?"

"Yes, there is. It's yes. The data does support Difalco's work. All Jonathan Blair's findings are consistent with Difalco's. Blair had concluded the same thing the day before he died."

"Then how come there's a long answer?"

"Well…" Baker finally crammed the muffin into his mouth, and Green had to wait while he chewed. "You've got to admire Miller's work. He's a genius. He's head and shoulders above most people. I couldn't figure out how he generated the simulation of Difalco's work and managed to make his numbers fit the way he wanted." He licked crumbs from his fingers. "There's a new book from a cognitive neuroscience conference in Denmark that I want to check, but I've had to order it up from McGill. The University of Ottawa library says their copy is signed out to: guess who? Our guy Miller."

The professor looked as if he had single-handedly uncovered the key to the mystery. Green frowned warily. "What's odd about that? Miller is doing research in the field."

"But the timing! The coincidence—a new book out, and he's got it. It's highly suspicious, don't you think? Plus, I've tried calling him to borrow the book, and he's not returning my calls. I'll bet he used that book to help with his simulations."

Melanie and the thousand dollars a day notwithstanding, Professor Baker was clearly relishing his role as computer sleuth. His eyes danced as his imagination took flight. Green cast about for some gentle brakes. "I thought you said he faked them."

"He must have, but how?" Reverence mixed with determination on Baker's face. A man not unlike myself,

Green thought, fascinated by the mystery of facts. "It's so damn clever, so well hidden. Just a couple of small changes in the algorithm, like a weighting factor here or a regression sequence there, and it throws Difalco's data off completely. But the real beauty of it is that Miller's own research data fit together properly too. He could have fooled Halton, me— hell, the whole scientific community! He would have been the one to go to Yale on a research fellowship, and no one would have known he was a fake. If Difalco hadn't stuck up for himself, and if Halton hadn't asked Blair to do an independent replication…"

"Blair wouldn't be dead."

Baker blinked. "Well, yes, there's that. But evoked potential word processing research might have gone off in the wrong direction for years. That's the point. Miller's that convincing." He shook his head ruefully. "I don't envy Myles the job of cleaning up this mess."

"He fired Miller already."

"Well, yes, but Myles was supposed to present this research in Stockholm next month, and this is going to be a major blow to his credibility. Plus, Yale won't want to touch him with a ten-foot pole now. It's going to be a long while before his work is credible again."

"Was it credible before?"

"Oh very. And potentially very useful too, which of course was what he wanted."

"What do you mean?"

Baker seemed to hesitate as if he had overstepped his bounds, then reached for another muffin. "Well, you know we are often influenced in our choice of career by personal problems. Wilder Penfield, the great pioneer in brain surgery, had a sister with epilepsy. Halton has a son in an institution, brain-damaged from birth. Myles was a graduate student at Berkeley at the time."

Green masked his surprise. "I only knew about the two daughters."

Baker shook his head as he chewed. "He never talks about it. Some deep dark secret, I gather. But it's his driving force, so to speak. That and, let's face it, he's ambitious as hell."

Twelve

Afterwards, Green was so deep in thought as he arrived back at his office that he failed to see Marianne Blair's executive assistant lying in wait outside his door. Peter Weiss seized him by the elbow and spun him around.

"You haven't answered any of my calls."

Green shook him off. Around the squad room, heads turned curiously. "Do you want the case solved or do you want me chatting on the phone?"

"From what I hear you've been busy sleeping with witnesses."

"Actually, I was up all night watching a suspect."

Weiss wrinkled his nose as if smelling a foul odour. "An Arab. Yes, I know."

Green hesitated. Weiss must be getting his information from somewhere else. He hoped it was Jules. "A Canadian, Mr. Weiss. Of Lebanese origin."

"CSIS should be informed."

Green rolled his eyes. "This has nothing to do with international terrorism, or with Mrs. Blair for that matter. This is about Jonathan's girlfriend."

"Then you're naïve, Inspector," Weiss retorted. "If it's an Arab, it's political. If it's a Jew, it's political, if it's a black, it's political—"

"That's your problem," Green snapped, pushing past Weiss into his office. "I'm just investigating a homicide, and so far, the only politics involved are the ones I have to play with you guys. I don't mean to be rude, and there's no disrespect implied, but you're wasting precious time. I'll phone Mrs. Blair myself." He picked up the phone as if to convey his sincerity. "I'll tell her all I can. But I have several urgent leads to follow up, and that's where I can help her the most."

Weiss glowered in the doorway, searching for a toe-hold of authority. When Green began to dial, he spun on his heel and stalked out, flicking at the sleeves of his linen suit as if to rid himself of the taint of crime. Green's tone with Marianne Blair was more diplomatic, but his message much the same. After dispensing with her as quickly as possible, he flipped hopefully through his stack of phone messages, but none was from Sharon. He called home but got the answering machine. It's still early, he told himself. She could still be at the beach or at a friend's, especially if she didn't have to work until the evening. Full of hope, he called the ward where she worked, but the ward clerk told him Sharon had called in sick earlier in the day and requested a few days off. The woman was surprised he didn't know and asked if Sharon was all right, because she had sounded strained and upset.

Green hung up, fighting a sense of foreboding. It was time for some serious damage control. He had to explain the necktie, but to do that he had to find her. That meant calling her friends, all smart, capable nurses like herself, who thought he was cute but entirely unreliable as a life partner. It meant calling his in-laws, who had been keeping their fingers crossed ever since their career-woman daughter had finally reeled in this rather unlikely marital prospect—Jewish at least, but a divorced policeman who'd forget to eat, sleep or change his clothes if no one was there to stand over him. His mother-in-law's screech would echo all the way from Mississauga, and his father-in-law would have them both packed on the next plane up. Green shuddered. Could he face that? On top of Lynch, Weiss, Marianne Blair and all the other naysayers on his back right now?

Closer to home and easier to drop in on without inventing excuses was his father, whom Sharon adored. She knew he stayed alive only for the moments he could spend with his son and grandson. She would never leave town without visiting him to say good-bye, and no matter what excuse she gave, his father would know the truth. For a man who sat alone in his apartment all day watching TV, Sid Green had an uncanny knack for reading people. He would know if Sharon were leaving for good.

But Sid Green's knack for seeing through people might prove tricky, Green realized as he knocked and breezed into his father's living room, trying to look cheerful. Sid looked up from his chair, where he was watching some indeterminate soap opera. There were spikes of bristle on his chin which his razor had missed, but at least he was still trying to shave, Green thought.

"What's going on?" his father demanded irritably. Any change to his routine, no matter how pleasant, seemed to irritate him.

Green held up a paper bag. "I brought you cheese bagels from Nate's. You hungry?"

Sid said nothing, but watched his son suspiciously as he slipped into the tiny kitchenette to heat up the food. Sensing the heavy silence, Green stalled in the kitchen, looking for an oblique approach to his inquiry. But as it turned out, he didn't need one. Returning to the living room, he found his father's rheumy eyes fixed on him knowingly.

"Sharon was here."

Green kept his expression neutral. "Oh, really? When?"

"She already bought me cheese bagels from Nate's. She made some for her and me, but she didn't touch her own."

"Did she...say anything?"

Still Sid held his gaze balefully. "She brought me some new pictures. Mishka, don't do this to me again."

Green blinked. "Do what?"

"Chase her away. She will move to Toronto and take Tony away from me. When I am dead, that will be time enough to get a divorce."

"Hey, Dad, she brought over some baby pictures. Who's talking about divorce?"

Sid didn't reply, and Green felt his heart turn to stone. "Was she?"

Sid took a deep breath. "She took a picture from the drawer when she put her pictures away. She doesn't think I saw, but she took the picture of you with your mother at the river. That time you carried her down there just before she died."

Our last family picnic, on my twenty-first birthday, Green thought. Sharon had always admired that picture, but surely she knew how his father cherished it! "God, Dad, I'm sorry."

"I have copies. But why did she do that, Mishka? To have a memory of you together, for Tony, when she takes him to Toronto."

Green felt sick, but he forced himself to laugh. "She's not going to Toronto, Dad. I asked her to get that picture. I...well, I need it for something."

He didn't know how he was going to cover up that lie, but right now it was the least of his worries. He stayed a few minutes longer, filling the silence with chatter, but he knew his father was unconvinced. As Green left, he searched for a way to cheer him up. Depression and loss could be fatal.

Passing a pharmacy on his way back to the car, he saw a window display advertising gifts for Father's Day the next week. Some Father's Day, he thought grimly. My wife and son in Toronto and my father near his deathbed, full of reproach. It was then that he thought of how to explain the lie. Blown up and beautifully framed, the picture would make a perfect Father's Day gift. To a man mired in memories, it would be more touching than a hundred sweaters or dressing gowns. The problem was that if Sharon had indeed gone back to Toronto, he would have to steal yet another picture to make the gift.

Back in the office, there was still no message from her. Had she really left without a single word to him? Anger flared briefly. How dare she have so little faith! And so little appreciation of the pressures he was under? She'd seen him smeared in the press before, and she knew better than to believe a word they said! Surely when she calmed down in a few hours, even a day or two, she'd remember that. Reassured, he decided not to call anyone else, at least not just yet. If she still wasn't back tomorrow, he'd begin the search in earnest. But she'd be back. She'd stuck by him before, kicking and screaming but still there, through worse than this.

Having forced his worry into the back of his mind, he turned back to the phone messages that had collected. More than half were from the press, and he tossed them into the waste basket. Fat chance I'll call you bastards, he thought grimly. All you want is a juicy pound of flesh for the headlines. Carrie's murder and my tie had done nicely today, but what about tomorrow? In the absence of anything else, perhaps a nice little story about my collapsing marriage. Or my inability to protect witnesses and my failure to charge the suspect staring me in the face.

Contrary to popular opinion, nothing was staring him in

the face but reams and reams of information. To tease out the answer, to make sense of all the conflicting tides, could take days. The crux of the puzzle lay in the motive. Everyone else was betting on the Haddads. Sex and revenge were feelings the public—and his fellow cops—could understand far more easily than the panic of professional humiliation and lost dreams. On the surface too, the evidence clearly favoured Eddie Haddad—the knife, the bloody shirt, the lies about his whereabouts.

Sullivan, Jules and Marianne Blair were right. Most policemen would have arrested Eddie on the spot. So why was he holding back? On a mere hunch, based on the panic in Eddie's voice and the earnest look in his eyes? Or was he, as Sullivan the pragmatist often accused him, winging out into the wild blue yonder, seduced by the complex psychic web of Halton's group? There was a mystery there, as fascinating and sinister as any he'd encountered, but perhaps it was irrelevant. Perhaps Blair's murder was a mere lucky coincidence for the student who had perpetrated the fraud. Green hated coincidences, the enemy of deduction, but sometimes they were true. Sometimes the obvious suspect was the right one.

But just then a shadow blocked his doorway, and he looked up to see Brian Sullivan leaning against the frame. He tossed a file down on Green's desk.

"Well, buddy, if you were looking for an easy answer to our problems, you can forget it."

* * *

"There's not one fingerprint in Carrie's whole apartment!" Green echoed incredulously.

Sullivan shook his head. His hair stood in straw tufts, and his eyes were red from rubbing. "Nothing useful, and no fibres or tissue we can pin down either. This killer's no fool. He anticipated all the angles." Sullivan sighed. "And that's not all the bad news, buddy. The black hair we got from the shirt? It doesn't match any of the Haddads. Not even Eddie's."

Despite the forensic dead ends, Green felt a surge of triumph. His intuition had been right! Better than all the computer scans, the forensic minutiae and the balancing of probabilities that formed the core of everyday detective work.

"It doesn't really mean anything," Sullivan muttered, dropping into the chair opposite. "I mean, it weakens the case against Eddie, but it doesn't kill it. One black hair...it could have been there for months."

"The shirt was washed."

"Spot washed, forensics says. Mike, it's staring you in the face. The kid is as guilty as hell."

Green wavered. He remembered the neat little bullet hole in the centre of Carrie's forehead and felt a hard fist form in his chest. He rose. "Maybe you're right. Maybe—"

The phone shrilled at his elbow, making them jump. Green pounced on it, hoping it was Sharon, but instead the gravel voice of the desk sergeant came through.

"There's a Mr. Pierre Haddad down here, Inspector. He insists on seeing you."

Raquel's uncle was tight-lipped and grim as Green ushered him into an interview room near his office, and when he spoke, it was obvious he had rehearsed the speech carefully.

"Inspector Green, you notice I have brought no lawyer with me. That is because I want to cooperate with the police. My sons and I have done nothing wrong, and we trust that the Canadian justice system will not betray us. I know that the knife and shirt from the murder were found in my garage. I know that my son Edward has lied about being home with us that night. We have talked about it and I believe his explanation. I also believe that you are an honourable man and did not put the knife there. So I appeal to you, as an honourable man, to listen to our side of the story. There can be only one explanation. The Haddad family has been framed."

Although he had just been thinking the same thing, Green tried to look sceptical. He arched an eyebrow. "Framed? Why would someone do that?"

Haddad looked at him as if he thought him a complete fool. "Obviously, so you would blame us instead of him."

"I mean, why you?"

"Perhaps someone saw the boys arguing with Jonathan Blair earlier and took advantage of the situation."

"A pretty long shot, Mr. Haddad. They'd have to know who your sons were, who Raquel was and her connection to Jonathan, and they'd have to want Blair dead. Not many people fit that bill."

"Probably only one, Inspector. The murderer."

Green continued to play devil's advocate, using Haddad to explore the theory. "It leaves a lot to chance, and it implies Blair's murder was a spur of the moment thing. When the killer sees a chance to blame your sons, he goes off to the library and sticks a knife in Blair's gut. That's another thing—the knife. He had to get himself a Bedouin knife."

Haddad waved a hand in dismissal. "Those things are everywhere."

"But he'd have to buy it. The fight with Blair was at six-thirty. Many stores are closed at that hour on Tuesday, and even so, it probably would take him more time to hunt one up." Green shook his head. Detective Gibbs had not yet been able to find where the knife had been bought, and Green knew that if it took Gibbs this long, it would take the killer even longer. "This was much longer in the planning, I'm afraid."

"Then it was planned to blame my son Eddie," retorted Haddad.

Green analyzed the implications. "For that, the killer would have to know an awful lot about your family."

"Raquel could have told anybody about us. That is how the killer could know everything. Even that we did not want her to see Jonathan Blair."

Green took the reasoning one step further. For this frame to work, it was equally important that the family know about her affair with Jonathan. The killer needed the Haddads to make a fuss and to make public their hostility towards Blair. Yet the Haddads said she never talked to them about her friends.

"Tell me," he asked as casually as he could. "How did you find out Raquel was seeing him? Did she tell you?"

Haddad took a deep breath. The faint pink of shame tinged his cheeks. "Jonathan wasn't the only one. There were others before. When Raquel came to this country, she seemed to go wild. She is so beautiful. The men, everywhere, they chase her. She liked it. She saw how the Canadian women do what they want, go out with boys, choose whoever they want, and she wanted that too. Even before I knew about Jonathan, I decided to send Raquel back to Beirut when her courses were over. But then I found out they were going to move in together."

Green hid his surprise. Certainly Jonathan's mother knew nothing of such plans. In fact Jonathan had told his father only days before his death that he was coming back to Vancouver, perhaps for good.

"What makes you think that?" he demanded.

"I found a note from Jonathan to Raquel. It was a—a..." Haddad flushed. "A love letter. Disgusting. Jonathan talked about getting an apartment next week. That made up my mind for sure."

Green frowned. "Where did you find this note?"

"Last Sunday night my boy Paulie found the note on the front walk. She must have dropped it on her way in. When I read it, I said that's enough."

And that's when the phone calls to Lebanon began, Green thought to himself. "Did you ask Raquel about the note?"

Haddad nodded ruefully. "Tuesday afternoon, at the university. That was the argument you know about. I asked her about the note and I told her about Lebanon."

"What did she say about the note?"

"She said it's not true. There is no note. Jonathan and her are not…together. But Raquel always lied to me. Hid things from me."

Green's antennae began to quiver. "Do you still have the note?"

Haddad reached into his pocket and extracted a folded sheet of paper. He held it a moment in trembling hands before reluctantly handing it over.

> *My Darling,*
>
> *I can't stay away from you! I grow hard just writing this note. I want you, I need you, and I'm sick of sneaking around and grabbing stolen hours with you. To hell with your uncle. To hell with my mother and the stuffed shirts we work with. We're going to do it! I'll tell my mother I'm taking a trip, we'll get that place and we can stay in bed for the rest of our lives! I can't believe I'll be able to fuck you whenever I want you. Which is always! Only one more week! Hold on, baby. I am, hard as it is (just the way you like it). I love you madly!*
>
> *Jonathan*

*　*　*

Sullivan reread the note, then held it up to study it from a distance. They were sitting in Green's office, having thanked Pierre Haddad for his help and promising to get back to him. The plastic evidence bag crackled in Sullivan's hands. Inside was an eight-by-eleven sheet of standard white computer paper.

"Pretty impersonal way to send a love note," Green muttered. "Looks more like an office memo."

"People who do everything by computer operate like that. I get lots of memos just printed by computer. Nobody bothers with writing anymore. At least the guy signed it."

"Right…" Green rested his head in his hand. "But you've got to admit, it's pretty damn convenient. Hardly anything we can match it to, to check if Blair really wrote it…and this business of it 'accidentally' dropping on Pierre's front walk. Give me a break."

"You're saying it's a plant?"

Green swivelled to face Sullivan. "Let me ask you this. What would be your reaction if you found a note like this from Lizzie's boyfriend?"

Sullivan grinned. "Lizzie's only sixteen. I'd kill the guy."

"But if—"

"What every father'd would be, Mike. Furious. Just like the Haddads. I'd probably try to send her to my sister in Alberta."

"So this note would be almost sure to provoke a reaction?"

"Absolutely. He pushes all the buttons—crude sex, defiance of parents…just wait till you have a daughter, Mike. You'll want to protect her from the likes of us till she's thirty-five!"

I have a daughter, Green thought with a sudden pang. A daughter and a son, but perhaps I'll never get to know either. He forced the idea out of his mind with an effort. "This killer is clever, Brian. Look at the frame!"

"If it is a frame," Sullivan reminded him. "The only thing

we have to substantiate that theory is one black hair. And that could belong to Eddie Haddad's girlfriend, for all we know."

"But it doesn't. It belongs to the killer."

"As they say, tell that to the judge."

Green swivelled his chair back to his desk and stood up. "Let's get this down to Paquette and see what forensics can find. Then we'll take it over to the documents guy at the RCMP lab and see if it's really Blair's signature. Maybe then we'll have more than one black hair."

Green had hoped to get the note analyzed quickly, but just as he and Sullivan were crossing the main lobby towards the Ident Unit, Deputy Chief Lynch emerged from the elevator. Clutched in his fist was a newspaper. Oh fuck, Green thought to himself.

"Green! Get over here!"

Green sent Sullivan on ahead to Paquette's lab and steeled himself to face Lynch, who propelled him into an empty waiting room and slammed the door behind them.

"I don't need this shit!" Lynch flung the tabloid down on a chair. "I put myself on the line for you. I promised the bigshots you could deliver, and what do you give me? This!" He stabbed the front page with his finger.

"It's not worth wasting our energy on, sir," Green replied, although he knew it sounded lame.

"Wasting our energy?" Lynch echoed. "That's all you can say? The press calls us all a bunch of whores and incompetents, with you topping the list—"

"The press tries to sell papers. They do whatever it takes, you know that, sir. If they don't have facts, they make them up. I can't control what they print."

"You could if you'd answer their calls!" Lynch shot back. "Or answered Media Relations' calls. Or mine! If you told anybody what the fuck you were doing, then maybe it wouldn't look like nothing."

"What do you want me to do? Answer calls or solve the case?"

The Deputy Chief shoved a finger in his face. "Listen, sonny, this is not Adam Jules you're talking to. I don't give a fuck about your homicide record. It doesn't do me bugger all good if you're sitting on your ass letting this Arab bastard run around loose. Pick him up before I assign the case to someone else."

Green could feel the hairs rise on the back of his neck. Gritting his teeth he counted slowly to five. "He's not guilty, sir," he said when he dared.

"Not guilty! What are you, God? The way I hear it, the case is open and shut."

"The man was framed."

Lynch turned purple. "You working for the defence now, Green? Do I have to make myself clearer? Arrest the guy."

"Sir, we'd look stupid if—"

"We'd look stupid?" Lynch seized the paper and threw it in Green's face. "What do you call that! You've got till the end of the day to lay a charge in this case, or you're off it!" He spun around and slammed out of the room.

In the silence that suddenly fell, Green could hear his own heart thumping. He retrieved the loathsome newspaper from the floor. He had never seen the Deputy Chief so angry. He doesn't give a damn about the truth, thought Green bitterly. He just wants to look good, and heaven help the person who messes that up. I bet if I solved the case tomorrow, he'd be the first here for the pictures. My best buddy.

Fuck him, he thought, shoving the newspaper in the trash. What Lynch thinks isn't important. What's important are the facts.

With that in mind, he went out to rejoin Sullivan. He ran

into him just emerging from Ident's corner of the building, teasing Paquette over his shoulder as he left.

"That was fast," Green said.

"Not much to analyze." Sullivan waved the note. "There were only three legible prints on it. Haddad's right thumb and index finger and his son Paul's right thumb. The rest are just smudges, but nothing at all like Blair's."

"Hah!" Green cried, the adrenaline still pumping from his clash with Lynch. "Don't try to tell me Jonathan Blair wore gloves when he wrote his love notes."

"No, I won't try to tell you that. It's fishy, that's for sure."

Green strode down the hall. "He's smart, but he's not as smart as all that. He couldn't find a way to put Blair's prints on the note so he had to leave it blank. Stupid mistake. Now let's see how good he is at forging."

They battled the last of the Saturday shopping traffic as they made their way over to the RCMP Headquarters. Drivers baking in the heat honked and sat on one another's bumpers. Inching east along the Queensway, Sullivan glanced over at Green, who was staring out the side window.

"So what did Lynch want? More of the same?"

"He wanted to show me today's headline."

Sullivan grimaced. "Yeah, I saw it. But people don't really believe everything they read."

Green nodded mechanically. The adrenaline rush had begun to subside, leaving a shakiness and a sick feeling in the pit of his stomach. His earlier optimism had deserted him. What if the newspaper was right, and he never solved the case? What if Sharon had finally given up? What if he had finally destroyed, through his own self-absorption, the last of the affection that had kept her with him?

Was there any way to get it back? He felt the ache in his

stomach as he remembered the years before he had found her. Not as years of glorious sexual adventure, but as years of hope and pain and disappointment, looking for the one Great Love of his Life. A family, children, a place to come home to—how much he had wanted those things then! As an only child, with his mother dead now and his father a frail old man, he dreamed of being surrounded by family that would chase out the loneliness he had felt all his life. After a string of romantic failures, he had thought Sharon was the one. But maybe it was his destiny to be a loner, to have nothing but his work, his colleagues and moments of physical release when he needed them. Would he never move on? Would he never grow up? Was he destined to fail every woman who felt something for him? The ache tightened his chest and stung his eyes.

God, get a grip, Green! he scolded himself. You're wallowing in self-pity because you haven't had a decent meal or a decent night's sleep in days. You feel guilty about Carrie, and rightly so. And your marriage has hit a rough patch, that's all! Is anybody's marriage perfect? Sharon's working too hard, I'm working too hard, the baby's exhausting and the damn apartment's too small! We can fix all that.

He took a deep, cleansing breath and raised his head just as they turned into the RCMP parking lot. "The best thing we can do, for all our sakes, is solve this damn case."

The documents expert at the RCMP lab took only ten minutes to compare the 'Jonathan' on the note to one on a memo Blair had written to Halton. During that ten minutes, he didn't say a single word. The silence was broken only by the rustle of paper and the shuffling of his footsteps. When he finally spoke, it was like a gunshot in a deserted room.

"It's a tracing. Pen pressure's too even and the hand was moving much too slowly. There's a minute tremor in the lines which you only get if you're moving slowly. A good likeness in terms of letter formation. A quick glance, even someone familiar with his signature—they wouldn't notice anything wrong."

* * *

"I knew it!" Green pounded the dash of Sullivan's old Chevrolet. "I knew it was a set-up. Eddie Haddad a cold-blooded killer? Give me a break."

As Sullivan steered the car onto the Queensway entrance ramp for the short hop from the RCMP Headquarters back to the Elgin Street police station, the sun was sinking deep into the murky western sky. Heat still hung over the city like a wet sponge. Sullivan lowered the visor with a sigh. "What next? Do we pick up Miller or go home?"

Green squinted ahead into the hazy red glow. "I never did like Miller as a suspect."

Sullivan groaned. "Who else, Mike? Difalco? Rosalind Simmons, maybe? Or how about the cleaning lady?"

"How about Halton?"

"Halton." Sullivan shook his head in disgust. "Ask yourself the first question in a murder investigation, who stands to gain by Blair's death? Miller. He fits all the criteria. Brains, inside knowledge, access to Blair's computer, motive in spades and no alibi for the night of Blair's death. He said he was alone in his office at his computer all evening. No one can substantiate that."

"That's the point. Wouldn't someone as smart as Miller have set himself up a better alibi if he were planning to kill someone?"

"Miller's a genius, but in street smarts he's a real dud. He's obsessed with his research, and you know as well as me that obsessions can blind a guy. And with his history of mental problems—"

"I know it fits, but it just doesn't sit right," Green said. "Blair was upset by his discovery about the data tampering. He was thinking of leaving Halton's program. Why?"

They were nearing the Nicholas off-ramp, which led to Green's apartment. "Mike, where are we going?"

Green wasn't sure he'd be able to get food past the sick knot in his stomach, but the half-eaten bagel he'd managed at noon was long gone, and dizziness was setting in. If he wanted to keep going, he had to eat. "Nate's Deli. I need to think."

Sullivan groaned as he steered the car off the Queensway onto Nicholas Street. "This is the third meal I've eaten out in a row. Mary will kill me."

Green waved a distracted hand. "No, she'll kill me. She always does. Miller's guilt would never have made Blair feel like quitting Halton."

"But Halton has nothing to gain by knocking off Blair. Miller was the one screwing up his program."

"Yes, but Blair was the one threatening to blow the whistle."

"Mike, that doesn't make any sense. You're right, you need food—your brain cells are dying. Why ask Blair to look into it if he didn't want the truth known?"

Green scrambled to keep ahead of Sullivan's logic. This was how they worked best together—Green making his wild intuitive leaps and down-to-earth Sullivan trailing along with the safety net. "Because Halton was passionate about his research, the same trait that makes him such a good suspect. He had to know the truth so that his future research would not be based on a lie. But then he asked Blair to keep it quiet, and Blair refused. Which would have really screwed up Halton's bid to work with Yale and finally play with the big boys. He had to knock the kid off. It fits, Brian. It's convoluted, but it fits."

Waiting behind a string of cars turning left onto King Edward Street, Sullivan gave him a long exasperated look. "I think Miller fits better. Come on, Mike, face it. You just like to see the big guys fall."

Green grinned. "What do you want from a scruffy little kid from Lowertown? I admit Miller's past strikes a chord. We're both working class, inner city Jewish kids. But I don't give you a hard time every time you go sappy over some Irish Valley boy—"

Sullivan laughed. "Oh, not much."

"How about Difalco? He fits the profile perfectly. Now there's a guy we can both dislike. Rich, arrogant, spoiled…"

"Yeah, but he's got an alibi. Plus no motive."

Green snorted. "Lateral thinking, Sullivan. That's exactly what makes Difalco and Halton suspicious. This killing is brilliant and premeditated. Whoever did it would have set himself an airtight alibi."

Sullivan manoeuvred the car off Rideau Street into the parking lot of Nate's Delicatessen. For a moment he was silent as he concentrated his energies on squeezing the oversized Chevrolet into the last tiny space on the congested lot. Then he turned to Green.

"But Halton's alibi does give us a small problem. Half a dozen sailing cronies place him in Toronto five hundred kilometres away. I'd say that was pretty airtight."

Green shook his head. "Not if you look at the timing. Yesterday I double-checked his story with his sailing buddy from York University. Halton was out sailing on Tuesday, that much is true. But according to Dr. Trent, he insisted on an early dinner, passed up his usual double martinis, and left shortly after seven. A fast driver in a good car could make it in under four hours. Halton has a BMW. It's cutting it close, but it's possible."

Sullivan laughed. "With wings."

They swung open the door to the deli and felt the blast of air conditioning. Both heaved a sigh of relief. Nodding to the waitress who approached, they headed towards the back.

"Brian, don't forget this killer is smart! Do you think he'd go to all the trouble of setting up this frame and not give himself a decent alibi? Miller's a sitting duck! He left the whole evening wide open, with no one to substantiate his story!"

Sullivan eased himself into the booth and picked up the menu. "Come on, a guy like Halton's much more likely to get someone else to do his dirty work."

Green froze half-seated, his thoughts racing as he suddenly remembered Difalco and the stolen files. "Two people! Each supplying only half the picture. One who had the motive, the other the means and opportunity. And who else but the golden boy? Brilliant, Brian! That's it!"

"Mike!" Sullivan waved the menu wildly. "Food!"

But Green was already across the room.

Thirteen

Green fled the delicatessen in a burst of inspiration, only to stop dead in the parking lot when he realized he had no evidence. He sent Sullivan to get his car while he pondered a plan of attack. Tackled together, Halton and Difalco were unassailable; Halton had the perfect alibi and Difalco no motive. Green had to split them apart and undermine their mutual trust. If either could be made to see that their interests differed or if Green could find a crack in that trust, he might have a chance.

He could try a frontal attack on Joe Difalco, pointing out that Blair too had once been Halton's trusted soldier. He could try to appeal to Difalco's macho need not to appear as a patsy, but he doubted Difalco would crack. For one thing, Difalco was wily enough to recognize hot air when it blew his way, and for another he knew that as the actual killer, he stood to lose much more than Halton, no matter what deal he cut.

Similarly, any confrontation with Halton would be laughed right out of the ring. Halton would know he didn't have a shred of evidence to back up his claim. A shred of evidence. That's what he needed. Some sort of leverage to hold over them, if not to force a confession, which Green knew was unlikely, at least to panic one into betraying the other.

The evidence was not in the research files, that much Green knew. Dr. Baker had analyzed it all, and everyone had come up blameless except David Miller. But somewhere, someone had to know something. No murderer was so lucky as to leave no tiny miscalculations behind.

Blocking out Sullivan's muttered curses as they drove back towards the station, Green pondered again the sequence of events and jotted notes in his notebook:

1. Sunday— fake note typed on Blair's computer.
2. Saturday night—note planted on Pierre Haddad's front walk.
3. Monday evening—Blair completes formal statistical analysis proving Miller wrong.
4. Monday evening (before or after above?)—Halton drives to Toronto.
5. Tuesday morning—Blair asks for urgent meeting with Halton.
6. Tuesday night—Blair murdered.

Whoever killed Blair had to have known on Saturday that Blair was going to complete his analysis on Monday. Halton had chosen to go to Toronto on the very day Blair needed him the most! Definitely odd, thought Green, feeling that familiar rush when the scent is strong. But how would the killer have known? By breaking into Blair's files himself to keep an eye on his progress? By running his own analysis on the side? Only Halton would be in a position to do that easily, for he had all the office keys and all the computer passwords.

Alternatively, Blair could have told Halton the results earlier. Every researcher, long before he runs his final formal analysis, keeps an eye on trends in the data and runs preliminary tests to satisfy his own curiosity, as well as to determine how many more subjects he has to test. Blair probably knew a week or two earlier which way the data were leaning, and perhaps in all innocence he had relayed his impressions to his boss.

Green held his breath, his mind racing along these lines. Jonathan's friends had found him increasingly moody in the week or so before his death. He had told his father on Sunday before his final statistical run that he was unhappy with how things were turning out. Unhappy about the statistical findings, or about Halton's reaction to them?

Maybe he had told his father more than that. Maybe he had given Henry Blair some small detail which had held no meaning for Henry but might be the key to the case.

Green looked up excitedly just as Sullivan was approaching the Rideau Canal on his way towards Elgin Street. Looming ahead were the gothic green spires of the Château Laurier, the majesty of Wellington Street and the Parliament buildings behind. On impulse he asked Sullivan to drop him off and sent him home to have dinner with his family, with instructions to stay near a phone in case he was needed. At least Mary should be pleased.

Henry Blair was alone at a table in the corner of the dining room at the Château Laurier, looking forlorn and out of place in his rumpled sports clothes amid the chandeliers, leaded glass and creamy linens of the elegant hall. He picked at his Lobster Newburg, a nearly-empty bottle of Chardonnay sitting in a silver bucket at his elbow.

He spotted Green from across the dining hall and his face lit with anticipation. Struggling to his feet, he offered a shaky hand and inquired if Green had any news.

"We're certainly closing in," Green replied, taking the seat opposite and drawing out his notebook. Blair offered him some wine, which Green reluctantly declined, before emptying the bottle into his own glass. The scent of lobster and Madeira floated up to tantalize Green's nostrils and he felt his stomach contract.

"Marianne tells me it's some Arab relative of Jonathan's new girlfriend."

Green shook his head. "I would have told you if we had been definite. By the way, did Jonathan talk to you about his…ah, love life?"

Henry Blair gave a wry smile. "He was pretty private and I've always respected that. I knew about Vanessa Weeks, of course. I met her at Christmas when Jonathan and she came out to Vancouver for a visit. And I knew he'd broken up with her, which didn't exactly surprise me."

Green frowned. "Why not? Everyone else was surprised."

Blair nodded with an air of weary wisdom. "I guess I've a little more experience with ambitious women. They're challenging, but somewhat hard to live with in the long term. You… kind of have to bury yourself."

"Did Jonathan tell you why he broke it off?"

"He was vague, said something about it not being the right time for him to make a serious commitment, but that sounds like a euphemism for just getting fed up with it, don't you think?"

"Did he seem sad?"

"Sad?" Blair took a long swallow of wine. "Yes, he did. That's why I thought he may just have been unable to cope with her. You can't stand them, Inspector, but it's not easy to be without them either."

That applies to life with any woman, Green thought wryly. Whether ambitious or just plain stubborn. "Did he mention anything about a new girl?"

Blair pushed a piece of roasted zucchini around his plate, untasted, and Green followed its progress with absorption, longing to snatch it from his fork. "After Marianne told me about the Arab suspect, I remembered that he had said something about a girl a couple of weeks ago. Rachel, wasn't it? He said this girl was after him, and she wasn't easily discouraged."

"So from what you could tell, he wasn't interested in her?"

"Not at that time. But last Sunday his attitude seemed to have changed. He sounded much more sympathetic to her. Concerned in fact, now that I think of it."

Green leaned forward, the zucchini briefly forgotten. "Concerned in what way?"

"Well, that she was another pawn in the power game, just like him."

"Pawn?" Green echoed in surprise. "What was he referring to? Who was she a pawn of?"

Blair looked across the table with bleak, heavy-lidded eyes. "I don't know. He didn't actually say much, but from the general theme of the discussion, I'd guess it was Halton."

"Are you saying Halton was using her?"

"Oh no, I…" Blair looked blank, then surprised as if an idea had just occurred to him. "Do you mean taking advantage of her? Goodness, that could be what he meant. That would certainly be Halton's style."

"You're saying Halton fooled around with his female students?"

"I suspect Myles fooled around with everyone. He is a man of enormous sexual appetites."

Green pondered the implications as he watched Henry Blair abandon the grilled zucchini and busy himself with the wine. A creamy morsel of lobster claw lay forgotten at the edge of his plate, and Green's fingers itched. In the lengthening silence, Blair would not meet his eye. Green remembered his allusions to Marianne Blair and some secret from Halton's past.

216

"Did those appetites include your ex-wife?"

Blair set his wine glass down hastily, splashing some wine onto the tablecloth. Clumsily he mopped at it with his napkin. "I'm sure that's quite irrelevant to the subject at hand, Inspector, and Marianne would have your head if she knew you'd asked it."

Green shrugged. "Much of what I ask seems irrelevant, but I need to know as much of the big picture as I can."

The waiter approached Blair's elbow and discreetly removed the plate. Green watched the lobster go with silent longing. Blair waited until they were alone and then folded his hands in his lap, his composure restored. "What precisely are you after? Why did you come to see me?"

Green leaned towards him. "You know something about Halton that you're sitting on. Something unsavoury about his past. I'll tell you frankly that I'm considering him a suspect in your son's murder—"

"What!"

Green waited patiently. He knew that once the outrage had spluttered out, Blair would come face to face with the question he had posed. All he had to do was wait. After a couple of minutes and a deep gulp which drained his wine glass, Blair calmed himself sufficiently to shake his head. "You are right about there being something unsavoury in his past, but I assure you it's quite in the past and it certainly has nothing to do with my ex-wife. A woman, yes, but not—"

"Henry! Inspector!" A commanding voice hailed from across the room and both men looked up in surprise to see Marianne Blair charging towards them through the tables, eyes sparking. Her grey hair protruded in irregular spikes, and her brown skirt flapped in her wake.

Through the room, conversations trailed off. Leaded glass

partitions divided the dining hall into intimate cubicles, but Green could still see heads swivel at the tables along her route. Marianne Blair seemed oblivious.

"Marianne to his rescue, as always," Henry muttered, reaching for his wine glass, only to discover it was empty. He put it down with a sigh and raised his head to face her as she reached the table. But her eyes had skewered Green.

"What on earth are you doing now! Wasting taxpayers' money as well as time?"

More heads swivelled. While Green was counting to ten and formulating a reply, Henry Blair jumped into the breach. "No, Marianne. The worthy inspector thinks Myles Halton may have killed our Jon."

She was struck dumb for a moment and groped blindly for a chair from the next table. "Ridiculous," she managed once she had fallen into it. "Myles thought the world of Jon."

"He also has a violent temper," Blair replied. "You know that even better than I."

Mrs. Blair flashed her ex-husband a quick look. Of puzzlement or of warning, Green wondered, and in the next breath she answered the question. "I'm sure the inspector doesn't want us wasting his time airing petty grievances from the past."

"I'd hardly call Darlene a petty grievance, Marianne. Nor that poor son of his."

"Myles has paid his dues for that a hundred-fold!" she shot back, giving Green a faint inkling of what their marriage had been like. "He's made it his life's work, as you well know."

"Yes, well it shows what a guilty conscience can do," Blair sniped drily. "Still, I suppose one should be grateful he has a guilty conscience. It raises him above the level of your common psychopath."

"Henry, enough!" Mrs. Blair slapped her hand upon the table, making the silverware jump. She glowered at him, jowls shaking and brows drawn low together. Looking at her now, Green noticed that she had touched her cheeks with blush and her lips with a shade of pink that almost matched her coral silk blouse. Almost, but not quite. Once again, her attempt at fashion coordination, although expensive, fell just short of the mark.

"Are you saying Myles Halton is responsible for his son's condition?" he probed blandly.

The two stopped their verbal ping-pong to gape at him. Mrs. Blair thrust her chin out pugnaciously, and her ex turned to her as if to ask for permission. Neither said a word.

"How?" Green pressed. "By smashing up the family car while drunk? No. A violent temper, you said." Still, the Blairs sat tight-lipped. An idea dawned. "He beat the kid. Too hard, one too many times."

Mrs. Blair glowered, but Green sensed her hesitation.

"That's it, isn't it!"

She was now shaking her head vigorously. "No! You've got it all wrong!"

"Well, he's got it half-right, Marianne."

"All right!" she snapped, swinging on her ex-husband. "You're determined to tell him, aren't you! You never could stand Myles. He was too brazen for your tastes, never played the gentleman's game quite well enough. So here's your chance to get even."

Blair shut his eyes against her venom. "Marianne, I'm doing this for Jon. Someone has murdered our Jon."

Her jowls quivered, and the flame died from her eyes, leaving them bleak. Her hand trembled and half-reached for Blair's before drawing back to clutch the top button of her blouse. "Do you want to tell him?"

His voice was unexpectedly tender. "No, you tell him."

She glanced around the room, for the first time seeming aware of others. Behind the glass partitions, dinner conversation had returned to normal, but nonetheless she lowered her voice. "Only a handful of people know this story, and I want you to know that under any other circumstances I would never violate Myles' confidence like this. But Henry is right. Jonathan has to come first and avenging his death is the only thing I have left. I trust that you will respect the confidential nature of what I'm about to divulge and will not make public—"

"The public will hear only what becomes a matter of public record, at least from me."

She took a deep breath and twisted her button, searching for a starting point. "When I was at Simon Fraser University, I had a close friend named Darlene Etherington-Hughes. Darlene came from a wealthy Toronto family who had made their money generations ago in textiles. She was a very beautiful girl, but she'd attended a sheltered girl's boarding school and when she came on the university scene, she went a little wild. She was easy prey for the would-be Don Juans." Her wayward hand left the button and wandered down onto the table to toy with the packets of sugar. She studied the labels.

"Like Myles Halton?"

She nodded, her eyes intent on the sugar. "Myles and his fraternity brothers. By then he was in fourth year and a big man in the fraternity. Darlene and I were a year behind, and usually he went for the freshman girls. Back then he was a good-looking man—still is, but he's put on some weight. He was all muscle then, and his hair was thick, wavy and black. That and those blue eyes were a knock-out combination.

Anyway, Darlene was no small prize. Beautiful, old money, some brains, but she had the typical spoiled heiress ego, and when they started to date they fought like cats and dogs. He was used to blind adoration, and she wasn't the blindly adoring type." She raised her eyes from the sugar to flash Blair a wry smile. "We never are, are we, dear?"

He returned the smile ruefully. "Daddy's fault, I know."

It was an affectionate exchange, old and practised between them. There is still a lot of fondness between these two, Green thought.

"Myles was genuinely intrigued by Darlene," continued Mrs. Blair, her eyes back to the sugar. She had begun to split the packet apart along its seam. "She was rather a notch above his usual fare, and I think as much as Myles ever loved anyone, he probably did love Darlene. But he had some fatal character flaws, which are all Henry was ever able to see."

"They are rather looming, my dear."

She shrugged, not to be drawn into another ping-pong match. "Then more than now."

"What character flaws?" Green demanded. Hunger was sapping his patience. "A violent temper? An overdeveloped sex drive?"

She nodded with a smile. "Both. Plus a colossal ego and a fierce competitiveness. Myles always had to be number one, in his work and in his love life. He cheated on Darlene left and right, but he'd go mad with jealousy if another man so much as winked at her. One day someone did, and she winked back. A harmless flirtation at a party, that was all it was. Everyone had had too much to drink, and you know how those frat parties could get."

Green did not know. He had earned most of his university credits at night school, squeezing courses in part-time between his shifts on street patrol. "What happened?"

"Myles took the guy outside, beat him up, and then turned his fists on Darlene. Myles was a boxer, in fact, he could have been a professional if he hadn't valued his brains more than his brawn. When he turned those huge fists on petite Darlene, he broke three ribs and ruptured her spleen. The trouble was that she was three months pregnant at the time and had not yet told him."

Suddenly, the pieces fell into place. "And he damaged the baby."

Mrs. Blair nodded. "It was born severely brain-damaged. Myles was utterly distraught with himself. He has a strong fatherly streak which is evident in the way he treats his students, and he would have loved to have had a son to nurture. He married Darlene, mostly out of guilt, and pays the most expensive private institution in the States to care for his son."

"There were no charges?"

"Darlene never told anyone. Her family suspected, I think, but it was all neatly swept under the carpet with the marriage."

"And since then all his research has been directed at understanding the brain?"

"It's his life. He barely knows his wife and daughters. Henry here thinks that's just because he's a man's man, but I think it's guilt. The work is a kind of penance."

Across the table, Green saw Henry roll his eyes, but he wasn't so ready to dismiss the idea. He had seen the passion in Halton's eyes when he had talked of his work.

"What do you think he'd do if someone was threatening to take it all away?"

Marianne started to reply, then froze and stared at him in disbelief.

*　*　*

On his way through to the hotel lobby, Green stopped to buy himself three chocolate bars, and by the time he was through the front door, one was already gone. Instead of catching a taxi back to the police station, he decided to walk. The evening was warm and breezy, and it was an easy fifteen minute walk from the Château Laurier across Confederation Square and down Elgin Street to the station. He needed to sort out what he'd learned and plot his next move. Halton, he decided, was a man of some moral integrity but even more ambition. Not only to scale great academic heights but also to assuage a deep and haunting guilt. It was an odd prescription for murder, but a powerful one nonetheless.

Outside the Château he waited at the light to cross the first portion of Confederation Square, then hugged the eastern side of the square past the National Arts Centre, Regional Headquarters, the new spiffy white Court House and on past the trendy shops and eateries that graced the gentrified Elgin Street. Couples strolled hand in hand along the sidewalks, peering in shop windows and exclaiming over menus.

Munching his O'Henry and deep in thought, Green barely noticed them. If Halton had used Difalco as his accomplice, how had he motivated him? Falsifying data or cutting ethical corners was one thing, but cold-blooded murder was quite another. Was Difalco that Machiavellian? Had Halton told him that if Miller's research fraud was exposed, they would all go down, not just Miller? Academic trust was fickle, and once lost, impossible to regain. Would that have been enough for Difalco, or would he have said 'Nice knowing you, Professor, but I think I'll switch to McGill'?

Without a more powerful incentive, Green suspected he'd

choose the latter course. Halton might have promised him the Yale position, and that would have been a tempting plum in the highly competitive university job market, especially for a white male who hardly qualified as disadvantaged. Or he could have taken him into his confidence and told him about his shameful past and his brain-damaged son. He could have impressed upon him the broader humanitarian implications of his research and its potential to help millions. He could have dangled dreams of international glory and admiration, a page in history, maybe even a Nobel Prize. And he could have hinted at the darker alternative, that even if Difalco jumped ship, Halton would make sure that his name was ruined too.

That combination of soul baring, promised glory and threatened ruin might have been enough. Difalco was a complex man, full of cynicism on the surface but underneath, Green suspected, capable of great passion. His needs would be complex, and Halton's own personal tragedy might lend a needed edge of humanity to motives that might otherwise seem no more than sordid greed and opportunism.

If that was so, how to crack Difalco? How could Green ensure that the man's desire for glory and his fear of humiliation would be better served by siding with Green against his idol?

Green pondered the problem all the way back to the station. He needed something tangible to hold over Difalco. Physical evidence would be nice, but he didn't have enough reasonable and probable cause for a search warrant and he wasn't sure what he would name in it anyway, other than Carrie's two sketches and Blair's wallet, which were still missing. Other bloodstained articles like shoes and pants might still exist, but Green suspected that Difalco would have long since disposed of anything that could connect him to the crimes. In the absence of hard evidence, Green would have to tinker with motive and alibi.

Back at his office he shuffled through his phone messages and checked with the desk sergeant, but there was still no word from Sharon. He called home but she was not there. I'm not going to worry about this, I can't worry about this, he told himself as he left yet another message on the machine. That made four in total, but it was better to appear desperate than to appear as if he didn't give a damn that she was gone. With Lynch's deadline and the work that still lay ahead of him tonight, even if and when he made an arrest, he knew he probably wouldn't get home before tomorrow afternoon. An answering machine might not be the most romantic medium for patching up a marriage, but at the moment it was his only hope.

The chocolate bars were finally getting into his bloodstream, and he felt his steadiness return. Leafing through files, he came to the report on Joe's alibi for the night of Blair's murder. Detective Jackson had tried hard to pin down times, especially between ten-thirty and eleven, but since the serious drinking had begun at eight o'clock and had continued unabated until two a.m., details had become very hazy by ten-thirty. Jackson had the impression that Joe's buddies were reporting more on his habitual drinking patterns than on their specific recollections of the night in question. The waiter recalled bringing drinks to their table regularly throughout the evening, but could not swear that Joe had always been there. The bartender recalled Joe speaking to him about the Blue Jays' game on the TV over the bar. It had been the seventh inning, and Jackson had verified that the seventh inning was being played between ten-ten and ten-thirty. The bartender further recalled Joe paying for the running tab of the group at two when the pub closed. Amidst considerable fanfare he had charged it to his Visa card, a claim which Jackson had also verified—$152.92. But between approximately ten-thirty and two, no one could consistently place him at the scene.

Here was the toehold he could use. Green glanced hastily at his watch. Three hours to pumpkin-time. He grabbed the phone and called Sullivan, who with any luck had had time to relax and put his two young sons to bed before being called back to duty. Fortunately Sullivan was by the phone expecting his call, and Green didn't even need the apology he had prepared.

"Brian, I want you to bring Difalco in for questioning. And do your Clint Eastwood routine—tall, silent and looming. I want him really freaked."

Sullivan chuckled. "What do I tell him?"

"Absolutely nothing."

*   *   *

Joe Difalco may have been spooked, but he was still clinging convincingly to the shreds of his machismo. He was wearing a sleeveless black T-shirt and skintight black jeans which showed off every ripple of muscle, and he slouched in the cheap plastic chair in the interrogation room with his elbows on the table and his chin propped in his hands, ignoring Sullivan as if he were a fly on the wall. The picture of boredom. He waited until Green had taken the chair opposite and given his standard preamble, then fixed him with lazy eyes.

"I want you to know this six-foot moose here you sent to get me doesn't scare me one bit. I came because I want to cooperate. I've done nothing wrong and I've got nothing to hide. Or fear."

Green smiled. "Oh? And why is that, Difalco? Your alibi's so perfect and your motive non-existent?"

Difalco shrugged. "Something like that."

"Well, think again, my friend." Green tossed a file on the table between them. "Your alibi is far from perfect, and as for motive...I have a little story to tell you. See what you think. Two guys both accuse each other of tampering with their research data. Halton hires Blair to find out which one is telling the truth. He needs to know which theory is correct, but if the deception ever became public, the scandal would ruin his project with Yale, his financial backing, and the credibility of all he has discovered so far. All those years of meticulous theory-building, wiped out by the mere whisper of the word 'fraud'. So he had to find out the truth, and he had to keep it quiet. Blair found out the truth, but he refused to keep it quiet. Refused to sweep it under the carpet and fix the fake results so that no one outside Halton's little research club would know. How does this sound to you?"

Difalco had begun listening with a bored air, but by the end, in spite of himself, he was sitting straighter, his brows drawn and his dark eyes alert. Now Green could see the intelligence in them. Difalco sat very still in the silence that followed Green's question, as if warily scanning for traps.

"Nice-sounding fantasy," he drawled finally. "But if you mean Miller and me, the only place I seem to fit is as the victim."

"Oh, it's not a fantasy, Joe. Halton has confirmed the whole sordid story of the disputed data, and Blair's role in it. Blair did find a fraud, and knowing Blair's ethical standards, he would not have supported a whitewash."

"No, that doesn't sound like Jonathan."

"Okay, so here's the next part of my story. Halton has a dilemma. Somehow he has to shut Blair up."

Difalco dropped his jaw as if to speak, then stopped himself. His dark eyes slitted warily.

"Halton can't afford to be directly involved," Green continued breezily, "because he has too obvious a motive. He needs an airtight alibi, and he needs the help of an absolutely trustworthy accomplice. Someone above suspicion, someone with no motive, someone with the physical skill and nerve to follow through, and someone whose dreams of glory match his own and whose fate rests just as precariously in Blair's hands as does his own."

At each point, Difalco's eyes widened further, until he could contain himself no more. "If you're talking about me, you're insane!"

Green leaned back with a satisfied nod. "Remember you don't have to tell me a thing. I'm just telling you about a theory I have. It was a pretty damn clever plot, I must say. The Haddad set-up was beautifully executed. Raquel had been your girl, and you knew exactly how her family would react. To be on the safe side, you set up the best alibi you could. You installed yourself with a bunch of half-wasted pals in the pub across the street, made sure you talked to the bartender just before you left, and made sure you paid the whole night's tab by Visa at the end. Nobody missed you for the half hour you were off murdering Jonathan Blair. You probably just told everybody you were going to the can."

Difalco forced himself to take a few deep breaths then tried to laugh. A shrill cackle emerged. "You got absolutely nothing on me. No way you can prove this shit."

"Well, now let me tell you about circumstantial evidence, Joe. It's when we collect a whole bunch of little pieces of a story—none of them by themselves mean a damn—but when we lay them all out together, with each piece fitting together, then there's no other logical explanation that fits all these little pieces. So here's what the jury is going to see, Joe. Jonathan finishes his research and tells Halton, who orders him to bury it. Sunday, Jonathan tells his father that he's disillusioned and wants to switch universities. Monday, Halton takes off to set up his perfect alibi. Tuesday, Jonathan is murdered and you've got a half-assed alibi that leaks like a sieve. Two days later, the eyewitness is murdered and her sketch of a dark-haired man with a mustache is stolen. And then the clincher, Joe. The clincher is when Halton asks you to break into Jonathan's office and steal the files so no one will ever know about the research fraud."

Panic had begun to dawn in Difalco's eyes, chasing out the bravado. "Halton didn't ask me to break—"

Green dropped the chatty tone and sat forward. "Don't you see how he's set you up? You're the one with the dirty hands, and he hasn't got a speck on him! But I know he's the mastermind behind this. You're the pawn, used and manipulated by a man who held your future in his hands, a man whom you looked up to and trusted. That's how a court will see it, Joe. It won't save you from jail, but it will shorten your time."

Difalco shoved himself back from the table, as if trying to flee from the idea. "But I didn't do it! Maybe Halton did, but look somewhere else for your patsy. Halton didn't ask me to do a damn thing!"

"Come on, I caught you red-handed stealing those files. You had no reason yourself to steal them, because they supported you."

"Yes, but I told you I wasn't stealing them. I thought they were some files I needed—"

"And I don't believe that bunch of crap for one minute."

"I don't care what you believe! I didn't kill Blair!"

"Joe, you're not hearing me. Halton doesn't give a damn about you. He's using you, just as he used Jonathan. Then look how he rewarded Jonathan's loyalty. Don't think for a moment he'll protect you. He'll cut you loose in an instant if it comes to saving his own skin."

Difalco's face flushed. "What the hell kind of person do you think I am? Do you really think I'd kill another human being in cold blood? I talk big, but come on, you know it's mostly bullshit. Okay, maybe I'm a bit of a screw-up and a cheat, and I take the easy way out, but I wouldn't do that for Halton for all the glory in the world!"

Green leaned forward across the table. "Then why were you in Blair's office stealing those files?"

Difalco glared. "I want to see a lawyer."

"If you didn't kill Blair, why were you stealing the files?"

"Fuck you."

Green banged the table. "Why, Joe!"

"Because I got a fucking e-mail message from Jonathan telling me my results were fake, that's why!"

The response was so unexpected that Green froze, fist in mid-air, and gaped. "What!?"

Difalco thrust his chair back further and snarled. "Goddamn it, you cops and your fucking attitude. Threatening, pushing people around, trying to get us off-guard. I got an e-mail message, okay? It was from Jonathan and it said 'I've replicated your study and Miller is right. We need to talk.'"

Green's mind raced as he tried to absorb this new twist. "When did you get this message?"

"Wednesday, the morning after Jonathan died. I don't check my school e-mail all that often. He sent it Tuesday evening, but I didn't see it till the next day. Then I freaked. I figured his results must implicate me somehow, so I thought if I just sneaked in there and..."

"How do you know the message was from Jonathan?"

"Because it said his name right on the—" His voice trailed off, and a puzzled look came over his face. "But that just means the person logged on using Jonathan's password. It could have been anyone who knew it. I wondered why the message said my results were wrong, when Halton told me later they weren't. I thought Jonathan must have been lying, but if someone else sent the message...but why...?" The puzzlement gradually faded from his face as understanding dawned. And with it, outrage. "Shit! I was used! You're right about one thing, Inspector. Someone manipulated me!"

In that moment of outrage, Difalco's eyes were clear and his face without a mask. For the first time, Green felt he was meeting the real Joe Difalco, a bright, passionate, deeply insecure young man with a lot to prove and an onerous image to maintain. Deep beneath the layered personae, there was a decent core. Joe's story had the unmistakable ring of truth; it was so bizarre and off the wall that he could never have pulled it out of a hat on the spur of the moment. But once again, it sent the mystery spinning in an entirely new direction.

"You're saying someone wanted you to steal those files?"

"Someone? That fucking Miller! He gets me to get rid of the files for him and take the heat if I got caught! Fuck, the guy's good! He was at the lab just a couple of hours ago, trying to pump us all for information about our research. Said he'd found a new book, and he was trying to track down how he'd been set up. But I bet he was looking to see how far he needs to cover his tracks, who else's research data he needs to erase."

Warning bells shrilled in Green's head. "Who'd he talk to?"

"Most of us. We've all fallen a bit behind with Blair's death, so we had extra work to do. Fuck that bastard!"

Green's eyes willed Difalco to focus. The young man was flushed deep red with outrage at being outsmarted.

"Joe, think carefully. Did anyone act strangely when he asked? Did anyone do anything unusual after he left?"

Difalco had been shaking his head. "No one except Miller himself. He was drooling over Rosalind Simmons, and he asked her to go with him. That's a first."

Fourteen

Green urged the Corolla on as they raced across town towards Rosalind Simmons' apartment building. Beside him, Sullivan was punching numbers on Green's cellular phone. Rocking to the movement of the car, he listened, then shook his head.

"No answer. Miller's not home."

"Damn!" Green pressed the accelerator closer to the floor. Sullivan hung on to the armrest.

"Don't kill us, Green. I'm sure Lynch will extend the deadline to one a.m."

Green shook his head impatiently. "This killer's cleaning up, and Miller's blundering around out there turning over rocks. I've got a very bad feeling about this."

"You still don't believe he's guilty? Even after this e-mail business? That was pretty clever, and Miller's the one who'd benefit most."

"I don't know any more, Brian. It's like a goddamn maze. All I know is that with all these people playing amateur detective, someone is going to get killed. Whether it's Miller or—"

A vague memory was tugging at his mind, a pencilled vision of frizzy hair and sharp, deep-set eyes. Suddenly it came loose. If he added colour to the hair and eyes…

"Rosalind Simmons!" he gasped. "That's who Carrie saw!"

*　*　*

The frizzy hair was pulled severely back into a ponytail when Rosalind opened her door, but the sharp eyes were the same as in Carrie's sketch. She didn't look surprised to see them, but not pleased either.

"With all the intrigue swirling around, I figured you'd get back to me eventually."

Green pushed past her into the room angrily. God, he was tired of fencing with this bunch! "What intrigue?"

"Who screwed up whose data, who fooled Jonathan Blair—?"

"I haven't time for riddles, Miss Simmons. What did David Miller want with you this evening?"

She moved in front of him as if to block his progress. "What business is that of yours?"

"The business of life and death," he shot back. "Now tell me."

She folded her arms over her chest. Behind her, he could see a small bachelor flat almost devoid of furniture. Nothing hung on the off-white walls, and the only hint of her own personality was the rowing machine in the corner.

"I'm not going to help you arrest him," she said. "He's a good man."

"He probably is. Just tell me what he wanted."

"Nothing. Just to talk. He's very depressed about what happened. I cooked him some dinner and he left."

"Talk about what?"

Her gaze strayed past him across the room and for a moment she seemed to waver. Then she shook her head. "It's private."

He knew she was hiding something, but was too tired and frayed to outmanoeuvre her, so he tried a more indirect approach. Walking around her, he settled into the corner of the shabby couch, which sat alone against one wall in a poor attempt to create a living room. It probably doubled as her bed at night. Sullivan remained leaning against the wall near the door, taking notes.

Green fixed his eyes on her. "What were you doing at the Morisset Library on the night Blair was murdered?"

She blinked, first at the abrupt change of topic and then rapidly as she absorbed the shock. She turned her back and busied herself straightening dishes on her makeshift shelf. "What are you talking about?"

"The question was plain enough. A witness saw you." It was a bluff, but he hoped his tone was convincing. Carrie MacDonald was no longer around to support him. "I'd also like to know why you didn't mention it to the first detective. It sounds suspiciously like withholding information from the police."

She fumbled a cup, almost dropping it. "I was so shocked—I mean, when I heard about Jonathan's death—I guess it just went right out of my head. We were all shocked, Inspector."

"Give me a break, Miss Simmons. I know you're far from helpless. You can take care of yourself pretty well, can't you?"

"I've learned to." She set her jaw and faced him defiantly. A woman who reacts to threat with anger. "What do you want?"

"The truth. What were you doing in the library that night?"

"Studying. Students do that."

"What time?"

"From nine till closing. Exactly the time Jonathan was killed."

"Did you see anything unusual? Hear anything?"

"No."

"Did you recognize anyone else there?"

She hesitated a fraction of a second. "No."

"Who?"

"No one."

"Bullshit." He took a guess. Another bluff. "You saw Dave Miller there, didn't you?" Her flinch told him he'd hit the mark. "He was there at that time and when you heard Jonathan was murdered, you panicked and decided not to mention you'd even been there. Isn't that how it happened?"

She was shaking her head fiercely. "Dave would never do anything! He's been set up!"

"But he was there."

"You're putting words in my mouth!"

"Miss Simmons, I understand your loyalty to Dave—"

"He's a gentle, honest man."

"So was Jonathan Blair!" Green retorted. "He didn't deserve to be murdered. If Dave Miller didn't kill him, trust me to uncover that. But if he did kill him, who deserves your loyalty more?"

She roamed around her barren room, straightening covers and wiping up imaginary dust. Finally, she began to speak. "Dave told me he was going to the library to meet Jonathan."

"When did he tell you this?"

"About nine o'clock that evening. I was just leaving, and I dropped into his office to ask if he wanted a bite. He said no, because Jonathan had asked him to meet him at the library later."

Green frowned. "You're sure he said Jonathan asked him?"

"Yes."

"Where in the library?"

"Just…" she shrugged, "just in the library, I think."

"So Jonathan was in his office that evening?"

She shook her head. "He'd been around earlier. He sent Dave an e-mail."

The e-mail trick again! "You mean from his computer to Dave's?"

"Yes. We did that to each other all the time. Silly little things half the time. Like 'Hi, you lonely in there?'"

"Did Miller ever verify the message really came from Jonathan?"

"I have no idea." Comprehension widened her eyes. "You think someone else sent him that message!" she gasped. "To get him over there, so he'd get blamed?"

Green's mind was racing. Pieces were falling into place, but the picture didn't make any sense! Groping for logic, he asked her to continue her account of the evening. Now that she knew he was considering Miller's side, she softened and came to sit by his side.

"I did go over to the library and hang around, but I didn't see anything. I was hoping…" She flushed, awkward with feminine wiles. "I was hoping to catch Dave when the library closed, maybe get him to go out for a beer afterwards. I saw him studying on the fourth floor."

"What time was that?"

"About ten-thirty. I saw Jonathan too, his nose buried in a book, scribbling furiously."

"When and where?"

She flinched at his sharp tone and twisted her hands in her lap. "Uh—after that. Maybe twenty to eleven? He was in a corner of the library, a place we'd never normally go."

"The Medieval Literature section?"

Surprised, she nodded. "He was so intent that he didn't see me."

The insight came to Green in a flash. Blair was hiding!

Trying to avoid all the colleagues who had suddenly turned up at the library. The question was—who else besides Dave Miller and Rosalind had he seen? "Did you see anybody else from your group?"

"Well, I didn't stay around. Soon the intercom announced ten minutes to closing, and I started trying to find Dave, but he wasn't in his carrel anymore. I realized I must have missed him, so I hurried to try to catch him downstairs." She flushed again, knotting her fingers. "I…I feel sorry for the guy."

Green had no time for sentiment. "And did you find him downstairs?"

"Well, there was a lot of confusion. The fire alarm went off and—"

"Did you find him?"

Reluctantly she shook her head. "But he said he left when the fire alarm rang. And I believe him. Dave is not like other men, Inspector. He's not capable of deceit. He's been trying to figure out himself how he was set up, and he says he's very close. He found a book in the library yesterday describing some recent research in Denmark on localizing functions in the brain."

Some vague memories stirred. Something Stan Baker had said in his wild speculations about Miller. And something Carrie MacDonald had mentioned when she first described her discovery of the body. Both had talked about a book. "Where is this book?"

She hesitated, avoiding his sharp gaze.

"Miss Simmons!"

Without a word she rose and went to her bookshelf, where she pulled out a thick, shiny volume. "Dave told me to hold it for him and not to let it out of my sight for anyone."

Green flipped through it, recognizing words like perception, sensory input and cerebral cortex, but little else. He was going

238

to need Dr. Baker's services again in a hurry.

"He said it was that important?"

She nodded. "He certainly got very excited. He was looking at the section on auditory processing, and he said he found exactly what the culprit did to the numbers. He said he just had one more person to talk to and I should keep the book just in case."

Green felt a chill. Had Miller known he was heading off to meet a killer? "In case what?"

She obviously had not sensed the same threat, for she shrugged with disinterest. "In case he got arrested, I assumed."

Green was just about to close the book and call Baker when a smudge of dirt caught his eye. Flipping on a stronger light, he took out his magnifying glass. On closer scrutiny it was far more than a smudge of dirt. Near the edge of the page, barely visible to the naked eye, were the clear lines of a fingerprint etched in blood.

*   *   *

Green paced the little fingerprint lab, tripping over Lou Paquette at every turn. Paquette sat at his microscope surrounded by fingerprint sheets and, in his utter concentration, not a sound could be heard beyond the faint wheeze of his breath. His hair was rumpled, and there was a smell of stale whisky about him, but he had dragged himself out of bed without complaint when Green had called.

"It's still going to be hard to connect the print to the scene," Sullivan pointed out on one of Green's passes. "The defence will claim that hundreds of students with hangnails could have touched that book."

"Not if the blood is Jonathan Blair's and the print is our

239

killer's." Green threw his hands up. "Lou, what the hell's taking so long! I thought you said it was a good print."

Paquette raised his head from the lens, his face ruddy from concentration. "It is. It's beautiful. I just can't match it to anyone. Not Miller, not Difalco, not the Haddads or Halton. It's not even Jonathan Blair's."

"Maybe it is just some student with a hangnail," Sullivan replied, rubbing his eyes wearily.

"Not that kind of coincidence." Green snatched the book off the table. "Not on the book both Jonathan Blair and David Miller found crucial to the research fraud. You two guys can go home, but I'm taking it over to the RCMP lab to see if Serology can tie the blood to Blair."

Green had to rant a little and threaten the wrath of the Police Chief, but he was finally able to cajole one junior serologist back into his lab to look at the bloodstained print. He gritted his teeth as the young man fiddled and measured and peered through his microscope before finally coming up with his verdict. Type A—Jonathan Blair's blood type.

"I could go further," the technician added nervously. "I mean, if you want. It's a pretty small amount, but I can get you some other factors. If you want."

"If I want?" Green shook his head in exasperation. "Of course I want. And I want DNA too. The killer's ID, and our whole case, hinges on this print. I need every piece of physical ammunition I can get."

Green glanced at his watch as he headed back out to the parking lot. Eleven-thirty. Half an hour to judgment day, and he was at a loss. Whose bloody thumb print had been on the book? Who had picked up the book as it fell from Jonathan's hand, and who had shoved it hastily onto a bookshelf on his escape route? And where was Dave Miller? Sullivan had checked out his apartment and had come up empty. Who was the one final person he said he had to talk to? And why? Was he just asking naïvely around trying to figure out the mystery of the vanished data, or had he seen the thumb print and put the pieces together? Had he gone off knowingly to a rendezvous with a killer, hoping to flush him out and so clear his name?

Green shuddered at the thought. This killer was far too clever and cold-blooded to fall for that, and in the ensuing battle of cunning, Green had no doubt what the outcome would be. But could he stop it? Yanking open his car door, he seized his police radio. He reached a weary Brian Sullivan just locking up his house for the night and ordered him to put out an APB on Dave Miller. Not to pick him up but to find him and keep him under surveillance.

Sullivan's weary voice suffused with energy. "Hey! Have we finally nailed him?"

"No. I'm scared to death someone else will."

Afterwards he sat in the driver's seat in the RCMP parking lot, his mind racing over possibilities, terrified that he was already too late. He was so lost in worry that he did not hear the shouts until the running figure was almost upon him. Startled, he peered through the shadows at the man scurrying towards him, glasses glinting in the lamplight.

"Jim Winkler, Hair and Fibre." The man stopped, breathless. "I was working late preparing a report for court, and I heard you were in the building. This afternoon I got to wondering about that hair we found on the shirt. You know—the one we couldn't match to anything? Well, just on a hunch I ran a new match, and you'll never believe this. Guess whose it turned out to be?"

Green was beyond riddles. "Who!"

"Jonathan Blair's."

*   *   *

It makes no sense, no goddamn sense! Green ranted to himself as he drove his car aimlessly through the deadened streets. The hair was on the inside of the shirt at the back of the neck. Exactly where it would be if the shirt had been worn and hair from the nape of the neck had got caught inside. How the hell would hair from the victim, who was in front of the killer and at least a foot away, have ended up there? Only if Blair had worn it, and that made no sense at all.

Unless…!

The thought so surprised him that he drove through a red light. Slamming on the brakes, he spun the car around and headed back towards the RCMP lab. It was a crazy, nonsensical idea, but the only one that fit the facts. There was one person who could perhaps tell him just how crazy it really was.

Twenty minutes later, shirt in hand, he was ringing the bell outside Marianne Blair's mansion, expecting to face the pinched sneer of her executive assistant. It was the only pleasure he took in rousing the household at this hour. But instead after a long wait, the door cracked open to reveal the cautious stare of Henry Blair. Blair swung the door wide at the sight of him. He was wearing the same mismatched clothes as earlier, but they were in rumpled disarray.

Green recovered his voice first. "I'm sorry to disturb you so late."

"No, no! It's quite all right, we were just ah…talking."

Marianne Blair appeared in the hallway behind him, her knobby hands clutching her blouse to her throat. She gripped her ex-husband's arm and stared at Green through questioning eyes.

"Is there news?"

He dodged artfully. "I'm getting close. I have one quick question for both of you."

"Of course, please come in. Henry was just…we were talking about Jon. Come, there's tea in the kitchen." Mrs. Blair drew Henry back to allow Green entrance and only then, in the brighter light of the hall chandelier, did he see the swollen redness of their eyes.

"Thank you, but I don't want to intrude," he mumbled. "I just wanted to show you this." He held out the evidence bag containing the black shirt. "Do either of you recognize this shirt?"

Marianne sucked in her breath with a sharp gasp. She took the bag from him almost reluctantly and stepped over to hold it under the stronger light of the hall chandelier. In the stillness, he could feel his own heartbeat as he waited. When she finally turned to him, her face was pale and her voice hoarse.

"This is Jonathan's. I bought it for him myself last year, to sort of liven up his wardrobe. Jonathan usually goes in for beiges and blues. But I haven't see it…oh, for at least two months."

It took him five minutes to extricate himself from their questions and to get back out to his car. A brief phone call to Sullivan turned up no trace of Miller. Sullivan sounded groggy and discouraged, but promised to continue the search and the stake-out of Miller's apartment. In the distance, the bells of the Peace Tower tolled midnight, each lugubrious chime like a further nail in his coffin. Green's sense of dread grew. Where could Miller be at this hour! Whom had he gone to see? Who could have held the final key to the mystery for him?

He sat in the dark, staring through the car windshield at the deserted Rockcliffe street, pondering all the pieces of the puzzle that fit nowhere. Why did the killer wear Jonathan Blair's shirt? Where did he get it? The image of Sharon and the photo suddenly flashed through his mind, and he held his breath as an answer slowly came into focus. Not Miller, not Halton, not even Difalco, but someone he should have seen right from the beginning, and for reasons as old as the hills. Considered in this new light, a number of niggling little problems suddenly made sense—why Jonathan Blair's sketch had been taken from Carrie's apartment, why his wallet had never been found, why his office and computer had been so easily accessed. Why the frame of Eddie Haddad had begun even before Jonathan's results were complete. Everything fit!

Shoving his car into gear, he tore out of Marianne Blair's driveway and down the hushed, mansion-lined street, barely missing an elderly gentleman out walking his Pekinese. He remembered that the apartment was a short hop across the Rideau River and up King Edward Street into the seedier student area of Sandy Hill. The little car squealed as he spun around corners and raced up deserted streets. Drawing up outside the apartment, he paused. He needed back-up, a search warrant, and an arrest warrant. But a life was in jeopardy and it might already be too late. In a life-and-death crisis, the department and the courts could be very forgiving.

There was no response to his knock and listening at the door, he could hear no sounds from within. Throwing procedure to the winds, he roused the building superintendent to open the door. The apartment was in darkness and a quick check of the rooms revealed it was empty. On the kitchen table lay a pharmacy bag, with a prescription receipt for Elavil stapled to the front. But the bag was empty.

Fuck!

Elavil was an anti-depressant which could induce a fatal coma with relatively few pills. Time was the enemy. David

Miller's home was just across the Queensway in one of the Lees Avenue apartment buildings, and Green decided it was faster to drive there than to call the surveillance team and explain. Careening into the apartment driveway, he spotted Brian Sullivan's old Chevrolet itself sitting near the front door. Beyond the car, just exiting through a side door and slipping around the corner of the building was a dark-haired man with a mustache. Leaping out of his car, Green raced to Sullivan's window and found him fast asleep at the wheel. Raging, he shook him awake.

"Grab that man with the mustache and call for back-up! No time to explain. I'm going up to Miller's."

The building was part of a massive, low-rent complex that had fallen into decay and squalor. Even at midnight the tenants hung over the balcony rails in the summer heat, shouting obscenities at one another. Beer bottles littered the lobby, and the stench of urine choked the airless halls. Through the flimsy walls, babies wailed and heavy metal rock music boomed. Green jumped over a drunk sprawled in the hallway and dashed for the elevator. How much time had the killer had? Goddamn it, if they'd been able to identify the fingerprint earlier, none of this would have happened! If only he hadn't felt sorry for Paquette that night and compromised his thoroughness. If only everyone on this case was not stretched beyond endurance. How long had Sullivan been asleep? Had the killer waited to be sure Miller was dead? Any delay increased the risk of capture, but leaving too early increased the chance that Miller would rouse enough to call for help. Green could only pray for a miracle as the cranky elevator jerked its way to the top floor.

He dashed down the dimly lit hall and pounded on Miller's door. No answer. Grabbing the handle, he thrust. The door gave and spilled him inside. A computer screen on the right wall washed the small room in a bluish glow which glanced off the fridge and stove in the opposite corner, but left the rest of the room in shadow. Green could just make out the dim shape of a bed against the far wall before he found the light switch. Murky yellow light filled the room, revealing a huddled form under the bedcovers.

Covering the distance in two leaps, Green groped for a pulse. Thin, but there. Thank God! He radioed 911, then returned to Miller. The man was unconscious and felt clammy to the touch. Green rolled him onto his back, loosened his clothing and checked his airways. As he searched his memory frantically for further first-aid techniques, his eye fell on the pill bottle on the bedside table. Beside the bottle sat an empty water glass. Green knew Miller's prints would be on it and no one else's. All other traces of the crime—the coffee cups, the drugged cake, whatever the killer had used to feed Miller the pills—would have been washed away. A suicide note, artfully dropped from the dying fingers, would be the perfect finishing touch. This killer, smart and thorough, would have added that.

Green scanned the floor, bedcovers and tabletops for a note without success. Then he settled on the computer. Of course! The computer was this killer's special trademark! Rising, he walked over to the screen, which had a display of multi-coloured brain cells. Tapping the space bar returned him to the file in use.

Dear Rosalind,

You are the only person I want to send a message to before I die. Now that I've lost my life's work, Professor Halton's respect, and my hopes for the future, I have nothing left to live for. My work was right and somehow Defalco tricked us all, but I have no hope of proving it, so what's the point? Maybe someday people will learn the truth. Thank you for your faith in me.

Your friend, Dave

Suddenly, Green heard a door slam and he glanced out the window. The roof of the twin tower opposite was directly in his line of vision and lit by a single searchlight above the rooftop door. Green saw a long shadow play across the roof, then as his eyes adjusted, he made out a small figure running towards the edge. The man's dark hair was on end, and in the floodlight his mustache was a jagged slash against his whitened face. Down below, three patrol cars converged on the building and screeched to a stop, sirens flashing. Green saw Sullivan talking to them and gesticulating to the high-rise.

The suspect was racing back and forth across the roof, peering over the edge as if searching for an escape route. The only exit was the rooftop door through which he had obviously come. Below, the police officers had sealed off the street exits and now stood gazing up at the building façade uncertainly.

Green grabbed his radio and called Sullivan. "Brian, he's on the roof."

"I've got a call in to the tactical unit."

The suspect had abandoned his aimless running and was turning back towards the rooftop door.

"No time," Green said. "He's going back into the building, and that means potential hostages and a half-dozen exits you might not know about. You've got to get up there right away."

Green saw Sullivan beckon to three officers and head into the building. "I'm on my way up," Sullivan said breathlessly. "What's his position?"

"He's still there, but he's thinking about the door. Quick!"

Down below, the ambulance and more squad cars

converged on Miller's apartment. The response to my 911 call, Green thought. He took one last quick glance at Miller and saw with relief that his breathing had not changed. Across the way, the suspect was reaching his hand towards the door. Time had run out.

Green crashed a chair through the window and pulled out his gun. "Police, freeze!"

The man jerked back and spun around, his hand shielding his eyes from the floodlight as he searched the darkness. Green kept his gun trained on him. "Put your hands on your head and back away from the door."

The man hesitated. Green gauged the distance from his window to the rooftop across the way. At least seventy-five feet. To his surprise, the gun was remarkably steady in his hand, but there was no way he was going to hit the man if he fired. If he could even bring himself to fire. He couldn't believe he was doing this. He'd never fired at a live target, and never hit anything at seventy-five feet.

But the suspect didn't know that.

"Back away. Right now!" Green bellowed, and to his great relief the suspect slowly turned away. Green had just begun to breathe again when abruptly the man launched himself toward the edge of the roof. Shit! In that instant Sullivan burst through the rooftop door, took a running leap in pursuit, and brought them both crashing to the ground.

Behind him, Green heard a commotion as the paramedics rushed into Miller's room. After briefing them on the Elavil, he turned back to the window. Sullivan was just hauling the suspect to his feet and hustling him toward the door. Handcuffed and dwarfed by Sullivan, the suspect looked fragile and harmless. Not like a deadly killer at all.

"Brian!" Green called. "Take the wig off."

Sullivan glanced over at him questioningly, then reached down to snatch the black wig from the man's head. A mass of pale blond locks slowly tumbled over the suspect's face.

"Gotcha, Miss Weeks," Green said to himself with a smile of satisfaction.

Fifteen

"My father's on his way up here, you know. You don't know trouble till you've met Dr. Lorrimer Weeks."

Vanessa Weeks sat in the interrogation room, her arms crossed over her chest and her chin thrust out. Gone was all trace of the panic that had driven her to contemplate suicide. Her eyes were steady and her tone sure. A damn good actress, Green thought, remembering her convincing portrayal of grief when he'd first met her. Only her pallor betrayed her fear. She had been booked and had spent the rest of the night in a tiny metal cell, but that seemed only to strengthen her resolve.

"I look forward to it," Green replied, tipping his chair back casually. "Would you care to explain what you were doing at Dave Miller's apartment last night?"

"I was worried. I went there to check on him."

"I see. Disguised in black wig and mustache."

"It's a dangerous building. I thought I'd be safer as a man."

"And the little detour up onto the rooftop on your way home?"

"There's no law against going up on a roof. If that's all you've got on me—"

"What about Jonathan's wallet and the sketch Carrie MacDonald drew of him? My men found them in the back of your bedroom closet. How did they get there?'

She said nothing.

"They're a poor substitute for the real thing, by the way. They won't love you back."

Her knuckles whitened, but she feigned disdain. "My father says he'll get that whole search thrown out of court, you'll see. You had no probable cause when you broke into my apartment."

He smiled. "Well, he can try, but judges up here are not that easily bullied. There was a life in danger and that Elavil prescription was in plain view, so the law's on my side. As for Jonathan's death, your alibi stinks. I had a female officer check out that university pool where you were supposedly doing laps. She was able to sneak in and out the back door of the change room with no trouble."

"Just because she could doesn't mean I did, Inspector. I believe I'm still innocent until proven guilty, even in this provincial backwater."

He sat forward in his chair, a cup of cold coffee forgotten at his elbow. He had been up all night, but he felt more alive than he had in days. His eyes held hers quietly as he played his ace.

"I saw Dave Miller this morning. He was still pretty groggy, but he wanted to tell me about his discovery. He'd found a new Danish book which showed yet another method of analyzing brain wave data that gives even different results. So maybe all three of you were picking up different parts of brain activity and Difalco's theory doesn't contradict Miller's after all. Both theories could be right. Or wrong. Quite amazing, isn't it, how little we really know?"

She had resolutely held his gaze, but now red flooded her cheeks. Her arms tightened across her chest as if she were trying to hold herself together.

"That's a lie!" she spat. "I looked at that book and I—"

Belatedly, she caught herself and clamped her jaw tight.

"You didn't read to the end. It was the last paper in the book."

She began to shake all over. "I'm not talking any more. Get out! Get the fuck out!"

Without warning she leaped up and flung herself against the door, bringing two police officers racing into the room. It took both of them to subdue her, and her curses echoed in the hall long after they had dragged her away.

*   *   *

"Boy, what a waste!" Sullivan exclaimed, shaking his head in disbelief. "A kid like that, with so much going for her, so much to contribute, and she's going to spend her best years behind bars."

After a few hours sleep and a fresh shave, Sullivan was in top form again but the long emotional night had finally taken its toll on Green. Slumped at his desk, he rubbed his eyes wearily.

"Yeah, she has a great mind, but people never saw beyond that, to the young woman who needed love and affirmation just like the rest of us. Perhaps even more than the rest of us. She'd been raised in a hothouse, made to grow up before her time, always expected to excel, to win, to be number one. The pressure was incredible. You know, rumour has it she broke her own wrist when she saw she had no chance of winning gold in tennis at the Olympics. That's how abhorrent losing was to her. I should have realized she wouldn't relinquish Jonathan Blair as easily as she seemed to."

"But she killed him because of the research, Mike, not because he'd dumped her."

"I think both things went together. I don't think she

planned to kill him at first. She just wanted Raquel out of his life, so she planted the love note for the Haddads to find. The sad thing is, I don't think Jonathan was as involved with Raquel as Vanessa thought. He just felt sorry for her because no one ever saw beyond the great body."

Sullivan guffawed. "You saw Raquel's picture. You honestly think Blair wasn't attracted?"

"Sure, he was attracted. In the heat of the moment he might even have slept with her. But what I mean is—it wasn't..." Green coloured. "It didn't mean anything. I think he really broke up with Vanessa because he suspected she might be involved in the research fraud. Then, somehow Vanessa found out he was investigating the fraud. My guess is on Sunday when she was in his office preparing the love note on his computer, she stumbled upon the data in his computer and she realized she was about to be exposed. I suspect she followed him around after that, trying to keep tabs on him and learn more about what he knew. Maybe she overheard him ask for a meeting with Halton, and knew she had to move. Her lucky break was to witness the fight between Jonathan and the Haddad brothers, and that gave her the idea for the frame. If she hadn't seen it, she would have figured out another way to kill him. Whatever it took, Jonathan Blair had to be eliminated before he met with Halton the next day."

"Yeah, but what about the knife? How'd she get it so fast? Last I heard, Gibbs checked all the gift shops and came up empty."

Green pawed through the papers on his desk, sending several skidding onto the floor. He pounced on one with a grin. "Gibbs, bless his obsessive-compulsive soul, didn't give up, and I have taught him well. Lateral thinking, that's what he used. He decided to check Middle Eastern restaurants, and what do you know! The Moroccan Nights on Bank Street found it was missing one of the decorative daggers that hang on the wall."

Sullivan shook his head. "Boy, what a cold cookie. To love the guy and wipe him out like that over some research—that's pretty warped."

"Yeah, and I think that's why she finally snapped. Ambition and success meant more to her than people. She'd defied her father in choosing Halton instead of Harvard, so she had a lot to prove. In the academic world you prove yourself by the significance of your research. You don't win a Nobel Prize by being wrong. Vanessa's work was based on Miller's theory. She thought Difalco's results contradicted Miller's and so put hers in question too."

"So it was her all along, not Miller, who tampered with Difalco's data."

Green nodded. "Difalco had almost finished his data collection, and naturally, he was beginning to crow. I think she got worried and ran some simulations of his work. When she found out his results were good, she broke into his raw data and altered his numbers. Then she suggested to Miller he run simulations, and of course the results weren't at all what Difalco claimed. And the rest is history. Miller checked Difalco's raw data, yelled fraud, Vanessa erased the data and Difalco yelled sabotage. If only she'd realized, as Miller did, that both theories could be right. Or both wrong. And that truth is the only important player in the drama."

"Yeah. But sometimes you get too close to things. Get too committed, lose sight of the big picture. But you wouldn't know anything about that, right?" Sullivan hauled himself to his feet and stretched luxuriously. "Well, I'm taking the day off, going to rebore the engine on the old Chev. Maybe it'll last another winter. By the way, Mary says that little house you two were looking at in Barrhaven has dropped its price. It's a steal now, she says."

Green avoided Sullivan's eyes. At this moment, even Barrhaven would be preferable to the future he faced. He'd just called home for the seventh time, and there was still no answer. "Yeah, well…"

"Uh-oh. Trouble in paradise? Sharon didn't like the press coverage?"

"Something like that. Plus I've been a self-centred ass."

"So what's new? She knew that when she married you."

Green cast him a reproachful look. "Yeah, but I've sunk to new lows since the baby was born." He traced slow circles on the desk with his pen. "Almost as if…when it was just Sharon and me, I knew I could always walk away. She'd be hurt, but we'd both find someone else. But with Tony—"

"You're his father for life."

"That's the thing. I should be." Green paused, thinking of Hannah. "And I've been wondering…it's almost like I want to hold him away from me. To tell him 'Don't expect too much of me so I won't fail you'. To insulate him." And maybe to insulate myself a bit too, he added but only to himself, for that was a frailty Sullivan would not understand.

"Lots of fathers try that route, as you know, and we pick up the pieces." Sullivan clapped him on the shoulder. "You're in the soup now, man. You've just got to learn how to swim."

Green's door swung slowly open. They both looked up to see Sharon standing in his doorway, Tony balanced on one hip. The baby's face split in a wide grin at the sight of him.

"Soup?" Sharon repeated, calm and unreadable.

Sullivan moved to the door. "That's my cue, folks. I'm off." He tickled Tony's toes, mouthed the word "swim" at Green and slipped past them out the door.

Sharon remained planted where she was. "I listened to your seven messages on the tape and I decided I'd better come talk to you personally. God knows when you'd come home."

He winced but said nothing. His seven messages had said it all. He was a screw-up, he was obsessed with his work, sometimes he couldn't think straight, but he loved her, he loved Tony, he'd go to the moon for her if she'd give him another chance. Now it was her turn. She shifted Tony on her hip, and her composure wavered. She studied the floor.

"I guess I haven't been exactly blameless in all this, Mike. I've been bitchy and always tired and preoccupied with Tony. The old body's all out of shape, and my breasts are still leaking milk. Not quite the girl you married."

"Stop it." He jumped to his feet and moved toward her. "Darling, nothing happened."

She backed against the door, whipping her head back and forth. "Don't give me that. Denials or confessions...I really don't want to know." Her voice quavered. "I know I can't compete—"

"No!" He gripped her by the arms. "You need to know. Nothing happened. Yes, I was attracted to her and yes, she came on to me. But I stopped it. She got my tie off and my pants undone, but I stopped it. Because I didn't want to lose us."

For a long moment she simply stared at the floor, but finally her mouth twitched slightly at the corners. "She got your pants undone? How much?"

He risked tracing his finger lightly across her hand. "If we weren't in my office and you didn't have Tony, I'd show you how much."

She sighed. "I'm just not sure it's going to work, Mike."

"I know I'm not much good at keeping my promises, but—"

"But you promise to change?"

He bit his lip; she wasn't smiling. She had heard all this before. "No, but—" he eased Tony out of her arms into his, "—I do want to try."

"That seventh message, when you promised me a new house…"

With his free hand, he reached for the phone. "I'll call Mary Sullivan right now."

She finally smiled her slow, wise-cracking smile. "You ought to be tempted more often, Green. I might get a swimming pool out of it next time."

Barbara Fradkin was born in Montreal and educated at McGill University, the University of Toronto and the University of Ottawa. Her work as a child psychologist provides plenty of insight and inspiration for her fiction. An active member of Canada's writing community, she is currently president of the Ottawa chapter of Sisters in Crime, an organization of female crime writers. She is also treasurer of the Capital Crime Writers, another mystery writers' group.

Barbara's short fiction has been published in *Storyteller* magazine and *Murderous Intent* magazine (upcoming) and has been anthologized in *The Ladies' Killing Circle* (General Store Publishing, 1995), *Cottage Country Killers* (GSP, 1997), *Winning Shorts* (GSP, 1997) and *Menopause is Murder* (GSP, 1999). *Do or Die* is her first Inspector Green mystery and her first work with RendezVous Press.

Barbara resides in Ottawa with her three children, two cats and a dog.

Also available from  RendezVous Crime

Northern Winters Are Murder
Lou Allin

The tranquillity of a northern winter is shattered by the mysterious snowmobiling death of one of Belle Palmer's friends. The ugly truth behind the accident reveals a twisted story of anger and revenge.

ISBN 0-929141-74-1, $12.95 CDN, $10.95 U.S.

Speak Ill of the Dead   Mary Jane Maffini

When crusty young lawyer Camilla MacPhee's best friend is accused of the murder of a vicious fashion columnist, the real killer may be the one on the run from her dogged sleuthing.

ISBN 0-929141-65-2, $11.95 CDN, $9.95 U.S.

Down in the Dumps   H. Mel Malton

Introducing Polly Deacon, a most unusual heroine, whose peaceful life is violently interrupted when she finds her friend's abusive husband lying dead in the town dump.

ISBN 0-929141-62-8, $10.95 CDN, $8.95 U.S.

Cue the Dead Guy   H. Mel Malton

In the sequel to *Down in the Dumps,* cabin-dwelling sleuth Polly joins a dysfunctional theatre troupe, only to uncover more murder and sordid histories in her country district.

ISBN 0-929141-66-0, $10.95 CDN, $8.95 U.S.